THE
LITTLE
CLOTHES

THE LITTLE CLOTHES

DEBORAH CALLAGHAN

Bedford Square
Publishers

First published in Australia in 2024 by Viking,
an imprint of Penguin Random House Australia,
Sydney, Australia

First published in the UK in 2024 by Bedford Square Publishers Ltd,
London, UK

bedfordsquarepublishers.co.uk
@bedfordsq.publishers

© Deborah Callaghan, 2024

The right of Deborah Callaghan to be identified as the author of this work has been asserted in accordance with the Copyright, Designs and Patents Act 1988. All rights reserved. No part of this book may be reproduced, stored in or introduced into a retrieval system, or transmitted, in any form or by any means (electronic, mechanical, photocopying, recording or otherwise) without the written permission of the publishers.

Any person who does any unauthorised act in relation to this publication may be liable to criminal prosecution and civil claims for damages.
A CIP catalogue record for this book is available from the British Library.
This is a work of fiction. Names, characters, places, and incidents either are the product of the author's imagination or are used fictitiously, and any resemblance to actual persons, living or dead, businesses, companies, events or locales is entirely coincidental.

Quotation on p42 from JM Barrie's *Peter Pan*.

ISBN
978-1-83501-114-0 (Paperback)
978-1-83501-112-6 (Hardback)
978-1-83501-113-3 (eBook)

2 4 6 8 10 9 7 5 3 1

Typeset in 11.5pt Bembo Std
by Avocet Typeset, Bideford, Devon, EX39 2BP
Printed and bound in Great Britain by
CPI Group (UK) Ltd, Croydon CR0 4YY

To Joc and Don

A baby born in a cup of tea
Sailed the rim on the back of a bee
When the tea was drunk
And the leaves were read
The bee had drowned
And the baby was dead

Grandma Joan

Chapter 1

Audrey Mendes caught a bus from the ferry wharf to the first strip of small shops. Candles, homewares and whatnot. She sometimes trudged up the sharp rising hill towards the western sun, past the Victorian terraces that had been renovated in the eighties when it was fashionable to expose the porous bricks, but mostly she didn't, and not today, although she worried she should have. She could feel the band of fat from belly to hips when she leaned forward to the cramped space behind the seat in front to stuff her jacket into her gym bag, remembering with some regret the medium pasta salad she'd eaten from a plastic tub while working through lunch. That she carried the heavy bag containing her cosmetics, little-used runners and a lightly edited novel into the city five days a week could surely be counted as exercise.

•

At the pub she chose two bottles of white wine from the fridge and waited at the corner counter next to the long bar where people had begun to order beers and settle. The banter had started.

'Mate, did ya see the game?'

'Yeah mate, whatta game!'

Another game was playing at full volume on the screen in the next room. Audrey could see people in there drinking with Friday-night abandon. One of the bartenders came near and she waved. A little wave, granted. He didn't see her. He picked up a phone from the back of the bar and started texting. He picked up a second phone and texted. He picked up a third phone and texted. It was as if he was shuffling cards, such was his sleight. And Audrey waited. She was sure that when he finished fiddling with the phones, he'd serve her. It was gloomy in the pub, she excused him, and it was hard to be seen in the small alcove to the side of the long bar. And she was short, even in her heels, and the bottle-shop cash register blocked her face. The music was loud. A young woman with crimson dreadlocks and deep dimples, also tending the bar, joked with the man who had three phones. Another bartender, sporting a bun on top of his partially shaved head and a tightly plaited beard with a tinkling bell on its point, said something and they all laughed explosively, parted and strutted. Audrey waved larger this time. No one came.

'Hello!' she said in a too-loud voice. 'Hello! Can I please get some service?'

She watched others being served at the long bar. A young man was offered a tasting of craft beer, a new brand from Marrickville. Audrey could hear the bar staff telling the slight but apparently riveting story of Manmaid, a microbrewery startup involving twin brothers Leo and Levi, an abandoned garage and a small loan that might one day lead to imagined riches. The customer screwed up his face in disgust. The beer wasn't to his liking. It most certainly was not! He turned to his female companion and

The Little Clothes

expressed his thorough disapproval by twisting his lips and sticking out his tongue stiffly. He was affronted. A second tasting of a different brand was poured to test his fine palate. The bar staff huddled, waiting on a verdict.

'Hello!'

Audrey waved again, this time in half circles almost as wide as a small sedan windscreen. No one turned to her. Still, she waited. She was a polite person but when she had excused them for long enough Audrey became irritated. After another few minutes she put one bottle on top of the jacket in her gym bag and the other in her handbag, and started to walk out of the pub. Past the manager who sometimes called her *love* when she smiled at him in the local supermarket. The manager who, with his wife, was raising his daughter in his place of work. He turned as Audrey left. The pudgy child was trying to press buttons on a solitary poker machine by standing on her toes and slapping her flat hand high above her head. Here we go, thought Audrey, he's seen me.

'See ya, love.'

She smiled tightly at the young father, who was wearing a trucker cap inside and backwards.

One block and a few houses up, Audrey put her bags down on her verandah and walked back to the street to see if she had been followed. The street was empty except for her neighbours, who were tinkering with their car, bonnet up. She had thought of them as the amiable village idiots since they had trick or treated on Halloween among the throng of neighbourhood children. Roy and his son Troy were dressed in party-shop Batman and Robin suits and she'd given them each a mini Mars bar from her generous basket of lollies. Audrey had been dressed up too. A crone in greenface.

Now she shut her front door, clomped down the hall to the kitchen, twisted the top off a bottle, poured herself a glass and kicked off the bloody high heels she wore to court when she accompanied the men to help keep track of their books, manila folders, trolleys and coffee orders.

After twenty minutes, she started to wonder if there were security cameras in the pub. She didn't think so. The police had knocked on the door when she first bought her house. There had been a residential break and enter a few doors down, at number 83.

'Go to the pub,' she advised the two young uniforms. 'They'll have cameras there.'

'They don't. We checked there first.'

'Oh, well, you'd think they would. Being a business. Especially round here.'

'If you hear of anything or remember any suspicious activity from the last few days, please call this number.' They handed Audrey a card and pocketed their notebooks.

'I will. Hope you catch them.'

They left through Audrey's wonky gate, already alert to lifting rather than swinging it, their hips swaying under the weight of their cumbersome weaponry. Guns, batons, pepper spray, handcuffs.

Yet maybe there *were* cameras now installed at the pub. The new owners had taken over just five months ago, keeping the managers on but permanently removing the seafood pie from the menu. She'd have to explain her actions to the police who would knock on her door at any minute. She'd be struck off. Who would employ her now? How would she explain her behaviour to her parents, who would be disappointed in their surviving child? Their thirty-eight-year-old single daughter. The lawyer. There was no

The Little Clothes

knock on the door, but she was unsettled and decided to go to the pub to buy another bottle. Perhaps take one bottle back in her handbag. She couldn't take the already opened bottle, though she briefly considered filling it to the top with water. No. Stupid! But how to pay for three bottles when she'd only have two?

In the pub Audrey chose another bottle and put it on the counter next to the stolen bottle. She waved.

'Hello!'

She waited. The bar was hectic now and the staff moving with purpose.

'Hi, can I get some service please?'

Customers streamed in and stood in ragged lines at the long bar. They had all the attention.

'Hello, can I please get some service?'

No one turned. No one glanced in Audrey's direction. She considered taking the bottles to the bar but the sign said not to. *Purchase all bottle shop items in the bottle shop. NOT in the bar.* NOT was underlined three times.

'Hello! I am now leaving and walking out with two bottles of wine,' she yelled. 'I'm leaving!'

And so she did. Back at home Audrey again waited for the knock on the door as she sat at the kitchen table looking at the three stolen bottles. She was discomforted and cranky. Resentful. She felt she'd been forced into an awkward position. By 9.30 she had stopped worrying and was playing Words With Friends with strangers, scrolling Instagram, and watching *Ozark* on Netflix.

•

Audrey wasn't sure where she was when she woke thirsty in the morning. Her throat was sore. Had she been snoring? She thought for a moment that she was in the office and had worn her owl pyjamas to work. Still clutching at the wisp of a receding dream, she sat up and saw an empty bottle on her coffee table, standing tall above an icecream bucket. She remembered the sketchy details of the previous evening. Maybe there *were* cameras in the pub and everyone knew what she'd done – but perhaps they thought she was as crazy as one of the unhinged meth addicts from the housing commission blocks around the corner. Just the same. Crimes, she thought, big and small, were a leveller.

Although the bottle shop opened at 10.00 a.m., Audrey decided to wait until it would be more appropriate to buy wine on a Saturday morning. When would that be? She watered the parched succulents, snipped chives from her garden for butter-heavy scrambled eggs, fed Joni a carrot and changed the hay, opened the bills, and read the gossip page in the newspaper.

Audrey had bought the dilapidated worker's cottage with the inheritance from her brother, Henry. A few years on she'd made some changes. Landscaping at the front and back. A new gate. 'A lot of money for a lot of white pebbles,' her mother had said when Rita and Eustace came to dinner and a showing. Recently Audrey had added a sleek custom-built wardrobe to the spare bedroom. Its soft-closing drawers, multi-tiered hanging spaces and pull-out shoe and accessories trays were a salve. This morning she didn't go into the spare room, but she could smell it. As enticing as a new car or just-baked cake. Fresh paint, wood and polish.

The Little Clothes

•

The pub was swampy at eleven. Two young men in black T-shirts, black jeans and ivory bum cracks were clearing the debris from the night before. There was a large wooden tray of hamburger buns and a box of waxy potatoes on the long counter. A keg was being rolled in and tapped. The drone of a leaf blower could be heard from the cheerless beer garden – a mossy place that served equally for milestone birthdays and wakes. The television was resting. The bar fly had not yet claimed his stool.

Audrey chose two more bottles of wine from a now sparsely stocked fridge. There was another job neglected, she thought. She went again to the small side counter and cleared her throat. The manager walked behind the main bar.

'Just these two, love?'

'Yes, but I was only charged for one of these yesterday instead of four.'

'Don't worry about it, love.'

'No, I want to pay.'

'So, you want me to charge you for four of these and one of those?'

'Yes please.'

'Okay.'

Audrey tapped her card with relief.

'Have a great day, love.'

'You too.'

The little girl ran to her father as he walked from behind the counter, squealing when he tossed her onto his bulging shoulder and started picking up glasses with his free hand.

'Bye, love.'

'She's growing up.'

'Yeah, three and a half next week. See ya, love.'

Audrey recalled the muted organic cot blanket and mauve toy elephant she'd chosen and wrapped so carefully in cream tissue with a tea-stain calico ribbon when Shay-Lee was born. The child's name now indelibly inked: Shay on the father's left forearm, and Lee on the mother's right bicep. The father would drape his arms round the mother's shoulders so the tattoos aligned and could be read in the right order by interested customers.

Audrey's gift had not been acknowledged even though she saw the parents most Tuesdays on Trivia Night, when an assortment of nodding neighbours took a table together. She remembered with irritation how Tom had brought his friend Elspeth with him last week without consulting the group, and how she hadn't known anything. They'd tried to be inclusive and made her their scribe, but she'd written Ireland as I-land and Audrey's namesake Tautou as Tattoo. Audrey had barely refrained from grabbing the pen. Elspeth hadn't eaten because there was nothing vegan on the menu, even in the vegan section.

'It's not really vegan, or even vegetarian. They use the same vat of oil for the fish and chips that they use for the mushroom arancini and zucchini flowers,' she said. Audrey tried to look attentive to the details of the vegetarian menu, a page to which she never strayed.

The cross-contamination on the grill, the virtues of canola, avocado and coconut oil and the problems of insufficiently cleaned processing and cooking equipment were all tabled. Every few minutes Audrey nibbled apologetically at her congealing chicken burger and was signalled twice by Marion that she had mayonnaise on her chin. She was relieved when the quiz started. But only after they had suffered Elspeth's exposition on orange wine, the only drop that would pass her perfect plump lips.

•

This afternoon there was another baby to celebrate. Audrey didn't want to attend Erin's baby shower. She'd said yes, of course, grateful to be invited, and less concerned by what advantage the others in the office might gain from going than how it might appear if she was the only one not to go, and now she really couldn't think of a polite or credible way out of the obligation this close to the event. Her mother couldn't be sick again. It would be like cursing Rita. The plumber, mechanic and electrician had been invoked too often. Audrey planned to go back into the pub after the baby shower to check again for possible cameras, but was also keenly aware that the guilty often return to the scene of their crime. Still, it would be much busier later and she knew it was unlikely she would be noticed as she peered at the cornices and corners.

•

'Audrey! Come in!' Heidi, the new assistant in HR, momentarily unrecognisable out of the office and her navy suit, greeted her.

'You're just in time for Playdough Baby. Also, grab an ice baby and put it in your glass. Go and get a drink over there. You have to catch up! The first one to melt their ice baby has to yell "My water broke!" Hilarious, right! Ours are almost melted so you might not win that one. We're all making a baby out of playdough. Just take a ball of dough. Any colour, although I think only white is left. Still, more realistic, right?'

'Not for everyone.'

'Oh god, Audrey, that's hilarious. Everyone's told me how funny you are. I've heard so many stories. When you're finished, put the baby in a cupcake holder. Make sure you put your name under the cupcake case first so we know whose is whose. The cutest one wins. Alec's going to judge them when he gets back from golf! Put your present on the table out there.'

Heidi, Audrey thought, should have been in hi-vis, holding airport runway paddles or AFL umpire flags. So many rules and instructions.

There was a ziggurat of gifts balanced on the table in the entrance like a late-stage game of Jenga. This was Erin's second baby shower since the wedding and before that there'd been the engagement party when the affair with Alec – a senior partner and married father of five mostly grown-up children – had finally been unveiled. They'd all suspected after the Law Society Ball, of course. Then came the unequivocal and bitter email sent to the whole company from Alec's wife, Vivienne, who didn't hold back. She had outed the new couple to a point where even sympathetic recipients found some of the details *unnecessary*. Audrey waited a hellish two months for a second salvo from Vivienne that never came. Perhaps she had no inkling about Audrey. Perhaps she didn't care. Vivienne was a remote figure. The elegant wife who didn't make her husband happy. Whenever Vivienne called Alec, 'Psycho Killer' started to play. In the first flush of her own entanglement with Alec, Audrey found the laddish joke very funny.

The Little Clothes

The engagement had been closely followed by a hens' night in a city club, where all the support crew wore tiaras that identified them, in cut-out plastic letters, as *friend of bride*. The stripper had been an embarrassment. Most of the women shimmied with Andre. Audrey did not shimmy and unfortunately found herself the centre of attention, urged on by a chorus of cries to step up and join in. She sat in her chair, resolute, even as Andre straddled her lap to everyone's amusement.

Erin held a spectacular first birthday party for Carter that Audrey managed to dodge because of the clash with her own birthday dinner arranged by her parents. Erin's bespoke invitations arrived with alarming regularity. There had even been a hastily planned wake for Boxy, allocated to Alec in the divorce. The yellowing dog lay in an open cardboard container in front of an arrangement of candles and incense suggestive of a spirituality that Audrey silently questioned.

Gifts were bought. Tickets and hotels booked. Clothes decided upon. Themed thank-you cards without personal messages followed. Did they like the pewter ice bucket? Well of course they did, Audrey reassured herself, they'd put it on their list. But did they know it was from her?

The destination wedding in Tahiti over three days had practically drained Audrey's savings along with a week of annual leave. She spent too much time in her bungalow in a panic. It was difficult walking alone into a room of partying couples. The worst moment was being the last to arrive after the four-hour photo-furlough between wedding and reception, and teetering in new block-heeled sandals in front of the other guests, who were all barefoot and loose. Audrey hid in her room after the beach ceremony, occasionally peeping out into the walkways to see what was happening and if the other guests were also in their bungalows. It was so quiet she was nervous. Had she missed some of the instructions? Later she found out most of the guests had gone to a spontaneous party in the resort bar where friendships had been formed. Alec's mother, the grand dame, sat on a high-backed rattan chair at the reception and received those who dared go near. Audrey did not dare. Her tropical-patterned clothes, chosen with such care, were now in unfortunate contrast with the subtle linens and pastels worn by Erin's younger friends and those of her newly minted mother-in-law.

'Wow, Audrey, you look very bright, very Tahitian!'

•

'Audrey, darling, come in. You're late!'

Now Erin was propped in the corner of the denim couch with her legs crossed, her slightly protruding belly nestled neatly in her lap. She reached one arm above her head and hooked it like a coat hanger around Audrey's neck. Audrey leaned down and obediently pecked Erin on the head.

'Look at me! I'm enormous!'

'Not really. You'll never be enormous. If I didn't know you are pregnant, I wouldn't know. If you know what I mean.'

Audrey was trained early in reassuring others about their weight.

'You are so sweet, Aud.'

'Not really.'

'God, you're funny. Have you got a drink? I wish I could have one.'

The Little Clothes

Audrey clinked her ice-baby caipiroska against Erin's mineral water.

The bridesmaids were hovering and shrilling, and Erin's mother, coolly elegant in Akira, was reading to Carter, instructing him in a slightly raised voice, 'Tell Granny Sue how many flamingos. Let's count them together.'

Alec arrived well after four and held court, as he did in the office. Audrey retreated to the bathroom. The tiled sanctuary was decorated like a spa, with the only light coming from a bank of votives. Who had the time to light so many votives? Well, Erin, obviously. Elegant dark-bottled toiletries and stacked linen-look paper handtowels lined the limestone bench. Gardenias cut from the garden were haphazardly bunched in vintage lead crystal vases. Audrey looked at herself in the mirror with anticipated disappointment. Must get to the gym more often, she thought. She washed her hands with Erin's fragrant pump soap. *Cucumber and patchouli, oils of Africa, fungi from ancient forest floors. Paraben free.* She dropped the handtowel into the woven Ikea wastebasket beneath the bench and then scrunched up three more clean handtowels and threw them in too.

When Audrey walked back into the party, Alec was judging the playdough babies. Had he put a rinse through his hair? All the women were attentive. Laughing ostentatiously. He wasn't saying anything that clever. Nothing to warrant the congregated fawning. Audrey thought Erin was the clever one. She had left the office and her work as a junior administrative assistant when she married Alec and started her own *curated boutique* line of sandals. Erin had given each of the female wedding guests a pair of her beaded slides, *Shore Print*, in diaphanous bags that had been placed on their beds in Tahiti. Audrey's navy raffia with silver beads were too small, yet she was thrilled to receive them and didn't want to upset Erin by asking for a different size. There were other goodies in a canvas welcome bag that was printed with a sepia photo of Alec and Erin. Miniature bottles of Krug Grande Cuvée, Panadol, palm-shaped chocolates, sunscreen, and a leather luggage tag stamped with the dates of the nuptial extravaganza. Who wouldn't want to be reminded of this event every time they went on a lesser holiday? And a lavish brochure outlining the three days of activities bookending the wedding, illustrated with more photos of Erin and Alec. The welcome cocktails, a tour of the pearl farm, the culinary adventure at the local market, the drinks party on a yacht at dusk, the recovery barbecue on the long, wide jetty, an open-top classic Land Rover circumference of the island, an eco-tour of the mangroves, and guided reef snorkelling, all enthusiastically described and encouraged above a discreet small-print mention of the extra costs for private and personal choices.

Alec and Erin arrived at their wedding on palanquins and were greeted as if they were rock stars, royalty, or Instagram influencers.

At the recovery party, almost everyone was tossed into the turquoise waters. Audrey was not. She did not want to be tossed, but she wondered why she wasn't.

Alec chartered a plane to take the wedding guests back to Sydney at the end of the celebrations. Audrey commented that Erin and Alec would lose all their friends and family in one fell swoop if the plane went down.

'They'd have to go to so many funerals.'

'Audrey, that is the most tasteless comment I've ever heard,' said HR Nadine from across the aisle. 'You have no filter.'

The Little Clothes

'I thought the same thing as her. It seems silly to put all your eggs in one basket,' said an uncle standing in the aisle, waiting for the toilet to be vacated.

Later, Erin agreed. 'I did think about it. I was going to drown myself in the resort swimming pool if the plane crashed.'

•

'I think I'll have to go for this one,' Alec announced, picking up a playdough baby. There were squeals when it was revealed to be Erin's. 'Well, she is very good at making babies,' he said, leering at his young wife.

'Go to Daddy.' Granny Sue pushed her grandson forward as a foil, seeking her own little bit of the limelight.

'Aaaawww, how cute,' the women cooed in unison as Alec reached down and ruffled his youngest child's lightly gelled hair.

'We're the only men here, son. We have to stick together.'

Everyone laughed again.

Audrey skulked around the walls and the fringes of others' conversations for twenty more minutes. Alec waved to her with the tips of his fingers when they accidentally made eye contact. She again fled to the bathroom and while there took her time to drip the liquid soap, Krasner style, over the limestone bench, before putting the bottle in the clown patch pocket of her Lee Mathews smock. She peered into the drawers. Erin had lovely handtowels and room spray ready for use. Audrey resolved to buy some small luxuries for her own bathroom and to tidy her shamefully cluttered and stained medicine cabinet. After five minutes someone rapped on the door. It was Granny Sue and Carter.

'Why aren't you joining in the games?'

'Fat poo-head!' Carter shrieked. Sue shushed him down.

'This is how you were in Tahiti! Why don't you mix in? My daughter tells me you're very funny. I can't tell.'

'Oh, just not feeling the best.'

'That's what you said then. Is it irritable bowel? You're always in the bathroom. I can refer you to my doctor. He's fabulous. He's a GP but he's also a naturopath and a reiki healer. Exceptionally gentle hands. His name is Tone. He fixed my scalenes in just three sessions with dry needling. He'll even do a filler or two. He doesn't take on new patients, but I can get you in.'

'Thanks, Sue. But I already have a GP. By the way, it's not irritable bowel.'

'Gluten intolerance?'

'No! I'm just shy!'

'What? What did you say? I couldn't hear you just then above the noise. The music is way too loud.'

'I said goodbye. And Carter, I'm sure Granny Sue wouldn't want you to be quite so rude to your mother's guests. Maybe too much sugar, Sue? By the way, there's no soap in there and a bit of a mess on the bench. You might want to take soap in for Carter's hands.' And his mouth.

'That can't be true. I dressed the bathroom myself.' Sue hurried into the glowing chamber, the remnants of her grandson's squashed blue-iced cupcake on the back of her red silk tunic.

Audrey was the first to leave. A grazing board the size of a small meadow had long since relaxed. The melange of nitrate-infused meats, dips, cheeses and dried fruits a fleeting table-to-bin amusement. Thank goodness it had been photographed and posted when it was fresh and the

The Little Clothes

individual components discernible and likeable. No one saw Audrey go. They were all playing pin the nappy on the baby, groping towards the wall when it was their turn, eyes covered with one of Alec's ties, arms outstretched, being guided back on course by the onlookers. In the foyer, Audrey took a Tiffany bag from the present table and kept moving seamlessly out the front door of the faux Hamptons villa and into her waiting Uber.

•

At home, Audrey opened the card from the stolen gift bag.

Love you so much girl. Your the coolest mommy ever you slay life I wouldn't of survived without you. Thank you for being there for all the times we've lived our best lives and also through the shit that we've survived together lmao. Only we know. I am so so happy that you will be a mommy again because Im your sister from another mister and that makes me an auntie two times hahah love you, Hanny XXXX. PS. Your my BFFL forever. PPS. Goddess.

What the hell? thought Audrey. Hanna! Recently promoted to junior partner Hanna. She'd confided in Audrey just months ago that she found Erin and Alec unbearable. She'd cried at the Marble Bar while Audrey bought the drinks. Thank god Audrey hadn't told Hanna about Alec and his nocturnal visits to her house when he was still married to Vivienne.

Audrey had gone to Nadine in HR in a frenzy of embarrassing tears, deep breaths and a barely suppressed flinty anger.

'I am way more experienced. I am older, I have worked here longer, I worked on Gilchrist and Aziz. I actually ran that case. Both trials. Now it's quoted everywhere as our great success. I wouldn't mind seeing how many new clients came out of that case. Which I ran for two years! More than two years!'

'Calm down, Audrey. Or come back when you are calm. And make an appointment next time. I'm busy and cannot anticipate or attend to your every grievance.'

'What do you mean by that? I never complain.'

'I wouldn't say never.'

'Fine. This'll take a minute. Tell me why. Why didn't I make partner?'

'Do you really want to know? The truth?'

'Yes, I do. That's why I'm here making an idiot of myself.'

'You're not considered a team player, Audrey.'

'I work longer and harder than anyone.'

'But not on the team.'

'Who is the team?'

'Come on, Audrey, you know what I'm talking about.'

'No, I don't. Give me an example of my not being a team player. Whatever that is.'

Nadine rolled her eyes. As if she had a long list to choose from. Which she didn't. Audrey Mendes was accommodating. Often browbeaten.

'Well, the photo session for the brochure, for a start.'

'The what? The photo session? What do you mean?'

'The company spent a lot of time and money securing the location for the photoshoot. Everyone was dressed and styled. You got hair and make-up. The clothes. Like everyone else. You actually looked quite nice. Everyone else thought it was fun but you mocked it. Someone had to organise all of that. It didn't just happen. My girls were here till midnight the night before.'

The Little Clothes

'God, Nadine, the brochure was a team-building exercise? Really? You believe that? The brochure was to promote the company. We non-partners were the unpaid models. And as if we don't all work till midnight and later when we have to. You and I are usually the last ones here. How many times have we turned off the lights together? I hardly think posing in hired clothes in someone else's glamorous office constitutes working. We're actually here to work as lawyers to help people through the legal system, then we charge them a whole lot of money because they can't do what we do and they are terrified of what might happen to them.'

'Audrey, do you really think you were an unpaid model? Why would they pick you for that? And don't you lecture me about lawyers and what we do. I have my law degree too and practised here before you started. Here's my personal advice, with my professional hat off, as a friend, Audrey – if you want to be in the boardroom, act like you want to be there, and go when you're invited. Show some respect to the people who control the boardroom.'

'Don't you control the boardroom?'

'What? Don't be sarcastic, Audrey. Don't even start.'

'But don't you? Control the boardroom, I mean? I've never been able to book it without your permission. You keep that green diary of the times for all the rooms.'

'Someone has to organise things, Audrey. Do you think coordinating the bookings is easy?'

Audrey thought it was probably fairly easy.

Nadine pushed back from her desk and Audrey marvelled again at how her bob was more helmet than hair: a blunt cut grazing her chin and framing the slash of red lipstick and heavily mascaraed lashes. Sitting on an ergonomic chair in a spacious corner office overlooking Hyde Park. Carla

Zampatti suit. Trembling hands betraying her. Photographs adorned the walls and shelves with dedications of love for Nadine from celebrity clients. Rascally politicians and the like. Many of whom Audrey had defended from her own partitioned workspace near a kitchenette on a lower floor.

'But what about my work? My record of work? I *have* been a team player. I've won many cases for our clients. The clients like me.'

'There you go, Audrey. Right there.'

'I don't even know what you're saying.'

'*You* have won cases? The clients like *you*? Grow up, Audrey. No one gives fuck-diddly-squat about what you did for which case. We are a team. We are not islands unto ourselves.'

Audrey was momentarily taken aback by Nadine's quote. Had she been reading?

'But I did win cases. I wrote the documents. I proposed the way through. I *did* do it with the team. I worked long hours well past midnight when the others went off to dinner. I *did* it. They almost never asked me to join them. Even when we were working as a team!'

The diners weaved noisily back into the office one night and gave Audrey a grease-spotted paper bag from Golden Century.

'Here you go, Aud,' Richard said, plonking the unwanted offering on her desk. 'We over-ordered. The dim sum is pretty strong but there's also a bit of sweet and sour pork and something green that no one ate. Still, you don't look like a greens girl to me. Come and join us in the boardroom for a drink before you hook into that.'

'Thanks, Richard, but I've already eaten and I have work to do.'

'Oh, come on, Aud, lighten up. Join us for a drink.'

Audrey had gone to the boardroom hating herself, but gratefully accepted a glass of warm wine with ice cubes after it was discovered the bar fridge had been turned off at least a day before.

'Fucking cleaner. I've told them not to unplug the fucking fridge for the vacuum,' said Alec. 'Probably didn't understand what I was saying. This is what happens when you let the peasants in. So, Audrey, what have you been doing all evening that held you back from joining us?'

'I had work to do. And I wasn't invited. My father is one of the peasants, by the way, so that probably explains the no invitation thing.'

'What are you working on?'

'You know what I'm working on because you asked me to do it.'

'Audrey, you are, if nothing else, funny.'

'Well at least I'm something.'

'I am going to have to ask you to leave, Audrey,' Nadine said now in a studied manner, shuffling and restacking her folders, paint charts, travel brochures and magazines. 'We can talk again later. I hope to see you at drinks for Hanna and Daniel tonight. In the boardroom. My advice, for what it's worth, is that you go to the drinks. And if you do decide to go, try to find your way there on time and congratulate the new junior partners. Unkindness does not become you.'

•

Inside the pilfered Tiffany box was a miniature silver comb with a delicate pink silk tassel. Ridiculous, Audrey thought. And then, It must be a girl! And then, Erin told Hanna it was a girl. Audrey felt she'd done so much better with her French linen cot set and giraffe rattle. Yet she hadn't been let in on the secret. She also wondered if Alec had told Erin about the affair. Was it even an affair? Why exactly had she allowed Alec to come to her house so many times? Why had she always welcomed him in, poured his favourite wine that she'd hunted down and refrigerated to the right temperature, and then not objected when he left her less than two hours later? Why did she think she loved him when he flipped her onto her belly, pulled her to her knees and shoved himself in?

'Can we talk, Alec?'

'About what? You know I can't give you a raise.'

'Us. About us.'

'I'm sorry, Aud, I'm not sure what you're getting at, and I have to be home forty minutes ago. Vivienne thinks I'm at a meeting. Maybe later in the week? Maybe we can have lunch at Machiavelli? The house pasta. You like that, don't you? I've seen you polish it off more than once.'

'Well, we'd have to be very careful. Those walls have ears. And eyes.'

'Trust me, Aud, no one would *ever* suspect *us*. Have you seen Vivienne?'

•

Back in the pub, Audrey plucked a bottle from the fridge almost without looking. Any bottle would do. Her purpose was to crane again in all directions looking for cameras. She couldn't see any. The nightmare of the wine was surely over.

'What are you up to, Audrey?' Standing at the long bar

The Little Clothes

and smiling across at her was trivia-night Lorraine. 'You're looking suspicious! What on earth are you doing?'

Audrey laughed brightly.

'Have you ever looked at these gorgeous decorative tin ceilings? I'm just getting my Saturday-night supplies! Trust me, I'm not interesting enough to be suspicious.'

'True. But come and join us. We're just over there. What will you have?'

Audrey, shorter now in Birkenstocks but still in her tiered Lee Mathews smock, peered around the till and into the main bar. Marion, Sean, Jeff, Tom and Elspeth were sitting at two cocktail tables. The group met on non-trivia nights? Without her?

'I don't want to intrude.'

'What are you talking about? Intrude? You won't be intruding. We just ran into each other. You are funny. I'm buying. What will you have?'

'Okay. Just one. A sav blanc. I've been out all afternoon. So just one quick one. I'll pay for this and come over.'

'Look everyone, it's Audrey!' Lorraine announced Audrey's arrival at the table as if she might not otherwise be seen or recognised.

'You sit here, Aud,' said Sean, offering his stool and going in search of another.

'Hi everyone. Hope I'm not interrupting anything.'

'Noooo,' they chorused. 'We just bumped into each other. So funny you're here too. What are the chances?' Audrey thought the chances were pretty good since they all lived in the neighbourhood and frequented the pub.

She was jolted to see Tom's hand on Elspeth's knee. A bony young knee. What had she been thinking – that he might be interested in her? In Audrey, plump and plain.

Older. Had he amused them with the story of the cake she'd taken to his house one Saturday afternoon?

'Audrey!' he had said. 'What are you doing here? This *is* a surprise. Wow, I didn't know you knew where I live. Is everything okay?'

'I saw you come here once when I was helping look for a missing cat. Anyway, I was just experimenting and made an extra cake. It's a mandarin sponge. I grow mandarins. I have a tree. My parents have one too. So, I end up with a lot of mandarins. Thus, the cake. I've also made jam. You don't have to take it – the cake. But there is jam if you don't want the cake. But you don't have to take the jam either.'

'Oh, Audrey, that's very kind. Look, the thing is, I'm a bit busy at the moment.'

Tom, in a too-small vintage Mexico Games T-shirt and smiling hippopotamus boxer shorts, had left the front door three-quarters closed behind him and kept running his hand through his messy hair. His beautiful messy hair. Audrey barely resisted brushing a dirty blond lock from his eye.

'Well, you really don't have to take it. I can give it to Wanda on the corner. I just thought I'd offer it to you first since you're closer.'

Dumb, she immediately thought. There were so many winding stairs to Tom's house she was still out of breath from the climb.

'Very kind, Audrey, but I'm not really eating cake at the moment and I don't want to waste it. I'm on a bone broth reset. I'm auditioning in a fortnight. A new quiz show, actually. They're making a pilot. Need to get myself right.'

'No problem. It's no problem at all. I'm sorry I've disturbed you. You might prefer some mandarins from the

The Little Clothes

tree? I'll see you at the pub on Tuesday and I'll bring some with me. Or some jam? The jam is great. I make batches of it. Are mandarins and jam allowed on the reset thingy?'

'No, not really. No sweet stuff. Not even fruit or stuff like fruit. Look, I'll have to say bye for now, Audrey. I'm in the middle of something.'

Audrey hadn't taken the cake to Wanda because she didn't think Wanda knew who she was. She only knew Wanda through the stories the trivia group had shared, recounting the woman's rants in the park about dogs off leash, uncollected dog shit and the stinking garbage bins being left out on the wrong nights by her neighbours. If the cake is going to be wasted, she thought, I will eat it myself. Clutching the round Tupperware container she had bought for Tom, Audrey walked quickly home and googled *bone broth reset* and *recipes for mandarin jam*.

•

As far as Audrey knew, none of the trivia group caught up with each other outside of the pub beyond coincidental meetings in the harbourside parks, at the Saturday growers' market or at the village shops. They'd all signed up on a sheet of paper, pinned to the pub noticeboard, to a local waifs and strays trivia group, now known as The East-Enders. Most of them strangers until the first night, when they not only met but won. They ordered celebratory sparkling wine and split the prizes, enthusiastically agreeing to do it all again next week. There were high fives. Audrey had studied flags of the world, capital cities, the constellations, and the lineage of Australian prime ministers in between.

Lorraine grandly invited Audrey to a *high tea* early on, but when Audrey knocked on the door holding a bouquet of peonies and wearing her best dress, Lorraine appeared bedraggled and confused in a stained brunch coat and slippers.

'When are the others coming?' Audrey asked, meaning Tom.

'I don't know. Who else would come? And why are you here again?'

'You invited me to high tea.'

'I don't think so.'

Lorraine found some stale digestives after fumbling at the back of a sticky food cupboard, while Audrey made cups of tea without milk, found a vase and washed the cascade of dishes in and around the sink.

'I'm not myself today,' Lorraine said through spilling tears.

'That's okay. I get it.'

None of the group had ever asked exactly where Audrey lived, and she happily left it vague after her dispiriting afternoon at Lorraine's. She had found Tom's place by physically stalking him one Tuesday evening after they won. Hiding in the dark against the wall at the bottom of the meandering stairs that led through his yard of weeds and ironic 1950s garden ornaments to the little liver-brick cottage, Audrey had contemplated, for twenty minutes, whether to ascend and knock. She leaned into the cool wall before dawdling home ambivalent.

'No, I won't stay for another, but thanks, Sean. It's been great to see you all. I've been out all afternoon at a baby shower, and you can't begin to imagine how that was! Plus I have a family lunch tomorrow, and who knows how that will go. Such is my social whirl.'

The Little Clothes

'Oh god, you're funny, Aud,' Lorraine said. Again.

'That's what I'm told. Anyway, I'm going to head home. See you all on Tuesday.' Audrey walked her arse off the high stool as smoothly as she could. She had no purchase on the tread beneath her dangling feet and manoeuvred with one cheek following the other, caterpillar style. A final humiliating little jump to the floor.

At home, she washed her hands and held up the cream matinee jacket she had bought at Marilyn and Miss Lou. It was her first purchase for the wardrobe in the spare room, the culmination of two weeks' careful consideration and some loitering in the David Jones childrenswear section at lunchtime, surveying their range so often she panicked that suspicion had been aroused. Not supposed to be there. A fish out of water. She had already placed her many purchases from previous years in the new wardrobe and discarded some, but this soft, perfect, tiny jacket was for now the shiniest jewel. She felt she too could unwrap little clothes and rattles at a party and anticipate a future with a baby. Audrey gloated over the knitted Dior baby jacket, size 000, before deciding where she'd place it. Finally, after moving other items, including some whimsical knitted toys – a puffin, a rabbit, an otter – she liked the way the jacket sat in its tissue nest against the freshly planed, sweet-smelling wood.

'That's a beautiful choice. A gift?' the cashier said, wrapping the little jacket .

'No, it's for me.'

'Oh. When are you due?'

'Sorry?'

'When's the baby due?'

'Oh, I get it. I just buy things I like when I see them.'

'Well, it's a great choice. Bound to become a family heirloom. Good luck with your baby. Looks like it will be soon.'

Chapter 2

'Come in, my darling girl.'

Audrey's father ushered her into the gloomy entry of her childhood home. She was comforted by the fusty smell of a house that was always closed and cooked in daily. Notes of lamb chop and sprouts. Faint whiff of cigarillo and gas fire. Her mother's Ma Griffe.

'How are you, sweetheart? It's marvellous to see you. You look as beautiful as ever.' Eustace Mendes kissed his daughter on both cheeks. He gently held her hands as if they were going to folk dance.

'Your mother is upset that you're late.' He winked. 'Nothing new there. I think you're three minutes late today. But I have been hearing about it for at least an hour.'

Eustace, now more Shar Pei than man. His face a pleasant pillowing droop. No fine lines. Just loose caramel flesh divided into two on each side. More of the same spilled over his shorts like sloppy pizza dough when he oiled up to work shirtless in the garden on summer afternoons. The presence of his daughter once a month allowed him to briefly pass the baton of his wife's scrutiny.

Audrey had not grown used to the shrine in the entry where the family telephone sat on top of the nest of carved tables. The shrine to her brother, Henry. There were other shrines. His bedroom, of course. There was also the shrine on the round glass-topped table in the sombre lounge room, where photos of Henry were flanked by two china display cabinets and other now-dead relatives in frames, smiling from the past into their futures.

'Hello Mumma.' Audrey tried to kiss Rita on the cheek but was, as always, held stiffly at a distance. Audrey pulled away as quickly as she was repelled.

'Aunty Ninnie!' Audrey leaned a little closer to her mother's sister. 'Where's Uncle Gary?'

'In the side passage trying to fix the lock on the gate,' said Rita for her sister. 'Your father has no idea how to do it. He thinks he's a handyman, but he is not. And what is that you're wearing?'

'It's new. I like it. Don't you like it?' Audrey did a little twirl to make the hem of her dress flare. To make her mother smile.

'You remind me of your Cabbage Patch doll. What was she called again?'

'Slumpy. Slumperina.'

'That's right. How appropriate. You think something concealing and flowing like a tent is slimming, but it isn't. A caftan always makes you look bigger.'

'You used to look pretty good in a caftan, Rita.'

'Ninnie, I did not. I looked like I'd been draped in curtains! Or upholstered by that bossy decorator woman you hired.'

The sisters cackled about the orange velvet and chinoiserie Nin had chosen for her lounge room two decades earlier.

'It's way too much fabric for me. I don't like a caftan. Let's face it, it's a beach cover-up. A pool party cover-up

The Little Clothes

at best. And where is Eustace? All that fiddling about. I'll need him to carve soon.'

'Mumma, pick on me but not on Dad. He's a brilliant handyman. Here, these chocolates are for you. I've chosen your favourites and some new ones. The white heart and the salted peanut caramel plus your usual, red velvet and the lemon curd.'

'Trying to make me fat.'

'No, Mumma. I thought you might like them. Anyway, you're not fat. Definitely not fat.'

Rita was a bird. Twiggy arms, frail wrists and chicken-bone legs jutting from beneath her half apron, truncated by balding sheepskin-lined slippers. Her sparse grey hair in a skimpy ponytail tied with an elastic band beneath a fraying scrap of paisley. She was a woman who had been hungry all her life in pursuit of thinness. Her bones now brittle and sore. Rita had told Audrey early and often that middle-aged women grew a basin and then spent the rest of their lives filling it.

'Women cannot eat carbs after forty,' she had told her daughter. 'You just can't. So don't!'

Forty seemed a way off and Audrey resolved to make the best of the time she had.

'You know who would have loved them?' said Rita, mottled knuckles to hipbones, pugilist's chin. No one responded. It was a worn path. They let her answer. 'Henry. That boy could really eat chocolate. What an appetite. He could eat anything.'

'Well, Henry could also *do* anything. He was a special person. With his tennis and paintings and shows. And handsome. So handsome.'

'He was, Nin. He could do anything. You are so right.'

'Come out and say hello to your Uncle Gary.'

Nin scooted her niece out the kitchen screen door into the garden. A plain space made into a sinuous labyrinth. Eustace's masterpiece. The flat double suburban block now an oasis of maturing fruit trees, palms, ferns, orchids, rhododendrons, clematis tumbling over a homemade trellis, paving stones bordering beds of hydrangea, azaleas, aquilegias, fuchsias, brugmansia (suaveolens and sanguinea), nicotiana. The vegetable troughs and raised stone herb beds brimming with heads of lettuce, nasturtiums, tarragon, tomatoes, mint, Vietnamese mint and thyme. A pond with water lilies, rushes and sedges surrounded by stands of feathery grasses. Flowering ginger.

'Audrey! My favourite niece!'

'Only niece,' said Audrey, reciting her much-used riposte from the family script.

'How are you going? Got a boyfriend yet?'

Audrey turned to see Nin shaking her head vigorously with eyes widened in warning to her hapless husband. Nin finally swiped her finger across her throat to shut him up.

'Nah. Don't need that in my life. And even if I did, he wouldn't need Mum in *his* life.'

'She means well. She loves you, Aud. She's so proud of you.'

'Yeah?'

'We're proud of you too.'

'Thanks, Aunty Nin. How's Scottie?'

Nin pecked at the air as she spoke, nodding and shaking her head in little unprovoked bursts of defiance. Lips pursed.

'Not so proud of him. As I'm sure your mother's told you, he hasn't called by for at least three months. Got the girlfriend and her family in the posh suburb. Living in their

The Little Clothes

granny flat with Sienna. It's not so much about me as it is about Gary. Still, Scottie will be back when he needs money.'

Lunch was different now. Scott and Henry weren't there. When they were children at Sunday lunch they sat together on one side of the table, with Audrey closest to the kitchen to help with serving and clearing. The two mothers opposite, with Grandma Joan stoutly filling the space between her tiny daughters and telling her tales of foreboding. 'I hope I'm still here at Christmas,' she'd say, raising her glass of sherry. And at Christmas, while Eustace carved the bird: 'I hope I'm still here next Christmas.'

Gary and Eustace sat at either end. Audrey had liked it like that. Henry and Scott made it fun. They sneaked Eustace's whisky into their soft drinks, once put whoopee cushions on their fathers' chairs, always teased Audrey about her boobs when she had started to change at eleven, and made their mothers' eyes water and dance with their jokes. The mothers animated just by the presence of their glorious sons. Nowadays Audrey felt she was having the monthly family lunch in a nursing home and her life was passing her by. She felt trapped. As trapped as Henry was in his old bedroom. Suspended like the lemons in preserving jars lined up on Rita's pantry shelves. The lemons from the abundant tree that Eustace tended along with the others. Mandarin, avocado, bay, lime and mulberry.

'Mum! You made empanadas!'

'I always make empanadas.'

'No, you don't. I haven't had these for ages.'

'It's true, Rita. You don't make them anymore. Remember when you made them for my wedding? At least two hundred of them, Audrey.'

'Hang on, Nin. That number keeps growing. I think it might have been closer to fifty.' Eustace, leaning against the broom cupboard in the kitchen with a beer in hand, tempering as always the pre-Sunday-lunch prattle while Rita scurried and darted.

'Eustace, I'm talking about my first wedding.'

'Oh, sorry, Nineveh. I always forget. I do remember the empanada store at the school fete. That had to be at least four hundred.'

'Well, I've made them today,' said Rita. 'Although they're not my best. Not of wedding standard.'

'Oh my god, I can't wait.'

'Well, don't eat too many. They're fattening and I made them for your father. It's his food, from his childhood. And there's roast chicken with the trimmings, and Nin has made the lemon delicious pudding from *our* childhood. Audrey, could you please light Henry's candle? You know, Nin, your lemon pudding is wonderful, but what about Mum's? I've never been able to make it like hers. So light and moist.'

Audrey suppressed a snort, thinking about Rita's handwritten collection of recipes in a now stained and tattered exercise book, where almost every cake had the word *moist* in its underlined title at the top of the page. As a teenager, she had joked about it with Maggie. Even now, when the friends dined out together, they sometimes asked waiters if a dessert on the menu was moist. Then they percolated like the schoolgirls they were when they first met.

'Well, I hope mine is passable today. But Mum's was the best, for sure. I think it's all about your mother making it for you and serving it. Scottie always insisted I butter his toast

The Little Clothes

and put just a little scrape of Vegemite, the way he likes it. Gary could have done it just as easily or Scottie could have done it himself but he always wanted me to do it.'

'She still does it for him,' said Gary. 'When we see him. Which is never. Anymore. And if he thinks I'm going to him, I'm not. Why he left lovely Lisa, I'll never know. She was a beautiful girl. Ended his marriage for what?'

'Go to him, Gary. Don't be a stranger to your son.'

'Rita, he is the stranger to me. Scottie will have to come to the mountain.'

Audrey didn't light the candle but stretched across the counter to pluck one of the delicate half-moon pastries. She took a bite through the middle before landing a smaller crescent back on the plate. 'Delicious, Mumma! Really delicious. Oh my god, this is so good. I have to learn to do this.'

'Don't spray everywhere, Audrey. We have serving utensils for a reason. And plates and napkins. You know who really liked empanadas?' They let Rita answer. 'Henry. He loved them. Boy, could Henry eat empanadas.'

Audrey nudged her aunt. Nin elbowed back with less subtlety. Rita, mildly tolerant of their mockery, shoved dishes at them to take to the table.

'Mumma, this is hot! You burnt me.'

'Don't carry on, Audrey. Is Nin complaining? No. Only you.'

'We don't all have your Teflon fingers.' Audrey knew Nin would never complain to Rita.

Rita ignored Audrey. 'Sit down, everyone. Start before it gets cold.'

'So, Audrey,' Rita began. 'Have you been getting out? Have you seen Maggie?'

'Yeah, of course. I've told you that. We meet for dinner. She comes over. I cook. She eats. We go out to the theatre. To the movies.'

'Is she seeing anyone?'

'No, I don't think so. Not really. Why?'

'Oh, well, I always wondered about her. And you. About the two of you.'

'Mumma. Don't start that again.'

There had been a time in Audrey's late teens when Rita casually left pamphlets and books on her daughter's bedside table. More as a line of inquiry than as an acknowledgement or comfort.

Audrey had said to Maggie, 'She's got the wrong kid.'

And Maggie: 'Are you sure she doesn't know about Henry?'

'My mother knows what she chooses to know about her son.'

'I'm sure she'd tell me if there was someone special,' Audrey said now, 'and then I promise I will tell you. She's just come back from New York on that fellowship exchange thing at Memorial Sloan Kettering and she's working at RPA in oncology. She's busy saving and extending lives. They're doing all this amazing stuff with cutting-edge cancer drugs. Maggie's leading a team of researchers.'

'Now there's a girl who shouldn't wear a caftan.' Rita turned to her sister.

'Who?'

'Audrey's friend Maggie. She shouldn't wear a caftan.'

'Really, Rita? What's this sudden obsession with caftans?'

'I'm just saying she's a big girl.'

'Muuummm! Stop!'

'She's another Cabbage Patch doll. What was the name

The Little Clothes

of her doll? I've forgotten. You made them talk to each other in those squeaky voices when I was trying to drive.'

'Pashie. Short for Passiona.'

'See!'

'See what?'

'She named her doll after a soft drink.'

'Come on, Rita, that's cute.'

'Big girls shouldn't wear smocks. That's all I know. Or drink soft drinks.'

'Okay. Point made, Mumma.'

Audrey offered to clear the table when the elders were engrossed in their reminiscing and red wine, arguing gently about whether they would play canasta or mahjong. They would play neither, she knew. As a child she would have been commanded to leave the table after sitting under it behind the draped cloth with Henry and Scott, pinching their parents' ankles. The three cousins ran off together, laughing at how their plan had worked, to hide in the bush close to the house where they caught tadpoles in the creek as toddlers: the two mothers sitting on a rocky outcrop in the earliest days, ready to grip a bicep and lift a sopping child, finger to thumb, who had slipped on the hairy moss beneath the cold flowing water. Later the creek was for swinging from the fraying rope where the high-school boys gathered to pash Debbie and Kylie Hornby and smoke. In the early days, opera wafted from the Johnson house on the road above, an enchantment in the late afternoon.

Audrey went to a primary-school birthday party at the Johnsons', recently sold as a postmodern beauty, but back then just a house, and she had never forgotten the surprise and stench of stale urine in the uncleaned toilet, and the birthday boy's exotic mother; her raven hair, pinned with a real camellia, rippling over her trembling bosom and hips as she sashayed from room to room with cakes and games and party prizes while her toad-like husband sat in his body odour and bad temper on a grubby Wegner cowskin chair.

'Why aren't you joining in?' he asked Audrey in his fruity, pompous voice, tapping his pipe into the overflowing ashtray.

'I like to watch.'

'So do I,' he said, smacking his lips and hooting uproariously before tapering to a wheeze. He reached into his pocket for a handkerchief to dab his rheumy eyes and spittled lips. Audrey saw the speckles of blood and where the cloth was puckered and caught on dried phlegm. Fifty cents fell to the floor.

Audrey bent down and gave it back.

'That's for you. For being a good girl.'

She was pleased to have gained the attention of Mr Johnson, but her heart's desire was Mrs Johnson, with her red camellia, curves and voluptuous merrymaking.

When Rita arrived to take Audrey home the father had stood at the door, his nicotine-stained fingers firm on Audrey's shoulder. Pressing her down. Minutes earlier, while the candles were being lit and blown out at the dining table, Mr Johnson sat across from the shy birthday boy and dropped his arm to the side of his chair to cup Audrey's bottom where she stood next to him in the clamour of jostling children. When she did not react, he reached further beneath, pushing with a long yellow fingernail into the fabric of her underpants.

'What colour are they?' he whispered in her ear.

'White with blue roses,' she said, helpfully curving her

hand around his hairy auricle to block the din of the hip hip hooray.

'Thank you so much for having her. I hope she behaved?' Rita beckoned Audrey out the door as if they were being a bother to the Johnsons.

'She was a delight.'

'I doubt that. What do you say, Audrey?'

'Thank you for having me, Mr Johnson.'

'The pleasure was all mine. Did you get a sweetie bag?'

On the walk home Rita said, 'Well, that's an interesting family. You'd think the boy would have come to say goodbye. Did he like his present?'

'He didn't open them. They were about to. I was the first to leave.'

'Well, I'm sorry you missed out but it's late. Not great organisation on their part. Tomorrow is a school day. It certainly takes all sorts.'

Audrey thought about liquorice allsorts and the homemade crepe-paper lolly bag in her sweaty palm, staining her fingers red and smearing her party dress. In the dark, away from streetlights, she dropped the bag off the edge of the narrow footbridge to be carried downstream by the rushing creek.

•

Henry, Audrey and Scott thought they knew everything about each other. And they knew a lot. They had been giddy, rolling down hills in Centennial Park and sand dunes on Malabar. They'd smoked weed in the bush cave, procured kissing partners for each other and complained in tandem about their parents. And mimicked them. Scott did a brilliant Eustace and Audrey was strong as Rita. Henry did a burlesque riff on his grandmother Joan, Tennessee Williams–style. 'Comin' Aunt Joan, comin' Aunt Joan. Time for the six-o'clock sherry shake-up.'

Now Audrey was cast alone. The spare. The creek given over to a freeway. She stacked the dishwasher, handwashed the pots and pans using the caged soap cake, and folded four empanadas into a tea towel. She put the little bundle into her bag on the kitchen bench and went up the threadbare floral stairs to Henry's room.

•

Rita had been busy with candles, certificates, ribbons, medals and trophies. A reinvention. A makeover. A photographic resurrection of the perfect son. Rita containing her grief in Kmart do-it-yourself frames. No photos of Henry with his friends after high school. The bed remade with dinosaur linen. Rita had tidied and rearranged her dead son's room for years. Picking at lint and plumping the pillows, swishing the feather duster over the trophy shelves. Twirling the cobweb broom in the ceiling corners. Straightening the drawers and smoothing the doona. More recently, switching on battery-powered candles each evening as if Henry could be guided back home to his childhood. *Second star to the right and straight on 'til morning.*

Audrey remembered her brother differently. At twenty-five, in silver vinyl shorts and combat boots, waxed chest. At Mardi Gras. Handsome at Scott's wedding and sockless in unexpected blue suede moccasins, his best man's suit a perfect slim fit.

The Little Clothes

Henry in the navy singlets cast off by Eustace. 'Henry, why do you wear the clothes I worked hard in so that you didn't have to wear them? I want you to wear a suit and tie in an office. A clean job. Well paid and respected. I don't understand it. You could do anything.' Eustace shook his head and looked at his handsome son with curiosity and a little sadness.

'It's just not me, Papa. I won't ever work in an office. I think I want to be an artist. I think I am an artist.'

Audrey remembered Eustace being embarrassed by his son's declaration. It confused her. She *knew* her brother was an artist. But her father felt the title of artist should be for others to judge and not self-proclaimed. And certainly not at such a young age. Eustace had said as much when he put his arms around Henry and kissed his son on the crown.

'Henry, that can be a hobby. An interest. Like my garden. But you need to earn a living.'

After Henry's sold-out first show, a modest gallery prize and the magazine profiles, Eustace said less but clearly nursed his fatherly fears. Audrey watched him cut out the articles and slide them into a plastic sleeve. He urged both of his children to remember that 'Output is more important than inspiration'. And that 'Having the idea is the easy part'.

Henry in his paint-splattered camo school pants. Sometimes paired with Eustace's work singlets. 'Henry, you hated those pants!' Rita said. 'I could barely get you to wear them to the bivouac. Now I never see you out of them.' She had laughed in the kitchen while she peeled potatoes over the sink, shaking her head at the magnificence of her extraordinary boy.

Henry once called his father on his trek home from a

compulsory weekend cadet camp. Two buses, a train and another bus.

'Papa, can you pick me up? My boots are getting wet.'

'That's what they're for, Henry. They're army boots. Men wear them in trenches and deserts in war. They get wet, they get dirty. We'll see you when you get here.'

Rita had driven to her son against the ardent protest of her husband. Audrey broke ranks with her father in rare support of Rita. She always wanted her brother back in the fold. And still did.

Henry had invited Audrey to sit at the French bakers tables in his Surry Hills rooftop studio with his friends on Friday evenings to drink and smoke and talk while he finished preparing a simple stew or ragout from chuck or shin that had been slow-cooking for at least eight hours in the adjoining kitchen. Redolent with chilli and smoked paprika, sweet spices. A crock of lentils and rice. The wide, deep pots often fed up to twenty. Audrey sometimes went.

In Henry's studio, once tidied for a magazine photo shoot, there was an assemblage of animal skulls, spilling ashtrays, sketches, charcoal sticks, crayons, feathers in jars, tubes of paint, clean brushes in washed tomato tins, bongs, rolls of paper, stretched canvases, motorbike parts, half-finished paintings behind drop sheets, Henry's Ducati that he brought up in the quaking industrial lift, sequinned tops, wigs, high heels, sketch pads, papier-mâché faces and phalluses from past Mardi Gras floats, polaroid photos taken on previous Friday nights around the tables where people gathered in his orbit.

'Audrey!' Rita had cried out when she saw her daughter in some of the polaroids stuck behind the kitchen door. They'd come together with Nin to clear the studio almost

The Little Clothes

two months after Henry died, because the lease would soon be up. 'You came here? When did you come here and why didn't you tell me? What are you doing in this one? And who is that? You're dancing!'

'He was my brother and best friend, Mumma. I like to dance.' Audrey Mendes was a wonderful dancer. Unexpectedly light on her feet, rhythmic and sensuous. Like Mrs Johnson. All twitching hips and come hither.

'Well, you get that from your father. I can't dance. I'm not convinced you can either. You never could at those ballet classes I sat through at St John's. You were like a Greek statue.'

'Well, I like dancing. We had good times here.'

'I never came here. I don't even understand this place. What is this place?'

'Henry's studio. You know that. He painted here. He sanded the floors and built a new kitchen, put in these shelves. It's the old caretaker's residence. His friends came on Friday nights. Henry cooked for them. He did a stew and sometimes a biryani. Even paella for birthday parties. He was a good cook like you, Mumma. There was dancing out on the roof when it was warm. In summer.'

'I get that, but what is all this?' Rita flung her arms wildly in all directions and started howling like an animal until Nin grabbed her and held her hard. Arms around Rita like a steel belt.

In a fog of stale bourbon, Audrey had gone to the studio the day after Henry's death and removed evidence. Loose photos, glittering costumes, bags of weed, a little cocaine, and some recent sketches and paintings of Angus, Henry's last muse. There were still plenty of traces. She'd forgotten to clean the mirror of telltale lipstick, take the books with margin notes, the magazines, the polaroids. There she was, caught mid-swirl with beautiful boys wearing booty shorts, and, in another photo, grinning from behind Henry, who was holding Angus in his arms. Audrey had also taken Henry's Le Creuset cooking pots with her that day. Her heroic sorting, lifting, carrying up and down in the shuddering lift, ferrying things to the car, fuelled by shock. The pots seemed both meaningful and useful. She looked around for a letter or note about Henry's intention to end his life and why he had decided to do so, but she didn't find one. She had the locks changed the next day. She had no idea how many of Henry's friends had a key.

Long before she saw the polaroids, Rita had banned Angus from the funeral that was held in the school chapel with a guard of honour formed by teenaged cadets in full military regalia on a steamy Sydney afternoon, who had been instructed in their part by the school. Eustace was nobbled too from speaking at his son's funeral. Everything had to be correct. There was no room for mess or surprises that might befall them, such as Eustace in tears. He who loved his son. Rita had never felt fully part of the school. They were not a paying family. No other families lived where they lived. She was apologetic in demeanour whenever she walked through the towering heraldic gates. Still, Rita had felt it was proper to go to the school when Henry died. To do the right thing and possibly be welcomed and recognised as the mother of the brilliant Henry Mendes. Audrey wanted to protect Rita from further hurt but was unable to thwart her mother's grand plan.

She had watched Rita offer herself up in the past. Preparing the choir breakfast on performance-for-parents day according to a flow chart of six steps that was handed

The Little Clothes

to her by the outgoing choir mother, who turned up at the breakfast to exasperatedly smooth the tablecloth, check on Rita's use of the urn, and to corner the choir master. Rita had come home fizzing with indignation that day. Her story, told several times with different fidgety details, went on and on from dinner till bedtime.

The whole family had run an empanada and salsa store at the school fete, next to the always popular sausage sizzle staffed by the alpha fathers, all hollering and jocular. Dads wearing their jokey barbecue aprons over lycra left on from the morning ride, serving sausages and onions onto rolls that had been ordered and prepared by the mothers. Each father hooting louder: 'There you go, sweetheart. Help yourself to sauce. And what can I get for you, little lady?'

A dab hand with the Singer, Rita had sewn costumes for *Guys and Dolls* the year Henry was cast as Nathan Detroit. Her exasperation at the sewing machine each evening for weeks disturbing the household. For seven years Rita had scraped out and cleaned the lockers of stickers and chewing gum and unidentifiable mouldy mounds, ready for next year's incoming boys with all their hopes and expectations. Audrey and Maggie had gone with her at the beginning of the holidays and carried the cleaning supplies in a bucket in exchange for an afternoon at the bowling alley. Rita joined the P&C committee, participated in the school's fundraising for Black Dog and Wayside Chapel. Still, she couldn't cut through and she didn't know why. There was something just out of reach that she didn't understand until later. It eventually came to her that she was in a competition when she overheard a conversation one Saturday at the school tennis courts. 'I'm surprised she can afford to send him here when you see how she's dressed.' 'Scholarship, darling.' 'Oh, I didn't know.' Henry was easily winning all the tennis trophies back then. Rita worried for weeks afterwards. What was wrong with how she had dressed to sit on the edge of the school tennis courts on Saturday morning? 'I had my new navy tracksuit on!' she said to Nin, indignant and querulous over the Sunday lunch. 'You know my tracksuit, Ninnie. You were with me when I bought it. It's lovely. Plus my sneakers with the silver trim.'

No one asked Audrey to speak at the funeral. And she did not speak up that she'd like to. The chaplain, who never met Henry, spoke. A teacher who had briefly taught her brother stuck to a script about school prizes, running races, tennis wins, teams, politeness and academic results. It was as if grown-up Henry had fallen off the face of the earth. Which he had. The school jazz choir sang 'Hallelujah' in dubious harmonies, making Audrey and Maggie turn abruptly from each other to avoid hysteria that might not be contained, when the lines of laughing and crying would surely be blurred. Henry had founded the jazz choir with a devoted music teacher. It was a refuge twice a week at lunchtime. It had been agreed at the school that the less said about suicide the better. They didn't want to influence others. Didn't want to start a contagion or sully the school's reputation and frighten the paying customers. The suggestion that they rename the jazz choir the Henry Mendes Choir was swiftly blocked.

So Henry had passed. He'd been lost. His death was sudden. He was gone. A much-loved son, not only of his family, but also of the school.

At the wake, the tea and cakes were brought and served by the school-committee women to hungry boys who hadn't known Henry. Rita was attended to in the corner of the

The Little Clothes

room by a flurry of mothers who later delivered Pyrex dishes and disposable tin trays of lasagne to the front step, despite the distance they had to travel into uncharted territory, for exactly a fortnight after Henry died. Audrey watched her mother become small and brittle and inconsolable. Rita would not allow Eustace to come near her. Ever. If he came to her, or put his arm around her, Audrey knew her mother might not survive.

•

Audrey surveyed Henry's bedroom. There was one framed photo of Henry and Audrey laughing on a play park tractor. Perhaps it was the only photo of herself in the whole house, she thought, when she came across it behind some of Henry's early sketchbooks leaning against the lower shelf, where she foraged for things that Rita might have disregarded. It was only recently that Audrey had been able to walk into Henry's room, which was still an untapped spring of misery. She accidentally cut her finger on the edge of the wire stand at the back of the cheap frame as she grabbed the photo. A shock of stinging pain. She pressed her finger against the laminate bookshelf to stop the flow. Then picked the frame up and cut her finger again. She made a squiggle pattern in blood on the shelf and wrote *Henry* with her index finger. When she got to 'u' in her own name the fluid congealed. She used the hem of her cheesecloth dress to wipe the shelf. Then she took the framed photo and walked calmly downstairs to put it in her tote bag on top of the empanadas.

'Audrey, what have you got there? And where have you been? Nin left twenty minutes ago. We called out.'

'Just an old book from my bedroom.'

'Oh. My sewing room. You should take anything else you want soon. All those books can go. You have too many books. Who needs to keep all those books when you've already read them? They're dust catchers. I need the space. You must take some empanadas too. You don't eat properly. What's that? Blood on your dress. How did that happen? You need to soak it before washing. Or throw it out. It doesn't flatter. Maybe give it to Maggie. And what on earth are you doing with your hair these days? I can book you an appointment with Renee.'

'You never spoke like that to Henry when he grew dreadlocks.'

'He was young. That was a stage. Now you're almost forty you can't have stages. Especially not with your hair. Pick a style and stick with it. Pick and stick.'

'Mumma, I'm only thirty-eight. And I have a hairdresser.'

'Well, go and see them. Where's that blood coming from? Are you hurt?'

'It's just a paper cut from work. Keeps opening up. I noticed a couple of Henry's sketchbooks up there in his room. I'd like to have the one with the drawings of Scott and me. Henry must have been about eleven, twelve, when he did them. He was already so good.'

'He was a genius.'

'He wasn't a genius, Mumma. Just precociously gifted and already on his way in the art world. God, I miss him.'

'He would have given that all away eventually. He had so much more potential. Anyway, you really shouldn't be up there poking around. Of course, you'd like to have the sketchbook. But I already gave you a painting.'

'I gave it to Angus. I thought he should have something.'

The Little Clothes

'Angus, Angus, Angus. Well, you shouldn't have given it to him. Now you don't have one.'

'I do have a few, Mumma. Henry gave me some and I took two from his studio when I went to lock it up, the day after... he... you know. After he did it. It's the sketchbook that is more meaningful to me. I think Henry would have liked me to have it. I think it would be right to frame a page for Scottie.'

'Do you, now? What makes you think that? Scott didn't even bother coming to the funeral.'

'That's not true. It wasn't that he couldn't be bothered. It was that he couldn't. He was too sad. Henry was his best friend.'

'Henry was everyone's best friend according to you. Well, he was my son. My flesh and blood. There are some things in life you have to do even if you don't want to. In any case we've barely seen Scott since Henry died. Just that awkward afternoon at Nin's, and Christmases. We haven't even met whatshername yet. Sierra?'

'Sienna.'

'He'll probably be on to the next one before we clap eyes on Sierra.'

'Sienna. He came to Dug Out for the real wake.'

'Stop it, Audrey! Why do you keep on about the real wake? The *real* wake? Really, Audrey. I'm tired of hearing about the real wake. Why is that real and the family's wasn't? The school honouring your brother and his contribution there, when the so-called *real* wake was probably just a bunch of misfits drinking in a dingy bar. I'm right, aren't I? But you can't bear it. He went to the private school and you didn't. Well, he earned it. That's why he went. We couldn't afford it for either of you. You were still given every opportunity.'

'That's not it at all. Henry was not that person. The boy you wanted him to be. And you know it. And I took my opportunities, Mumma, and I appreciate what I was given. And I have never resented Henry. Except for leaving me. That I can't forgive!' Audrey was surprised by her sudden tears and trickle of snot. 'Look, Henry left his stuff to me and I know you took a lot of things from his apartment, which I completely accept and understand, but I'd love to have the sketchbook.'

'I'll think about it. I can't believe you speak this way to me, Audrey. It hurts. Don't you think I've lost enough already?'

Rita put six empanadas into a plastic container and handed them to her daughter with an air of resignation as she ushered Audrey towards the front door and onto the PebbleCrete driveway. She'd made it clear over the years that Audrey Hepburn was her inspiration when she named her daughter. Rita and Nin were spatchcocks, with their mutual nerves and angles. Audrey was more like Eustace. Fleshy and plain. Sturdy and kind.

'Hang on, I'll be back, Mumma.'

'Audrey! Where are you going now? Your father's waiting to say goodbye. It's almost five o'clock, for goodness' sake!'

'It's fine, Rita. She'll come. There's no hurry.'

'Audrey! Audrey! Where have you gone? She was just here. Honestly, that girl. All her sneaking around. We're waiting for you! Your father's waiting.'

'Just left my cardigan and some books upstairs, Mumma. Thanks for lunch. I love you both. I'll call.'

•

The Little Clothes

On her way home, Audrey realised she needed to stop for petrol. Her favourite and least favourite day of the month was over, and she felt giddily free of obligation. She pulled in behind another car at the nearest petrol station and filled the tank. By the time she turned towards the shop to pay, the car in front of her had gone and a short queue had formed behind her.

'Hey love. Can't you see there's a queue here? Can you pull in over there while you pay? Or are you gonna block the pumps for the rest of us?'

'Talk about selfish! What a bitch.' Another one joined in through his window. Audrey saw a woman in the passenger seat and the worried faces of little children peering from the back.

'What?' Audrey looked around to check who they were talking to. She was shocked to confirm they were talking to her. 'Sure, sorry. I'll move right now.'

'Wow. Thanks a lot, sweetheart!'

Audrey pulled up near the shop as directed. The shop for two-day-old traveller pies, soft drinks, three-for-one chocolate bars, crusting egg and lettuce sandwiches, lotto tickets, gift cards and *Woman's Day*.

Her head pulsed. She was shaken. Strangers had verbally abused her for no reason. They had called her a bitch. She couldn't summon the nerve to get out of the car. So Audrey sat and waited and wondered what to do. In police dramas the detectives always looked for CCTV footage at the service station to chart the trajectory of a crime spree. But did it exist? Were there cameras recording every numberplate that came and went? Would they have captured what had happened? And would they catch her if she drove off now? She remembered working on a case where the onus was on the petrol station owner to provide a USB with the footage of a non-paying customer to the police and no action had ever been taken. She couldn't bring herself to go inside the shop. She'd risk it, she decided, and drove away without paying, fantasising that the idiot who yelled at her would have to pay for her petrol and his own. She looked into her rear-view mirror, but no one was following and soon she was back in her house on the couch. The phone call or knock on the door would come. She was sure.

It didn't.

Slowly Audrey settled and turned the pages of Henry's sketchbook.

It was just as it had been when Henry sat on the bank of the creek, drawing with charcoal while Scott and Audrey, shin-deep in water, caught tadpoles and frogs in Rita's jars on summer afternoons. For a moment, Henry was still there.

Chapter 3

After Henry died, Audrey took up the reins for her bewildered parents and put her own grief on hold. Eustace was granted extended sick leave and eventually permanent retirement with a reasonable tranche of money given on negotiated compassionate grounds after forty years of employment in the canning factory. It was plenty, he said, when combined with his superannuation, to fund the simple way in which he and Rita lived and planned to keep living. They paid the remaining mortgage on their house, took a cruise, booked by Audrey, to South America to visit the sisters and cousins, then flew home, and set about their new daily routine, with Rita in the house and Eustace in the garden. They sat together in the house for meals and television. Eustace slept in Audrey's old bedroom at the beginning but soon converted the shed in the backyard to accommodate his needs. Rita made no comment so he knew she was agreeable, but the new arrangements troubled Audrey. Her family seemed to have disintegrated.

The shed suited Eustace. He was able to rise from his single bed, without disturbing his easily startled wife, to brew the first muddy coffee of the morning on the gas ring next to the red vice clamp on a bench he'd assembled years ago from discarded railway sleepers. He lit his first cigarillo of the day and often thought about his childhood and why he had come to Australia and whether it had worked out. He had shared these thoughts and more with Audrey. Henry's death had unravelled father and daughter so completely, yet they came to know each other differently and better through grief. Slowly, in listening and small gestures, each attended to the other's wound.

Sometimes Eustace woke thinking he was in Isla Negra with his parents and sisters. Still close to his dream, he thought they were all still there. The girls, his mother and father, in the stone house with the enveloping timber verandah. It was a mild jolt when he knew his circumstance. There had been decades of toil and displacement, longing and duty. The loss of landscape. The pain of regret. What might have been? The joy of his children. Then sorrow, and the tedium of late middle age. He had come this far, he had told his daughter, so he would keep on going.

On warm mornings, from his step, Eustace watched the sun rise and touch the tips of the avocado tree. Audrey sometimes saw him there when she stayed the night to keep her parents company. Eustace had long ago made a wire hoop on the end of a long stick to hook the avocados down from June to November. Some were used in a rotation of dishes known to Rita. Others were given to the neighbours and to Audrey, who all followed Rita's advice and handwritten recipes. Tuna slices in avocado halves with capers and creamy dressing; avocado and papaya ceviche; avocado salsa in lettuce cups; pickled avocado with marinated mandarin slices; moist avocado chocolate cake, and so on. Eustace often ate half avocados splashed with Paul Newman's vinaigrette, which he kept in a bar fridge with his beer and heart medications. He was able to shower outdoors next to the shed, comfortably shielded by the garden. Eustace washed his own sheets and clothes, which Rita later retrieved from the washing machine to hang on the Hills Hoist before folding and placing them on the front step of the shed for her husband to put on the Ikea shelves that served as his wardrobe. Rita never went into the shed. Not so much to respect her husband's privacy, but because that was where Henry had hanged himself. The rhythm of the days seemed to suit them both and was only interrupted by their monthly Sunday lunch with Audrey, Nin and Gary; occasional visits from neighbours; shopping; medical appointments – colonoscopies, mammograms, bone density scans and the like; and their annual Open Garden showing, where Nin and Audrey sold tickets and Rita and Audrey served the biscuits and tea. Together, Eustace and Rita skirted each other.

•

Audrey spoke to Angus almost every day for a year after Henry died. His neediness gave her a little taste of the power she had never had in a relationship. She was the sister of Henry. He was gone and she assumed the mantle. She was in charge. The gatekeeper of the stories. With Angus she planned in meticulous detail a fitting wake at Dug Out. She the approver, he the chorus of suggestions. After the wake Audrey bestowed on Angus the photos and drawings she'd retrieved from the studio. The evidence. Then they talked several times a week about the shared and urgent question of why. In that pursuit she was able to be especially omnipotent, drawing on a life of knowledge and knowing. She knew many things that Angus didn't. She became the authority on Henry and his death. Later, when they awkwardly discussed the inheritance of Henry's things and those he'd apparently promised Angus, including savings, she had the upper hand. She listened selflessly to Angus in his petulant grief, then listened some more and gave unsought advice about counsellors and getting out and about again. Meeting someone new. And finally, when the embrace with her dead brother's lover became cloying and tiresome, and when they began to quarrel, she gave Angus some of her own money to use as a bond on a rental apartment, a box of paperbacks with Henry's observations in the margins, a diary of Henry's from his time with Angus, and an erotic painting that Rita had easily discarded.

Chapter 4

In the office on Monday morning there was a fuss. Not the usual Monday-morning loathing or sharing of weekend stories and photos; more an urgent atmosphere, an anticipation, as if there was going to be another announcement of a merger or takeover that might happily keep them all from their obligations for now. Audrey could see her colleagues speaking animatedly to each other in unexpected groupings. She put her sensible salad – prepared for the first day of her brand-new disciplined self-care regimen – into the fridge in the kitchenette near her desk and settled in to work on *Barden v Coulter*. She was on team Coulter. Always the defender.

'Audrey!'

Heidi, now immediately recognisable back in the office and her navy suit, towered over Audrey's partitioned workspace.

'Heidi! How are you? Great party on Saturday.'

'I know, right? Erin and Alec are so much fun. Everyone told me they give the best parties. They were right! It went pretty late. Got a bit wild. We started bopping to this band called Fleetwood Mac. Alec ordered pizza for everyone. Carter threw up and that made Sue throw up. Erin has those tiny pop-up plugs in the bathroom sinks and there was a bit of a problem because they couldn't wash it all down. What a pity you left so early.'

'I had something else to go to, something else to do and then something all day yesterday with my family, so… glad I missed the vomiting bit though. Was Carter okay?'

'Yes. He was put to bed. They sent Sue home in an Uber. By the way, you also missed the real drama.'

'There was more? Heidi, I really have to get to work. Maybe later.'

'Well, this'll only take a minute. While we were eating the pizza, we decided Erin should open her pressies. And it turned out that Hanna's present… you know Hanna, right?'

'Yes, Heidi, I know who Hanna is.'

'Well, her present was missing. And it was Tiffany!'

'Tiffany from paralegal?' Audrey was leafing through a document on her desk.

'No! Oh god you are funny, Audrey. Not Tiffany the person, Tiffany the brand!'

'Okay. So sorry… sorry, Heidi. What are you telling me?'

'That the present Hanna gave to Erin was stolen.'

'Sorry?'

'It was completely gone. Disappeared. And it was Tiffany.'

'Are you sure? There was a lot of activity in that house. It might have fallen down under the weight of the other gifts. Maybe Carter flushed it down the toilet.'

'No! We all checked everywhere a thousand times. I feel terrible because Nadine put me at front of house.'

'Oh god, Heidi, don't let Nadine do that to you. You weren't *front of house*, you were a guest at a party in a private home.'

'Do you mean that? I feel terrible. Hanna is so upset.'

'I'm really sorry that happened to you, Heidi. Nadine

The Little Clothes

can be awful. Careless with other people's feelings. I'm sure it will turn up. Everyone was a little bit crazy one way or another at that party. I mean Fleetwood Mac, really?'

'So you know them?'

'Yes, I know Fleetwood Mac. Anyway, I have to get on with this stuff that's been dumped on my desk. Apparently I'm due in court this afternoon. I have a load to get through before then.'

'Sure. Sorry. I'm sorry to bother you, Aud. Don't you want to know what the present was?'

'No. Probably something silly. Babies just need food and love. Not Tiffany. Any fool can keep a baby alive. Teenagers and adults are the real challenge.'

'Okay. All right. Are you okay? You say some weird things, Aud. Anyway, it was a comb. A little silver comb. How cute is that?'

'Very cute.'

'The terrible part is that Hanna described the comb when it went missing and how it had a pink tassel. Pink! It was supposed to be a secret and then everyone knew and Erin was crying. It was a bit of a mess. Erin had agreed not to tell anyone the gender of the baby but she must have told Hanna. She'd been planning a gender reveal next weekend. Just a casual barbecue for the family and her close friends. Erin hadn't told Alec the gender. But she'd told Hanna. Alec left. He walked straight out and got in his car. He'd been drinking. Erin was worried about him. Nadine says it's hard for Erin. That she's still young and Alec is full on.'

Audrey hated herself for feeling hurt that she hadn't been invited to the gender reveal. She didn't want to go to the endless silly parties arranged by Erin but she did want to be invited.

'Heidi, you have to let me get on with this. Come back any time to talk later if you need to. I should be back by six. And don't get caught up in their drama.'

'I'll be going home by then.'

'Well, any other time. I really have to get started here.'

•

'Audrey!'

'Hanna!'

'How are you?' Hanna peeped around the edge of Audrey's space and then slid in along the return and half sat on the corner join.

'I'm well. How are you?'

'A bit upset, to be honest. You weren't there later on Saturday night at Erin's, but I think I kind of accidentally started this fight thing between Alec and Erin. It was so stupid. I didn't think. I tried to call Erin all day yesterday. She didn't pick up or return my calls.'

'Hanna, I've got to get going here. Sorry. I'm in court this afternoon and I have sooo much to do. Try not to get caught up in their drama.'

'Can we get a drink later?'

'I don't know what time I'll be back or what I might need to do after court.'

'Aud, I really need you. I was wondering if you could call Erin for me? She totes adores you.'

'I'll text you. Okay?'

'Yeah, okay. What are you in court for? What case?'

'Hanna! You have to let me get on with this. You must have work to do too.'

Audrey turned back to her brief. Her phone rang.

The Little Clothes

'Audrey!'

'Nadine!'

'Have you got a minute to come upstairs and talk?'

'I don't have a minute, as it happens. All of my minutes are being consumed by other people who seem to want to gossip.'

'What are they gossiping about?'

'The accidental gender-reveal.'

'Not funny.'

'A little bit funny. Anyway, I have to get going. I'm due in court soon and I'm not across all the notes from Alec.'

'Well, it's Alec I'm calling about.'

'Nadine, I have to work. Why don't you slum it and come downstairs later if it's that important?'

'He came to my apartment from the party. He just turned up and was sort of crying and he started to grab at me. At my tits, if you must know.'

'Actually, I mustn't know. Please don't tell me.'

'He was ranting about Vivienne. His kids. They don't talk to him. It's so sad. Don't you think it's sad? I really felt for him.'

'Sounds like he felt for you too.'

'You are so inappropriate, Audrey. Everything's a joke. His kids won't talk to him. It's terrible.'

'Nadine. I have to go. Can we do this later?'

'You can be so cold, Audrey.'

'I'm just busy, Nads. I'll call you after court.'

'Okay. But I'm dying here. We just ran that workshop about appropriate behaviour in the office and then Alec's groping me in my own house. He's my boss, for god's sake.'

'I hope you sent him home to Erin in an Uber.'

'Aud, he stayed the night.'

'Nads, I'm going right now. I'm putting my fingers in my ears. Do not give me any more details. Talk later.'

•

'Audrey! It's Alec.'

'Alec, I know it's you.'

'Can you come to my office to prepare for court? I'm worried about this one. I've got the barrister – it's John Bollard, by the way – arriving in twenty to give his initial thoughts. Some perspective.'

'On my way, Alec. By the way, just a thought, one of mine – thoughts, that is – do you think Bollard is the best person to give perspective on this particular case?'

'I'm looking for his legal guidance, Audrey, based on precedent and his expertise, not his gender politics. Have you had coffee?'

'No, I'd love one. Large flat white, two sugars.'

'I meant could you bring coffee. Just ask someone.'

'Isn't Dinah there? Can *she* do it?'

'She's busy.'

'Sure.'

'Regular flat white, no sugar. Dinah will have a latte. Bollard is long black, according to his PA.'

'Daniel.' Audrey peered over the partitions of three workspaces. 'I have to go to Alec's office. Can you get coffee?'

'I have also been summoned. I'll have a regular oat milk latte. No sugar, but a honey sachet would be great.'

'Fuck off, Daniel.'

'Right back at you.'

Audrey joined the coffee queue downstairs.

The Little Clothes

•

'Where have you been, Audrey?' Alec said. 'We've been waiting. You should have asked someone else to get the coffee. Where's Heidi? How many goddamn people do we have to employ around here to get coffee?' Alec appealed to the ceiling with upheld palms. 'John, you know Audrey. She ran the Aziz case.'

Audrey put the cardboard tray of coffee cups on Alec's desk and shook hands.

'No honey, Aud?'

'Sorry, honey, I forgot.'

'Okay, let's get started. Thoughts, Audrey?'

•

'Nads, it's Aud. Just finished. You've probably left. I'm back here in the office. Alec's gone for a drink with Daniel. So if you still want to talk, I'm here. Otherwise, I'll see you tomorrow. I'm going to leave quite soon.'

'Hanna, it's Aud. I'm back from court so if you still want to talk, I'm here. But I'm leaving soon.'

'Heidi, it's Aud, just calling to see how you are now. Hope you're okay.'

Audrey knew no one would listen to her messages so late in the day. They'd only read texts, so she'd done her duty and the messages would be there for them tomorrow. She caught the bus from the ferry wharf up the steep hill. She privately called it the Ape Run when she walked it because her knuckles were so close to the path. She knew she should have walked because she was on a new self-devised program to get some exercise and eat less. *My salad is still in the fridge* at work, she thought with self-disgust. I drank four coffees with full-cream milk today, I ate lunch with Alec and Daniel at Speed and Sloane and ordered the fillet with bearnaise and frites when I could have had the light salad with turmeric tofu dressing. I will begin again tomorrow, and I won't have dinner tonight.

She changed into her Tinker Bell nightie, poured a substantial glass of wine and lay on her couch in time to watch Leigh Sales bayonet Barnaby. She stroked Joni in her lap and fell asleep.

•

The magpies and kookaburras called at birds' first light. Audrey sat up in the fuzzy dark trying to work out where she was. When it became clear, she stepped around tiny mounds of rabbit poo and went into the kitchen to drink some water from the tap, bending the pull-out hose towards her mouth. Joni sat on the far corner of the rush mat eating her night faeces.

'Well, that's lovely,' said Audrey, scooping up the white Rex rabbit, stroking the lengths of Joni's ears before delivering her into the cage in the back garden. The white pebbles rolled under Audrey's bare feet, making her walk in a sharply punctuated pattern of tentative small steps and accidental tiny slips.

As she turned to go back into her house, Audrey saw a bald pate next door. Just the top of a head. The bit of an egg you tap with your teaspoon before scooping a shallow dent for toast soldiers.

'Hello! Hellooo!!!'

She walked to the fence, still in her nightie, and called

out again, catching full sight of her new neighbours through the gaps. First she saw the dog, and then the man. The dog was muscular and thickset. The sort of dog Audrey recoiled from on the street. The sort of dog that dumbfounded owners might defend on the evening news after a mauling. No one had seen the tragedy coming. It was a shock to everyone who knew the dog. A lovely dog who had been so gentle with the grandchildren.

The man was urinating on the lawn, tracksuit pants held up by a wide-legged stance, elastic waistband stretched across his mid-thighs. She watched as he finished and shook it out before she quickly retreated without being heard or seen. A welcome to the neighbourhood would have to wait.

•

The office was calm, and no one had returned her calls from the evening before. Nadine even stepped into the same lift and smiled without teeth. Tight and false. No other acknowledgement of Audrey's presence and no nod to the events or urgent phone calls of the previous day. There was a sticky note from Hanna on Audrey's partition wall. *All well. Drink soon. Hxxx.*

•

In the pub Audrey sat next to Jeff at the end of their usual table. Elspeth was running late, and Tom, at the other end, frequently and determinedly defended her empty chair as other contenders arrived and took up their corners.

'Hello Shay-Lee,' said Audrey, holding her hand out to the child standing at the edge of their table. 'You look very sparkly tonight,' she said, noting the too-tight Snow White costume and silver ballet slippers. 'Are you going to help us with the quiz?'

'No.'

'I wish you would. My name is Audrey.'

'Ordery.'

'Audrey.'

'Ordinry.'

'Do you know what, Shay-Lee? I have a rabbit.'

'What he name?'

'It's a girl actually. Just like you.'

'I not wabbit.'

'No, of course not. I meant a girl like you.'

'You have girl?'

'No, I have a rabbit.'

'What he name?'

'Joni.'

Shay-Lee ran to her father's side on the podium at the front of the room as soon as he announced the start of the quiz. She hugged his leg with one arm and sucked her thumb on the other side as he explained the rules and points and grounds for appeal before introducing the quiz master, Kevin, who ruffled his sheets of yellow paper with authority and a hint of drama. The father spruiked the waffle fries and the special: parmi with chips, a Greek salad and a glass of rosé for only twenty dollars.

Elspeth arrived looking harried and took her place next to Tom. They huddled with their heads together, whispering. Tom put his arm around her and pulled her closer. Audrey saw tears and wished she, too, could cry on Tom's shoulder. That someone sweet would pull her into their body. When the entire team ordered the special and

The Little Clothes

Sean went to buy a round, Elspeth started an unreasonably long discussion with Shay-Lee's mother about the vegan meals before ordering a Caesar salad without the dressing, croutons, bacon, anchovies, parmesan and eggs. Tom laughed apologetically. Sean joined in. 'So a bowl of lettuce then?' Others laughed too. Elspeth rushed from the table to the bathroom. Again, Tom was left defending her chair.

'She's coming back. It's taken.'

'Sorry, Tom, didn't mean to laugh,' said Jeff. 'Sean can be a funny bugger.'

'I'll go and see if she's okay,' Audrey offered.

'No! Audrey, we need you here.'

'Don't you dare go.'

'You're our brains trust.'

'Can you just go in, Aud, see if she's okay? Please.' Tom focused his gaze on Audrey. Large brown wide-set eyes, reminiscent of Jackie Kennedy.

Audrey enjoyed being needed. It allowed her to slide into the group from which she often felt excluded, and then quickly move into busyness to avoid too much contact. She especially enjoyed being needed by Tom. The choice was easy.

'I won't be long. I'll just check.'

'Oh, and number five,' she whispered to the table before she left, enunciating every word almost silently except for tongue and palate clicks, 'is brown snake. And six is Etch A Sketch.'

•

Elspeth was snivelling in an unlocked cubicle. Sitting on top of the closed toilet seat. Head drooped. Her thick brown rope of hair tied in a temporary knot. Tiny black dress revealing red lace between her legs. White Jordans. Marine eyes, streaming mascara. Rosebud lips. Audrey saw for the first time how exquisite she was and thought sadly that she herself would never be beautiful like that. She would never be with Tom.

'Are you okay, Elspeth?'

'I don't fit in. I really like Tom but I'm too young and I don't fit in.'

'Elspeth, you don't need to fit in with us. We're just a bunch of people who barely know each other. Most of us met here at the pub. We see each other once a week for trivia. Honestly, none of us "fit in". By the way, it's great to be young. Don't underestimate it. Don't waste it.'

'But I don't fit in with his TV crowd either. They're all so attractive and confident. So many ex-girlfriends. They all still adore him. They come to his house and take over the kitchen. They call him Tommy and Tomay and Tom-Tom. They tell their stories from the past. One of them showed me where to find extra glasses in his cupboard. They come through the front door and within a minute they're in the kitchen washing up as if I don't. It's like they think they can do it better. And one, who I've seen on TV, I think it was Scarlet, said she was staying, said goodnight, and went to the second bedroom. I sort of followed her. She knew where the spare blankets were. I didn't know where the blankets were. She called me Elise. I'm not in TV. I'm an office assistant. I met Tom in Woolworths at the self-service checkout. He helped me when the technology didn't work and we just got talking. It kind of went from there. I didn't know who he was.'

'Where were the blankets?'

'What?'

The Little Clothes

'Sorry, just wondering where the blankets were?'
'Why?'
'Oh, you know, I don't have spare blankets, but I wonder where people who do have them keep their spare blankets.'
'They were in a wooden chest at the end of the bed in his spare room.'
'Oh okay. Anyway, they're not confident. If they were confident, they wouldn't be always swivelling for attention. They need the constant adulation. The applause. They're narcissists.'
'Do you think so? They seem confident. I suppose you can be both. By the way, Tom really likes you. He says you're smart.'
'Does he? Really? He talked about me? Did he really say that? Look, they're not all narcissists. Tom seems nice.'
'He is. He says you've got a great job and that you know a lot of things. He also really liked a cardigan that you wore last week.'
'Look, I think we should get back out there, don't you? You can eat whatever you like. The seafood pie that used to be on the menu would have been perfect for you.'
'I don't eat fish.'
'Oh, sorry, Elspeth. Sorry. I'm thinking of a pescetarian. Sorry. Vegan, right? Plus, cream in the sauce. That wouldn't have been up your alley. In your wheelhouse, so to speak. God, it was an amazing pie though, with this incredible truffle potato crust and lots of dill. Don't you love dill? I miss that pie. I think about it a lot. I wonder if I could make it. I grow dill and I occasionally buy truffles at the growers' market and there's always truffle oil. I'm pretty sure I could do it.'
'I can't eat dill. I have allergic rhinitis that's triggered by most herbs and spices.'

'Sorry, Elspeth. That must make it very hard to choose from a menu. I'll let you sort yourself out, and I hope you come back to the table. Tom is really worried.'

'He is? He's so sweet.' Elspeth started to cry again.

Audrey looked in the mirror and ran her fingers through her thin hair, Rita's limp hair, trying to fluff it up. She took a lipstick from her trouser pocket and applied a beige gloss.

'See you back out there, hey?'

'You should wear more make-up. Eye make-up. You have a great face and beautiful eyes. You have turquoise eyes.'

'Really? Thanks, Elspeth.'

He likes me, thought Audrey. He's seen me. I have a great face and turquoise eyes.

As she was walking back to the table, Audrey saw a flash of Shay-Lee's yellow skirt around the corner of the restaurant booths. She was worried about the little girl running at knee height among the pub crowd with no one watching her. The father was joshing, chatting to the bar fly and showing off to the woman with crimson dreadlocks and deep dimples. The mother hurried between the kitchen and the tables with laden plates and dirty dishes.

Audrey tried to follow Shay-Lee but was blocked by a spreading crush of young men arriving for the Tuesday special. There wasn't much light. She found the little girl running around the beer garden.

'Shay-Lee!' she called, raising her voice above the din. 'What are you doing?' Several people in the beer garden turned towards the crazy lady.

'You make me sad. Too loud.' Shay-Lee held her hands over her ears and wailed.

The Little Clothes

'Is there a problem here? What's going on?' said the father, walking in behind Audrey.

'Oh, sorry. I'm here for the trivia. I just saw Shay-Lee earlier and then she disappeared. I thought she might have strayed onto the street. Sorry.'

'Oh, it's you. I didn't recognise you. You don't need to worry.'

'Of course not. I'm sorry. She's so sweet.'

'She is. Thanks, love.'

Audrey rejoined the trivia table, where Elspeth was sitting on Tom's knee.

'Audrey, we're not looking good. Where have you been?'

'Sorry, guys. Not feeling great.'

'Irritable bowel? Do you need a change of knickers? I always carry a spare,' said Lorraine. 'Your meal is getting cold, by the way. We've all finished.'

Audrey was practically paralysed with shock that Lorraine thought she might have soiled her underpants. That others had overheard and thought the same.

'Audrey, come on. Pay attention.'

'Okay guys, number 28 is Maddox with two ds and an x, Pax with an x, Zahara with an h in the middle, Shiloh with two hs, one on the end, Vivienne with two ns and an e, not the male spelling, and Knox with an x, in that order. Or you can swap the last two. Twins. I don't think that will matter. Otherwise it must be in order, Marion. In order, for the extra point. Maybe just put an arrow from there to there, and number 33 is *Wild Swans* by Jung Chang. Jung, with a J for James.'

'Ssshhh! Keep it down, Audrey.'

'Not Jung James. Jung Chang. Like Chang's noodles.

Get rid of the James. Cross it out. Quick, cross it out. Here, give it to me.'

'Pens down.'

Back at home with a third-prize voucher for 15 per cent off at the local nail spa, Audrey was happy. Tom thought she was smart! Her heart swelled, then contracted slightly as she wondered if he had heard Lorraine offering her a change of underwear. She brushed the thought aside, took her draped aqua cardigan out of the cupboard and put it on in front of the mirror, swishing and making various faces, wondering which one Tom would find most appealing. None quite captured what she was after.

After showering, she opened the day's purchase, a Burberry raincoat, size 000, and hung it in the spare-room wardrobe on a tiny white wooden coat hanger. A perfect little raincoat. For a rainy day. She had splurged and bought the matching bucket hat with Burberry checks, which she placed in the accessory drawer next to the Tiffany comb. Sated, she shut the soft-closing drawer and elegantly bevelled door, a pattern she'd chosen with care from the brochure and samples left by the interior designer who had come calling with her wares.

Audrey took some lettuce leaves and fresh hay to Joni, walking gingerly on the white pebbles, drawing the attention of the neighbour's dog growling and watchful at the edge of the fence. Unnerved, she dashed inside, lowered the blinds and bolted the door.

·

Wide awake and worried at 2.12 a.m., Audrey rattled with anxiety that she hadn't locked Joni's cage properly when

The Little Clothes

she'd been spooked by the dog. Then she realised she'd been woken by the smell of burning.

Hyper-alert, she put a jumper on over her pyjamas and pushed into slides before sniffing at the air. She couldn't place the acrid smell. Had she left the oven on? No. Oven off. She checked all her rooms, then headed to the back door with a heavy long torch in hand.

'This is a torch and a weapon,' Eustace said, checking the boundaries when Audrey moved in.

'Keep it near your bed so you can grab it in an emergency. And get a deadbolt on this door. Actually, I'll come and put it on myself.' He had done so the next day, also organising and paying for locks on all the windows and the installation of movement-activated lights at the front of the house.

Torch in one hand, phone in the other, Audrey tried to open the electronic deadbolt quietly, but it reverberated in the still of night, making her duck before she slid along the walls of her back verandah and onto the rolling pebbles. Safe on the soft grass, Audrey held her phone so that the light shone into Joni's cage, where the rabbit sat on her hay, alert and twitching. Pink nose, black eyes, one black ear. Audrey checked the cage that Eustace had constructed to find it was properly secured. Relief.

Beyond the fence she could see the flicker of flames, and she smelled what she thought might be burning rubber. She walked sideways like a crab across the grass, a gait that allowed her to bend low. She peeked through the gaps in the palings. There were four men by a drum fire. The dog rumbled, then barked in short bursts, straining on its tether, almost lifting from the ground with the effort.

'Shut up, you fucking mongrel,' growled one man, crushing an empty beer can in his fist, then throwing it against something hard. Audrey sat on the damp grass in the dark and watched, too nervous to move. The dog and Audrey now aligned in their silence. She couldn't tell which man was her new neighbour. 'All middle-aged men have heads like thumbs,' Rita had told her. 'They all look the same.'

'She was a mean cunt.'

'Mate, mean as they come.'

'I don't know how you put up with her. I woulda whacked her.'

'Oh, mate. Trust me, I did. Took all me money. Ran off. Took the kid. Haven't seen the little bloke for over a year. It's criminal. Don't even know where she is. But I'll find her.'

'Is that the best decision?'

'Can't trust women.'

'Nah. They're all trouble, mate. Give it away is my advice.'

'Too much trouble for no return. They want the money and the kids but not the rooting and the cleaning. My ex lived like a pig. Didn't lift a finger. So I gave her the finger.'

'Well, we need to work out a better way of doin' things, fellas.'

Audrey sat still on the cool grass, afraid of agitating the dog and revealing herself to the neighbour and his friends. As it became light, she woke with her head resting on her balled jumper. The fire next door was out and the yard deserted, except for the dog, now muzzled and heavily chained, asleep on a hessian sack.

Chapter 5

At the vet, Audrey held Joni's cage on her lap in the waiting room. When two snapping schnauzers in matching rose-gold puffer jackets were led in, she moved to the quiet space designated for cat owners.

'That's not a cat. This area is for cats,' said the woman already seated in the gated area. Crocheted orange beanie, red artisanal shoes, resin beads like boiled lollies in purple, orange, green and pink, cage on lap.

'Let's not do the crazy-old-lady beads,' Maggie had said to Audrey when they were twenty-something.

'I agree. Let's wear pearls. And let's check each other's facial hair. If we see a free-ranging white whisker on each other's chin, we'll say so and pluck it out. Begone, white whisker!'

'Agreed.'

Audrey turned, smiling, to the woman in the orange beanie.

'You're right. It's a rabbit.'

'As I said, not a cat.'

'What problem could you possibly have? It's a tiny rabbit. Look, she's so sweet. Just as frightened of dogs as your cat is. Probably more frightened. Rabbits are nervous creatures. Her name is Joni.'

'But it's not a cat. Have you read the sign?'

'I'm sure they mean rabbit, cat, guinea pig, mouse, bird with a broken wing, hamster, baby possum or blue-tongue mauled by a cat. Maybe even a ferret. Just not dog.'

'It's also about diseases.'

'Really?'

'Yes. Haven't you heard of myxomatosis?'

'If they meant that it would be on the sign.'

Audrey moved back to the main waiting space in time to see a man who might be her new neighbour coming out of the clinic with his bristling mastiff. The dog was immediately recognisable, with its absurdly studded fluorescent collar.

She flinched and added to her list of nervous creatures who might be permitted in the gated area: *Women who are afraid of angry men*.

'One of these twice a day,' said the vet. 'And apply the cream to the affected area once a day. Do the pill and cream at the same time just to make it easier for you to remember. It could be caused by some sort of pesticide being used near you. In a park or maybe by a neighbour.'

'Yeah, the neighbour. Might be her.'

'Good luck. Come back in a fortnight. Sophie will get you sorted. Another appointment in two weeks, Soph. See you, Maximus.' The vet scrunched the dog's ear.

'Audrey? Joni? Johnny Mendees?'

'Yes. Me. And Joni. Here we are in the main waiting room. Not in the quiet space reserved exclusively for cats,' Audrey quipped to no response.

'Hi, I'm Hayden.'

'Audrey. And Joni. Pleased to meet you.'

'How can I help you, Joni?'

The Little Clothes

'Audrey. Look, she just hasn't been eating. More timid than usual and generally lethargic. Her nose seems dry. Should it be wet?'

Audrey lifted Joni onto the examination table and stroked her more than she needed to, signalling how much she cared. Trying to engage the vet with her tenderness and dedicated pet ownership.

'Has anything changed? Diet? Environment?'

'Well, a small change has been a dog moving in next door. A rather nasty dog.'

'What do you mean, nasty?'

'Aggressive. Territorial. A presence. On the other side of the fence. Sniffing and growling along the boundary.'

'I think this is a gut issue,' said the vet, feeling along Joni's stomach. 'When a rabbit doesn't eat it's usually a bacterial problem in the gut.'

'Couldn't it be more of an emotional issue? Anxiety about the dog?'

'No. I'm pretty sure I know what this is. But we'll take some bloods and swabs and maybe we should keep her here overnight. Do a scan. Just observe her.'

'Really? A scan? Overnight observation? Is that entirely necessary?' Audrey imagined a nurse in a Florence Nightingale cap hovering over Joni's cage with a candle, looking for signs of malady.

'We don't have to. You can try some probiotics first. I can prescribe those, and you can see how you go. We'll give her an antibiotic injection today and then see how she is in a week. There's a prepared rabbit food we stock out the front. We have it made to our own recipe. Maybe lay off the carrots and lettuce or other vegetable matter for the next few days and just use the dry food.'

The vet kept glancing over his shoulder at the phone on his desk, suppressing a smile about what he was being sent.

'So, Soph will look after you. Soph?' Hayden called in the receptionist and they exchanged a look. 'Have this made up for Joni and make another appointment for a week's time. See you then, Joni.'

'Okay, Joni.' Back in the waiting area, Soph took over. 'Here are the probiotics, just use the dropper. Twice a day. It's all there on the label. Just squeeze the end of the dropper and—'

'Thanks. I know how to use a dropper.'

'A lot of people don't. Here's the name of the food Hayden recommends. Do you want to try that? It's over there on the corner shelf.' Audrey obediently grabbed a surprisingly light bag, noting the price. She'll want to be shitting gold ingots after this, Audrey thought, placing the bag, barcode up, on the counter, to help Soph.

'That's $538 altogether. That's the consult, the injection, the probiotics, the food and the ointment. And when is a good time for you on Saturday?'

'Sorry, there's ointment? He didn't mention ointment.'

'Oh, no, my bad. The ointment was a previous thing for someone else. Not for you. So, it's $502 all up. And Saturday? What time suits?'

'Was the ointment for Maximus? He lives next door, so I could drop anything in.'

Soph ignored Audrey's offer and waited with exaggerated false patience.

'The follow-up, right? 10.00 a.m. next Saturday?'

'Great. Too easy. See you then, Joni. We'll send a text.'

'It's Audrey. The name is Audrey.'

The Little Clothes

'Oh, what a cute name for a rabbit. So adorable. See you, Joni. Too easy.'

•

Audrey and Maggie met at Queen Chow on Thursday night. It was close to RPA, where Maggie had things to do later.

'My favourite patient is dying,' she had said to Audrey in the morning. 'I'd like to get back at some point. Just be there for him. There's nothing more I can do. He has no family. I'd like to be with him at the end.'

In the restaurant she handed Audrey a small wrapped box and a card. 'Happy Birthday, Auds. Love you.' They clinked martinis.

'Oh god, Mags, they're beautiful. I love them. I really love them.'

'They suit you. They screamed "Audrey" at me when I saw them. Very flamenco.'

Audrey held the red drops to her ears and wiggled her head. 'Too generous.'

'As if. Anyway, let's have the salt and pepper cauliflower, the steamed dumplings, that hot chicken. I think it's the hot and numbing. Half Peking duck and something green.'

'Perfect.'

'I can't have another one of these, but you can. I really do have to get back in a couple of hours. Maybe sooner,' Maggie said, lifting her pager from the table. 'I just wanted to see you on your birthday. I guess there was a lot of fuss at work?'

'No fuss. Very simple.'

'A cake?'

'No cake.'
'What then?'
'Nothing. But that's okay. It's sort of the way I prefer it.'
'What! Nothing?'
'Nothing.'
'Oh, come on, Aud, that's not okay.'
'It is okay if I say so. I loathe the cake hoopla in the office. Days of discussion about what sort of cake, individual dietary needs, who will pick it up, how to arrange the money from the petty cash, what's the best time for most people, who will clean up the plates after, cheap sparkling in plastic cups that's guzzled as if it's the Kool Aid. Everyone sings the sad birthday song, calls for a speech that is usually "Thank you", and then they grab their slices and fuck off back to their desks. The birthday person is obliged to stay till the end and so usually cleans up. I don't mind at all. Every anniversary is celebrated in our office as if it is the second coming. Last week there was a lunch, wait for this, for the six-month anniversary of when Hanna met Todd on Tinder. Todd Tinder the Terrible. Talk about drawing the short straw or swiping in the wrong direction or whatever it is you do on Tinder. I really don't need office cake. This is more than enough, seeing you.'
'What about your mum and dad? Today, I mean.'
'Nothing.'
'I don't believe it!'
'Look, thirty-nine is not a special birthday. Dad's been a bit unwell. Prostate problem. Aunty Nin called earlier. That was nice. Really, Maggie, I don't love birthdays as much as you do with your amazing family.'
Audrey exalted Maggie's family. In some ways they had informed her life as much as her own family had. Mainly

through the things she didn't have. So many of them, for a start. Eight siblings. The luxury of being able to choose favourites. The mother with a tall bottle of Dinner Ale on her side table every night as she watched the TV news and knitted in all weathers while directing her children to be quiet and scarce before dinner. The father sometimes striding through the house in white BVDs and a singlet. 'Nonie! Have you seen my transistor?' 'Put some clothes on, Mack. We've got company.' Maggie's mother would nod backwards to Audrey, who, behind Nonie's La-Z-Boy, liked to hear she was company for the grown-ups. There was a grandmother, the rarely seen Mrs Spannock, with her built-up shoe and shaftless stair lift in the two-storey granny flat at the end of the garden. Once, when Mrs Spannock was at the dentist, Maggie and Audrey sat on the stair lift together, Maggie on Audrey's lap. They jammed it halfway up. A deaf single daughter living below Mrs Spannock, oblivious to her mother's clomping, reported who had broken the lift. Maggie and Audrey had been grounded and made to apologise to Mrs Spannock. Pocket money was withheld in both households after Nonie spoke to Rita, who was *very* disappointed in her daughter.

Two ping-pong tables side by side beneath tablecloths accommodated them all at breakfast, when poached fruit, racks of toast, homemade preserves, and jaffles of tinned spaghetti and baked beans were devoured. The toaster on the table had a lengthy extension cord snaking from a corner that tripped the surprisingly numerous unwary, even though it had been plugged in for so long the cord was felted. Every stumble was accompanied by a 'Woah!', as if the family was at a rowdy sporting event.

In the evening, roasts, sausages, meatloaf, savoury mince and steak-and-kidney pie were served with potatoes, creamed spinach, carrots and peas in bain-maries, followed by tubs of icecream plonked down with tinned peaches and, sometimes, steamed puddings. Scones and jam and cream were served on Saturday afternoons after mass hair washing in the laundry tubs. The mould was scraped from the homemade preserves and used as a challenge by the father.

'It's penicillin. I'll give two dollars to the first one who eats it.'

There were more ping-pong tables in the triple garage where the siblings battled it out. There was a dartboard on the garage wall, quoits in the hall, croquet on the lawn, frisbees, hula hoops, yoyos and a putting machine that ricocheted every accurate ball back to the skilful player. There was a game of Scrabble on offer almost every night and chess for the asking. After school the brothers brawled on the grass, where Mack mowed a cricket pitch in summer. A piano was always being played. Or a trumpet. Recorders and cicadas competed in the bushy cul-de-sac enclave with duelling Victa mowers, and later ride-ons, as neighbours sought dominance in the common grassy areas and on the verges. Mr Royalston once toppled his ride-on and an ambulance was called, causing a flurry of excitement on a Sunday morning. There were bicycles hanging from the garage roof and an often-used rowing machine, totem tennis, a boxing bag, buckle-on rollerskates and a machine with a belt that Nonie would put around her bottom to jiggle away her arse with the flick of a switch while she read magazines and smoked Alpines. At dinner there were quiz questions. After dinner the losers washed and dried while

The Little Clothes

the winners gloated and snapped each other with wet tea towels.

'They can't be still,' Maggie said now. 'We never talked to each other. They just keep moving so they don't have to actually look at themselves or their children, or converse with each other. It's still like that today when my sisters and brothers bring my nieces and nephews for Sunday lunch. I've told you before that Mack used to plant a tree up the driveway for every new grandchild, with plaques engraved with their names and birthdates. Another fucking competition. I have been so close to driving into all the trees and flattening them. I might still do it. By the way, Frances named her twins Salvador and Matisse.'

'She did not. Why?'

'Maybe because Angela named her new baby Cosette Impala.'

'She did not!'

Maggie nodded with an expression of *You heard it here first*.

'Oh god, Maggie. It seemed Kennedy-esque to me. It was so fantastic because in my house our meals were dull. Rita talked while we all listened. Everything that happened to her during the day was an anecdote. I loved being with your family. All butting in. To me it was freeing to be among so many. I felt comfortably unseen while I watched the show. The furthest Rita ever went from our home was to Henry's school and your mother went overseas for so long on her own.'

'It was just eight months, when Auntie Jean was dying. You do know there are different versions of childhood unhappiness? It's a matter of who you are and where you land. Look, Nonie and Mack were fine. It's just that everything involved one-upmanship. Skiing trips were a nightmare. I hated the lodge all full of bravado and the hauling of endless equipment and sleeping in the bunk room with everyone. We had to hear how my parents helped build it every time we went there. You could see other guests sliding away at breakfast or ducking out of the games room when we arrived en masse. I didn't have what you have with your father. I loved having dinner at yours when your father spoke quietly and lovingly about his garden or about his childhood, while Rita was in the kitchen. I had a major crush on Henry. But who didn't? In my home there were no close relationships. Just noise and avoidance activity. It was a hive. We were too busy riding up mountains or kayaking to talk to each other, unless we wanted something passed at the table. My father was a bully, always barking orders and challenging all of us to beat him at things. Just last week, when I visited him in the nursing home, he said to me, "Don't think, Margaret. Empty your mind. Just say the name of your favourite book. Right now. Just say it straight up. Your favourite book. No thinking. First one that comes into your head." Maggie perfectly mimicked Mack.

'My mother finds a thousand excuses not to visit him anymore. For the first time in forty years she has some peace. She once told me, after we'd had a few drinks, that every time she got into bed she could feel his erect penis in the small of her back. Prodding her.'

'Oh my god. TMI.'

Audrey and Maggie had first met in the school library. Deep in the shelves, where they hid at lunchtime.

'Do you read?' Maggie had asked, looking straight at Audrey through a gap.

The Little Clothes

'Yes,' said Audrey.

'So do I.'

'Have you read *Rebecca*?'

'Yes.'

'How good is it?'

'And *To Kill a Mockingbird*?'

'Yes. Scout and Calpurnia.'

'Yes, and Raymond Chandler?'

'Who's that?'

'An old crime writer. I read them all sitting upside down on a big chair in a holiday house that was loaned to us by a friend of my uncle who reviewed crime novels. They had them on the shelf. I didn't go to the beach in the whole two weeks.'

'That's funny. I wouldn't have been allowed.'

'Nobody noticed. The others were all playing beach cricket. No one wanted me on their team. It's easy in my family.'

'*Little Women*?'

'Yes! Who do you like best? Jo or Meg?'

'Amy,' said Audrey.

'I love Jo. I want to be Jo.'

'A writer?'

'No, Jo. I just want to be Jo. Out in the world.'

The girls reached their hands through the shelf and touched palms. Less high five and more I see you. Each found by the other.

Later in the high-school halls there were comments.

'Fat lezzos.'

'Can you walk behind each other so we can get past?'

After Rita had been on canteen: 'Did your mother fuck someone fat?'

'I don't think I could go there,' said the boys at the bus stop. 'Might get suffocated.'

Everything seemed bearable because of their friendship. Not only bearable, but joyous.

'So, Aud, not seeing Alec again I hope?'

'God, no. I'm not a complete fool. He doesn't see me at all. I think the wedding invite was a pity invite from Erin.'

'I can't get over that wedding and what it cost you.'

'Well, if you ever want to see it close up, including drone coverage, there's still a website dedicated to it online.'

'Thanks. I'll keep that in mind when I'm scrolling through music biopics and Liane Moriarty soaps on Netflix.'

'There was a second baby shower the other day.'

'Marriage didn't stop him before. I still can't believe you went to the wedding.'

'Hah! I have to work with him. I get along with him in a blokey kind of way. You're right, marriage won't stop him. Age might stop him, stops everyone in the end. Plus another two kids and the financial settlement with Vivienne. I've heard she stood her ground. Someone even said *gouged*. I don't see it like that. All those years at home with the children. She's a lawyer too. Can you imagine a worse scenario? The divorce of two bitter lawyers. Did I tell you he's dyeing his hair?'

'No way. That's sad.'

'Plus, he describes himself on his LinkedIn profile as *internationally revered*.'

'No.'

'Yes.'

'Even if you were, you wouldn't say so. If you were internationally revered everyone would already know.'

'He also claims a whole lot of other people's achievements,

The Little Clothes

including some of mine. But I'm not seeing anyone, and definitely not Alec. As you know, he just stopped dropping round after he hooked up with Erin. We never talked about it. It's like it didn't happen between us. I'm happy for Erin. She's actually really sweet and smart. I quite like a guy who comes to trivia night. I've told you about him. But not anyone else, really. You?'

'Oh, the TV guy. He sounds attractive, but TV?'

'I know. You don't want to be with someone professionally trained in the art of deception. Anyway, he seems to be with a semi-permanent girlfriend. Apparently he liked my cardigan, but that might have been ruined by an audible offer of a change of underpants.'

'What?!'

'You had to be there. But I do like him. He's incredibly handsome and sweet. He saves a chair at trivia for his girlfriend, although she could almost be his daughter.'

'But not a chair for you, Aud?'

'No. Not for me.'

Tom's modestly famous years and telegenic good looks were largely behind him. Best known as an awarded long-running lifestyle show presenter, he had recently appeared in an ad or two, and done a stint on *Kitchen Capers* where he stirred and smiled. Now a possible quiz show was beckoning. His agent presented him as a future Sam Neill, although not many others had joined those dots.

'So, really no one on your horizon either? A handsome nurse? A doctor? Tinder?'

'I can't be bothered. I don't have the time to do the sorting. Online or in person. The result is always such a disappointment. I've been out twice with Colin, though, since I got back.'

'The bagpiper? I love men in kilts.'

'Yep. Same. He's a lovely person. Mostly does funerals now. Remember that poor kid at Henry's funeral trying to pipe us into the wake?'

'Oh my god, that was gutting. "The Skye Boat Song" in short wheezy bursts. That day… oh my god. What a contrast with the real wake. Anyway – Colin. Tell me about Colin.'

'You've met Colin. What you see is what you get. A sweet chubby man who brews beer, plays the bagpipes and cooks curries. Watches rugby. You get the picture.'

'Looks good from where I'm sitting.'

'I also have my work, my fecund sisters and all their offspring, my friends.' Maggie smiled at Audrey. 'I'm moving back into my house at the end of the month when the lease expires. There'll be maintenance to do. As you know, it's been a student house while I was away. I've almost paid the mortgage. Don't want to over-complicate things.'

'I get it.'

'So, how's chez Audrey? Any renovations planned? Travel plans?'

'Oh, that's right, I've got a new neighbour. I knew I had something to tell you.'

'Go on.'

'Well, he has a muscle dog.'

'A muscle dog? What do you mean?'

'One of those thickset menacing dogs that's been bred to fight and attack.'

'Aud, really? In your neighbourhood? Are you sure?'

'It's chained up at night to a verandah post. I can see it through the gaps in the fence. There's a speedball and a punching bag too. Hanging down from the edge of the verandah beam. My neighbour pisses on his lawn. Like the dog.'

'Well, that doesn't sound great. How do you know about speedballs?'

'The gym. Anyway, a couple of nights ago he had some friends over and they were burning stuff in a drum and drinking beer at 3 a.m. I went out there to check on Joni. It frightened me. How they spoke about women. Well, I think the friends, mainly. But I'm scared of him and of the company he keeps. And I'm terrified of the dog. Except when it's asleep.'

'Audrey, don't give it too much thought. I can see it's in your head. Churning you.'

'Maggie, he lives next door!'

'Look, maybe keep to your side and he'll keep to his. Does he own the house?'

'Don't think so. I think it's a rental.'

'Okay. You could talk to the agent.'

'I will if I have to. I love this cauliflower.'

'Same.'

'I wish I could make it.'

'You could figure it out.'

The friends said goodbye on the footpath.

'Bye, Amy. Love you, Amy.'

'Bye, Jo. Thanks again. For the earrings and everything. I'll call.'

'Happy birthday again. Let sleeping dogs lie, Audrey.'

'I will. Hope your patient goes well. Good luck tonight.'

'I think he'll be gone by the morning.'

'I wish I could say the same about my neighbour.'

'Audrey!'

'I know, I know.'

Deborah Callaghan

•

Audrey could feel the thumping music before she got out of the Uber. She could see the strobing lights on the sky and had to walk around the middle-aged shaved-headed male revellers manspreading from next door to her front gate. She momentarily tried to think of a collective noun for them. A skull? A thicket?

'Excuse me. I just need to get in there.'

'Excuse me. This is my house.'

'Can you please let me through?'

'Can you fucking move, or I'll call the police.'

'Ooooohhh. We're in trouble. Come on, sweetheart. Have a drink. Not very friendly. Specially since it's a house-warming and you're a neighbour.'

'Sure. Sorry. I just have to get through my gate. I'm helping in a medical emergency here. Cancer. The medics are following.'

Everyone stepped aside.

'Sorry, love.'

At her front door Audrey's hands were trembling so violently she couldn't get the key into the lock; and as soon as she did, with a calm and will dredged from her gut, she slammed the door shut, bolted it, and kicked off her shoes to run down the hall to the back of her house, grabbing the weapon-torch on her way through to unlock the back door. She stumbled across the pebbles and lurched at the rabbit cage, where Joni sat in her usual place on the hay eating the prescribed food that was now indiscernible, at a glance, from her droppings. Her neighbour's yard was pounding and heaving. The flames from the drum fire licked the ember-flecked sky. Orange on ink. A strobe light cut the party people

The Little Clothes

into slow motion. Men were techno dancing, holding their hands flat and half sliding them above their heads to Biggie. Two partially naked women wrestled in mud in a toddler pool in the middle of the lawn. The dog was tethered.

Audrey opened the cage and grabbed Joni, held her to her chest, their hearts beating fast against each other's, and took her inside. She locked every door and window, then curled up on her couch with the torch and tried to fall asleep to the thump, thump, thump, doof, doof, doof. Two or three cans and a bottle found their mark on her roof. Audrey repeated silently to the beat, *Let sleeping dogs lie, let sleeping dogs lie, let sleeping dogs lie.*

•

'Audrey! You look terrible. You look like you've been up all night. You okay?'

'Thanks, Nadine, that's put a spring in my step. I'm fine. What's happening?'

'Can we have lunch today? My shout.'

'Are you going to sack me?'

'What? God, no.'

'Well, what then?'

'Lunch. You and me.'

'I can't. Alec has blocked out my day, actually my fortnight, to work on this assault case.'

'He won't mind.'

'I think he might.'

'He won't.'

'Why are you so sure?'

'He's having lunch with Bollard.'

'How do you know?'

'He told me. By the way, he's not living at home right now.'

'What? Why?'

'You'll have to come to lunch to find out.'

'Nads, I don't really care why. That was just idle curiosity. I've got work to do. I've got my own stuff to deal with.'

'Well, aren't we all high and mighty. By the way, there's a stain on your collar.'

'Really, Nads?'

'Okay, a drink then. Six.'

'Okay, six. Come and get me.'

'Why don't you come up and get me?'

'Because then we'd have to come back down. I'll meet you in the foyer at six.'

•

At her desk, Audrey jabbed a number into her phone. 'Nads, forgot to ask just now if I can use one of the small meeting rooms this morning? I have to make some sensitive phone calls. For work of course.'

Audrey could hear Nadine opening the green diary.

'The Moisen Room is available. That's Small Meeting Room 3.'

Audrey snorted.

'What are you laughing about? You can be so juvenile, Audrey. Moisen was one of the founding partners.'

'I know. What did he do to have Small Meeting Room 3 named after him?'

'Maybe just be a founding partner with Alec's father? That I can't really tell you, although he does have an amazing house at Palm Beach. I was invited there once in

The Little Clothes

the early days with Alec. Alec's mother still has the family home up there. It's The Wren. A famous house. I remember there was this jacuzzi on Moisen's deck overlooking the ocean and Barrenjoey. They both got a bit handsy with me. Anyway, I didn't name the rooms. I just book them. Marketing named them and had them rebranded. So take it up with someone else.'

'Sorry, Nads. It's a joke I share with a friend. I know Marketing put a lot of work in.'

'Whatever.'

Audrey hurried to the bathroom to clean her collar, drying it with the hand dryer by leaning down awkwardly and inserting the point into the blast of hot air. She could feel her neck flesh rippling. In the Moisen Room was a newly hung portrait of Bill Moisen, in sepia. A much younger Bill than when Audrey used to see him in the courts and corridors. He was wearing a weathered polo shirt, collar up, standing on a jetty next to a vintage sloop, making Audrey think about Martha's Vineyard.

'Hello. My name is Audrey Mendes. I'm a lawyer. You're my local police station. There are some things happening next door to me that I need to discuss. Or even report.'

'Oh, okay. What's your address? And give me a minute, what was your name again?'

'Audrey Mendes. It's still my name.'

'Okay, what can I help you with?'

'A new neighbour has moved in and he has a menacing muscle dog, and he held a party last night that went very late and loud and there were half-naked women wrestling in mud and quite aggressive men who blocked the path into my house and the music they were playing was explicit lyric-wise and actually quite offensive.'

'Okay Ms Mendes, Mendees, can I call you Audrey?'

'Yes.'

'Were you or your property harmed in any way last night?'

'No. Although some cans and a bottle were thrown onto my roof after I went to bed.'

'That's not good. How many, do you think?'

'At least three cans and a bottle.'

'Are they still there? The cans.'

'And the bottle.'

'Yes. Are they still there?'

'I don't know. I came to work early. I live alone.'

'Perhaps we can see them from the ground?'

'I'm not sure. I didn't look. The footpath was pretty messy this morning with broken glass.'

'Anything else besides the cans, the bottle and glass?'

'Just the terrible noise, the lights, the strippers, the threatening music. The offensive lyrics.'

'Well, we'll come around and have a word with your neighbour. We can't censor his choice of music or entertainment, but we can get it turned down after a certain time. They can't throw things onto your property. They can't block your entry into your house. They have to observe the noise curfew. Did you call the police last night?'

'No. I didn't. I was frightened.'

'If it happens again you should call straight away. Just makes it easier for us to assess the situation if we're there when it's actually happening.'

'In fairness, when I told the men on the footpath I was there for a medical emergency, they let me through.'

'There was a medical emergency?'

The Little Clothes

'No. I made that up, so they would let me through. I needed to get into my house. I felt threatened.'

'Well, we'll still come around once we have a car free. Will you be at home?'

'No. I'm at work.'

'Is your neighbour there?'

'Not with me. Sorry, I don't know. I don't know if he goes out to work. I left in a hurry this morning almost before it was light. I catch the ferry into the city. I feel threatened by him. Look, I don't want him to know it was me who rang. So please don't have a word with him.'

'No, he won't know it was you. So he threatened you?'

'Not in words, but I felt threatened. Will you call me back?'

'Definitely will call you back. I have your details.'

Audrey worried for the rest of the day that she'd blundered. That her neighbour would know it was her. That things might get worse. Perhaps, as Rita would say, she had *gone too far*.

•

'So, Audrey, what have you been doing?' Nadine put an Aperol spritz and a bowl of nuts on the table and handed Audrey a glass of wine.

'Nothing much. How can you drink that stuff? It's like grown-up Fanta. Why is everyone suddenly drinking it?'

'It's delicious. Refreshing. Anyway, I don't think the Italians would agree it's a recent thing. I really need to talk to you, Aud. There's no one else who gets the whole landscape at work. The history, so to speak.'

'The history of old Bill Moisen and his rich private-school friends on their yachts?'

'Audrey, I want to be serious. If you can't be serious, we can finish our drinks now and leave.'

'Nads, I'm happy to listen but I don't want to get drawn into any work drama. I also want to say straight away, before you start, that I am fond of Erin. She has a lot to put up with, you know.'

'Well, that makes things awkward.'

'Sorry, but that's me trying to set a boundary.'

'Alec has been staying between my place and the Sheraton since the baby shower,' Nadine said. Blurted.

'Okay.'

'Do you want me to unpack that for you?'

'Probably not.'

'He's so miserable with Erin. She's too young and now another baby. He explicitly told her, and they agreed, no more children after Carter. She's been so duplicitous.'

'Hang on, sorry, Nads. I must take this. It's the police.'

'Is everything okay?'

'I won't be a minute. Get yourself another drink. I won't be long.'

Audrey moved to the deserted arcade near the bar, a place to pass through rather than linger.

'Okay, I can hear you now.'

'As I said, this is Constable Galen. I wanted to let you know we called on your neighbour and—'

'What's his name?'

'You don't know your neighbour's name?'

'No. He's new. Just moved in. Thus his house-warming party last night.'

'Sorry, I'm not able to divulge personal details. He

The Little Clothes

seemed a bit surprised by our visit and was able to reassure us that the party had ended at midnight. He believed he'd complied with the noise curfew and said he was sorry that anyone was disturbed but he thought the curfew was midnight, not 9 p.m. It's a common mistake. There was no broken glass on the street or bottles or cans on your roof that we could see.'

'You looked at my roof while he was there?'

'I'm just reporting what I have written down here as per your request for follow-up. I was not at the site address.'

'So he knows it was me who made the complaint? Or were there other complaints?'

'No other complaints.'

'Yeah, solidarity!'

'Look, apparently he was apologetic and sorry for any disturbance. He seemed reasonable. He runs a men's group.'

'A men's group. What sort of group?'

'Sorry, I can't say.'

'What about the dog?'

'The dog?'

'Yes, the aggressive dog.'

'Was the dog aggressive towards you?'

'It growled at me from its yard.'

'Ms Mendess, Mendees, Audrey, we cannot do much about a dog that hasn't attacked you.'

'Yet.'

'Or one that growls from the confines of the owner's fenced garden. And we can't enforce against a fully registered, tagged and appropriately restrained dog with no history of aggression. Call the council about any barking issues. But definitely call if you have any further problems.'

'Thanks. How do you know there's no history of aggression?'

'We haven't got anything on record.'

'Any record of the man?'

'We can't disclose that. But I can tell you… let me look here… he runs a group for men who are cut off from their families. Their kids.'

'Should I be worried?'

'Look, I shouldn't say this, but he is known to us.'

Audrey walked back into the bar.

'Is everything okay, Aud?'

'Let's do shots.'

'Thatta girl. I knew you had it in you.' Nadine perused the cocktail menu. 'Cocksucking Cowboy or Alabama Slammer?'

'Just vodka.'

'So, Audrey,' said Nadine, loosening to her disclosure. 'Alec has been at my apartment for the last six nights.'

'What exactly are you telling me and why?'

'As I said, you know the history.'

'History?'

'I mean I can talk to you. We've been in the trenches together a long time. Right? We've both been there through the three mergers.'

'Okay. Yes, we've seen a lot.'

'I know we've had things happen between us before.'

'Nads, don't worry about that. We're all good. I like you.'

'Audrey. I meant Alec and me, together. We've got a history.'

'Okay, and…'

'Okay, well we're kind of together again, temporarily, but I don't want to be.'

The Little Clothes

'What do you mean, *together*?'

'He's been calling in and taking me to dinner. Stayed more than once. We've done this all before, years ago. When he was married to Vivienne.'

'Okay.'

'But I want to get out of it. I've moved on. He's kind of hanging around and he's spreading across my couch watching the sports channel when I get home.'

'He has a key?'

'Yes, Audrey, he has a key. I know. Don't start. He gave me some money towards the apartment and when he did that I gave him a key.'

'Uh-huh. Why did he do that?'

'What, why did he give me money?'

'Yes.'

'He helped with the deposit and didn't want it back. I think at the time he thought it might be a bolthole for him.'

'How did he get away with that with Vivienne?'

'Alec has his own family funds, a fairly steady stream, and ways of hiding them. You do know who his family is, don't you?'

'Yes, of course. So, the problem is…'

'He's sort of moved in and he's asking what's for dinner when I want to rest and eat a bowl of pasta, or a boiled egg, or just a glass of wine and some nuts. I don't want to lose the apartment though.'

'But you own it, don't you? Has he said anything about the apartment? Is his name on anything?'

'No. But I feel sort of obligated.'

'Nads. That is your home that you own. Anyway, why isn't he at his own home with Erin? Why did you accept all that bullshit about his misery over Vivienne and his kids? Why didn't you tell him to go home? You have to fix this.'

'I don't know. He's my boss. I like him. We're old friends. He was so upset. I've been an idiot, haven't I? I was flattered, I suppose. I feel like I owe him. He got me started on my new career path, then helped me get my apartment. Look, I feel like a fool.' Nadine started to cry from the outer corners of her eyes, which she dabbed at with a shredded paper napkin.

Audrey reached across the table and put her hand on top of Nadine's. 'Look, Nads. I've been there with Alec too.'

Nadine looked up, startled. 'What!? Are you trying to be funny again? You and Alec?'

'Jokes. Just a joke.'

'I never get your jokes. So, what should I do? Can you call Erin and try and check things out? I want my life back. Erin will pick up your call.'

'Nads, you could have just asked me.'

'So you'll do it?'

'I'll try. I have no idea what's going on. Hanna will know the most.'

'Well, I only trust you. Can't stand Hanna. She's duplicitous.'

'Sure. We don't want any duplicity. Look, I can't drink any more. I need to get home. I've called an Uber. I'm going. Are you okay to get home? Can I call you an Uber?'

'I don't want to go home in case he's there.'

'Nadine, it's your home. You shouldn't feel you can't go home.'

'But he's my boss. What am I supposed to say?'

'I wish you'd said it when he first turned up.'

The Little Clothes

'I can't go home till it's sorted. Whatever it is. Can I stay at yours?'

'Mine?'

'Yes. Just one night till you call Erin?'

'Okay.'

'I packed some things this morning.'

'What is he going to think if you don't turn up?'

'I'll tell him I'm staying with a friend. He doesn't have to know the truth.'

'Gee, thanks. And what am I saying to Erin? Does she know he's been at yours?'

'I don't know.'

Audrey was pleased to have company. Even Nadine. She was still agitated about her neighbour and didn't want to go home alone either. It crossed Audrey's mind that two competent professional women should not be frightened to go to their own homes. Nadine was a welcome layer of comfort. If Audrey was going to be abused by the bald man or savaged by the dog, Nadine would be there to call the police, or an ambulance.

It was quiet when they arrived. No lights on next door. Audrey fumbled in her bag for keys.

'You need a smaller bag, Audrey. You need to know where your keys are. I always carry mine in my hand with the keys poking through my fingers. Like a weapon. Like knuckledusters.'

'Yes, Mum.'

'No, I mean it. You should know where your keys are. Is this really where you live?'

'No, I'm pretending. Yes, this is where I live. Why?'

'It's just not what I thought.'

'You imagined where I live?'

Audrey finally upturned her bag onto the bench on her verandah, lit by the movement-sensitive lights, and sorted through the clutter of pens, coins, tiny notepads, loose credit cards, tampons, bra, hairbrush, AirPods, deodorant, peppermints, AirPod case, shopping lists on the back of used window envelopes, tube of SPF moisturiser, hand cream, receipts, a tissue and the keys. She opened the door and ushered Nadine inside with the most dignity she could muster.

'Sit down, Nads. A drink? Help yourself to wine in the fridge, or tea, or coffee. I just have to feed my rabbit.'

'You have a rabbit?'

'Yes. Joni.'

'Why?'

'After Joni Mitchell.'

'No. Why do you have a rabbit?'

The night was blank under a waning crescent when Audrey peered into Joni's cage and administered the probiotics. The rabbit was quivering. There was no movement next door. The dog didn't stir.

'So Nads, you can have my bed. I'll take the spare room.'

'God, no. I'll take the spare room.'

'No, because my bed has fresh linen, and the spare-room bed isn't made up. Also, most importantly, I have to call Erin and the connection in the main bedroom is sketchy. Almost non-existent. Good old NBN. I could almost throw a stone across the water and hit the city, but there's patchy connection in there.'

'Okay. What are you going to say?'

'I don't know yet.'

'Okay. I'll just head to bed. Which way?'

'Here, come through here. That's the bathroom in there

and this is the bedroom. Yell if you need anything. There's toothpaste and stuff.'

'Jesus, Aud. Your bedroom is worse than your handbag. Only bigger.'

'Nads. I'm tired. I don't need you to trail your white glove over my house. Stay or don't stay. But don't criticise. I didn't know you were coming. Otherwise it would have been perfect for you. And look, the lamp works like this. And the toilet seat in the bathroom is a bit loose. I'm going to call Erin now before it gets too late.'

'Okay. Thanks so much, Aud.'

'No problem. Do you need pyjamas?'

'You actually wear pyjamas?'

'Yes. Do you want some?'

'God, no. Yours won't fit me anyway. I'd be swimming in them. But thanks. Also, it's kind of weird but Alec hasn't called all afternoon or tonight.'

'Probably been in a post-court post-mortem bar somewhere. I'll come in when I've spoken with Erin.'

Audrey grabbed a glass of wine and went to the spare room that still smelled of the new wardrobe.

'Oh, hi… Alec. Alec! I didn't expect you. It's Audrey. I was just looking for Erin.'

'Audrey! How are you? Hang on, Erin's with Carter. I just picked up her phone. Erin! It's Audrey. Erin! Here she comes. See you tomorrow, Audrey.'

'Night, Alec.'

'Hi Audrey, what's up?'

'I'm so sorry to disturb you so late. It's nothing, really. I heard about the kerfuffle at the baby shower, and I haven't spoken to you since and I wanted to thank you so much for such a lovely afternoon and make sure you're okay.'

'Of course. Why wouldn't I be? If I could just get this baby out of me, I'd be fine. I'm booked in for a stretch and sweep tomorrow afternoon.'

'A what?'

'They stretch the cervix and kind of brush the amniotic sac. It brings on the birth.'

'Great. That sounds great. Brilliant. Good plan. Good luck, hey.'

'Thanks, Aud. You're so sweet. You would make a great doula.'

'I have no idea what that is and I hope it's not part of the stretchy thing. Everything okay with Alec?'

'Of course.'

'There was a bit of gossip.'

'Oh god, that office. Nadine, right? He was just staying at the Sheraton for a few nights because he's working on a big case and can't be around all the craziness here. If he stays there, he can walk to the office in a minute without waking everyone. Carter is at a difficult stage. Mum's here. It's crowded and I take up the whole bed. I don't blame Alec.'

'Shouldn't he be with you, Erin? So close to the birth.'

'Audrey, it's all fine. He's here now.'

'Okay. Good night. I'll look forward to the happy news.'

'Suppose you heard it's a girl.'

'I did. A girl is wonderful. A bonus. I'm glad it's a girl.'

'Pity it was revealed early.'

'Never mind. It doesn't matter. Seriously, I don't get the gender reveal thing. Whose business is it anyway? Just yours and Alec's. I think Hanna was pretty upset about that, by the way.'

'Yeah. Especially since she found the bloody present in her handbag after all the drama.'

The Little Clothes

'Really? She found it in her handbag?'

'I know.'

'Wow. How did that happen?' She bought another one, Audrey immediately thought with a flush of shame. She bought another one.

'God knows. It's all fine now. I have to go. Carter's screaming and Alec's watching cricket. Night, Aud. Come and meet the baby soon.'

'I will. Night, Erin. Night. Night-night.'

•

'Nads, it's me. Knock, knock. Can I come in?'

'I'm down here!'

Audrey found Nadine sprawled on the couch, drinking wine and watching *The Bachelorette*.

'Are you hungry, Aud? What were you planning for dinner? Should we order in?'

'If you want to. Go right ahead. I never order in. I can't bear how those delivery guys risk their lives for almost nothing. It's just modern-day slavery. Why people can't cook anymore and why everything is smothered in peri-peri sauce, I don't know. People even get bacon rolls delivered for breakfast, for god's sake. It's a bun with bacon and tomato sauce. Work it out, people.'

'Okay, Audrey. I get it. Spare me the lecture. I just thought we could share a pizza and a chat. You over-analyse everything.'

'I'm going to bed. Why haven't you asked what Erin said?'

'Oh yeah, what happened?'

'You already know he's gone home, don't you?'

'Sorry, Aud. He texted while you were talking to Erin. All's well that ends well though, right? Did she mention me?'

'Why don't you go home too, Nadine. I'll call you an Uber.'

'Sure. Not sure I could have slept on that mattress anyway. Oh, and by the way, I got great connection in your room. Maybe you should check your phone.'

Chapter 6

'Come in, my darling girl.' Eustace took his daughter's hands and kissed her forehead. 'I have been told, no, I've been warned, that before we can eat our lunch today you'll be sorting your books and things from your bedroom. into boxes. Makes me a bit sad.'

'I'll just pack it all up and sort it back at mine. How are you, Papa?'

'I'm well. Fit as a violin but I'd be better if we could go straight to the new seat in the garden and have a beer.'

'Too early, Papa.'

'Time means nothing. You're here. So now is the time. I have some native rock orchids in bloom. I'd like you to see them. Very pretty but shy little things. Like you.'

'I'll come out and see the orchids when I can. But first I have to help Mumma.'

'I know. How's work treating you?'

'Audrey! Audrey! Eustace, is that Audrey?'

'Hello Mumma, I brought some boxes.'

'Why are you standing here? Let's start. Eustace, switch the roast on in thirty minutes and keep an eye on it. And an ear out for Nin and Gary.'

Audrey's childhood bedroom was almost unrecognisable from any stage when she inhabited it. Rita had long ago rearranged and stacked most of her daughter's belongings in the wardrobe and a corner. Only the laden bookshelves remained as they had been. There were new fussy floral waterfall curtains made by Rita; her sewing materials in pull-out plastic bins; at least one hundred balls of wool arranged in colour gradations along the windowsill and a shelf above; a calendar marked with a few desultory appointments; framed photos of Rita and Nin as teenagers and brides; a macramé wall-hanging Audrey had made in primary school; Rita's laptop from 1996; a fax machine under a grey plastic cover; a filing cabinet containing yellowing tax returns, legal documents, a thick Henry file, letters from Eustace's family, utility bills from long ago; and a large framed painting of a sunset on the Andes, given to Rita and Eustace when they visited Chile.

'Okay, Audrey, let's start.'

'Mumma, I can do this on my own. You have things to do. I promise I'll pack it all away and I won't touch any of your stuff.' Audrey gestured to the sewing machine on her teenage desk and the fabrics, cottons and skeins.

'Oh, I thought we'd do it together. It'll be fun to do it together. Let's make a start. You can always come back during the week to finish.'

'Mumma, I want to do it today. I work during the week. I'm in the middle of a big case.'

'What about we start with your collection of foreign dolls? I'll hold one up at a time and you say yes or no.'

Rita opened a large box stuffed with tissue paper and unravelled the first miniature doll.

'Oh look, it's India. Do we like India? Are we keeping India? I don't know about that. Although her sari is very pretty. And there's that red spot. What does that mean? I'll put her to the side. Do you want India?'

'Mum!'

'What about Japan? I don't know about a geisha. What do you think? About a geisha. Do they just serve tea? Or is it something else? I can't work it out. Everything goes these days. It started with the Beatles.'

'Mum, stop. I want to take them all.'

Rita kept rummaging.

'Hang on, it's Russia. I always loved Russia. So mysterious in her furry hat. A spy! Do you think she's a spy? Oh my goodness, Audrey, it's Greece! Look at Greece! Are we keeping Greece in her little peasant dress? If I remember correctly there's a Greek boy in there too with his pom-pom shoes and white skirt. A red tassel on his hat. I love a tassel on anything, don't you? A doorknob, a curtain tie-back, a key chain. Such a shame the country's gone to rack and ruin. I've never been there but I think I would have liked it, except for the food and the climate. All that oily garlic oozing out of everyone's pores in the heat.'

'I find the food delicious.'

'Of course you do.' Rita swept her eyes up and down her daughter. Sitting on an ottoman she'd covered in a mauve and silver chintz, she kept diving into the box, unravelling it in a frenzy, the tissue piling up in front of her like fairy floss. She placed each doll on the end of the bed where Audrey sat.

'Oh, Aud, here's the lovely little Maori from New Zealand that Nin bought you. Her straw skirt is a bit worse for wear, maybe moths, but the feather cape is lovely. Very tribal. Very native. You have to keep that one.'

'Mumma! You can't say those things. I will take them all.'

'Don't be silly, Audrey. You should pick and choose. Who can stay and who can't?'

'Mumma. Just stop. I'm taking them all. Please stop unwrapping. Just leave them in the box.'

'Look, here's the African.'

'Mumma, there are more than fifty countries in Africa. And that's not counting the islands. They all have distinct cultures.'

'And the little Scotch girl in her tam-o'-shanter.'

'Scottish, Mumma. I'm wrapping them all up and taking the box.'

'Okay, be like that. You're not much fun, Audrey. That's your problem. I thought we might take a walk together down memory lane. Have a few laughs. Can we at least get on with the books?'

'I'm taking all the books too. I've brought lots of boxes. I'll pack them up today and I'm sending a couple of guys with a truck during the week when it suits you. They'll bring them to my place. Then you'll have all this extra shelf space.'

'Well, it doesn't suit me at all, I thought we'd do this together.'

'Mumma, you wanted this cleared. I'm here to clear it. I have the room at my house, and I came today to help you sort your sewing room. Can we rewrap all these dolls, please?'

'Oh, Audrey, look at the darling American doll in her stetson and cowboy boots. And the Swiss doll. How cute is she with her blonde plaits and apron dress? You have to keep Switzerland. You loved *Heidi* when you were little.

The Little Clothes

Remember she went to live with her grandfather? I think your father's boss, Mr Clarkson, brought this back for you when he went on his grand tour of Europe.'

'I remember *Heidi*.'

'I love these tiny perfect dolls. So delicate.'

'Mumma, I remember you showing me all those little baby clothes you bought when you were first pregnant.'

'Yes.'

'Before you had the miscarriage.'

'Yes.'

'I've never forgotten you shared that with me. It made me feel closer.'

'What on earth are you talking about?'

'When Dad took you to Nin's because you were bleeding. How Nin took care of it all. Went with you to the hospital. That you were a long way along.'

'I didn't share it with you. You found the clothes when you were snooping for your Christmas presents. I just explained why the baby clothes were there when you found them.'

'It felt like an important moment to me.'

'What? That I'd lost a child.'

'No. That you talked to me about it. That you saw it as some sort of failure, when it wasn't.'

'A girl. A tiny little girl. We only ever planned two children and now they've both gone.'

For a few seconds Audrey couldn't breathe, as if she'd been punched in the stomach. She wanted to protect her mother from realising what had just been said, so she started to wrap the dolls, jamming them into the box any which way, throwing the last tissue on top and shutting down any further discussion with a screech of packing tape.

'So now the books.' Audrey sat on the floor in front of the bookcase.

'Why do you want all the books? You've read them. They're yellow. They smell.'

'So you've said.'

'It's the truth.'

'These books made me. Saved me. They're my friends. I want to take them home. Look, here's *The Witch Doll*. The *Oxford Book of Poetry for Children*! "Tyger Tyger, burning bright." And *Rebecca*. I'm going to read *Rebecca* again. *Playing Beatie Bow*! You gave it to me in my Christmas stocking.'

'Did I? I don't remember that. I don't remember buying you any books. That was your father. I'm not sure it was good for you. Too many ideas. Anyway, what did you need saving from, Audrey? You had a home, a roof over your head, two parents, an education. I thought you were busy at work, so how are you going to do all this reading? Maybe just burn the lot.'

What *did* I need saving from? Audrey wondered.

'Mumma, I'm starting to pack them up. I'm going to hand them to you.'

'Oh, well, I can see I'm not needed.'

'You are needed. Just put them in that box.'

'I'll go and sort lunch out. Your father has probably burnt it.'

Rita fled the room, distraught. Audrey worried she might slip on the stairs. 'No socks on stairs!' Rita used to call out to her children as they dashed down for dinner. There was residual fear in Audrey whenever she descended a staircase.

She did a clumsy roll and push off the floor and went out to the landing to find that Rita was not sprawled at the bottom of the stairs with her legs at sickening angles.

The Little Clothes

There was no spreading pool of blood, so she continued to tape boxes and pack her books. Among them were her childhood and teenage diaries. Pink sparkly covers, furry synthetic aqua, lime-green plastic, glitter in water now congealed and mouldy, quilted purple. All locked. No keys.

Her autograph book from primary school was there too. *By hook or by crook I'll be first in your book*, Eustace had penned. *Make new friends but keep the old – new friends are silver, old friends are gold*, Rita had written, and added little butterflies and hearts and kissy lips around the edge. Audrey was startled to find an entry by Henry, his hand still so familiar. *Live fast, die young and leave a good-looking copse.* He never could spell, she thought.

'Audrey! Lunch! Audrey! Wash your hands. Those books are filthy. Wash your hands. Gary and Nin are here.'

•

After lunch Audrey went with Eustace to see the garden bench he'd been constructing in the shed and had now assembled in a circle around the base of the pink silk tree.

'It's beautiful, Papa. How did you work out how to do that?'

'A book from the library about making garden furniture.'

'Well, you're very clever. And I love the colour. I think it's watermelon. The black bolts are the seeds. You're an artist.'

'Thank you, darling. Let's launch it with a beer.'

'Okay. Are we smashing it or drinking it?'

'I think drinking, don't you?' Eustace went to the shed and returned with two bottles and an opener.

'Papa, I'm sorry I didn't come straight out this morning to see this. It's beautiful. Have you sat on it with Mumma?'

'What do you think?'

Audrey wasn't sure of her answer. Her parents' relationship was an infinite mystery. 'I think she's admired it from afar. Maybe from the clothesline. And I think you made it for her. And I think she knows that.'

'Audrey Mendes. Smartest in the class. Always were.'

Audrey and Eustace clinked bottles and drank their beer on the watermelon chair in the dappled light falling through the feather-leaves of the silk tree.

•

The boxes arrived at Audrey's house on Tuesday afternoon. She'd taken a rare, almost unheard of, afternoon off to receive them. When she was guiding the men into the spare room and showing them where to stack the boxes, her neighbour was watering his front lawn with a hose.

He smiled at Audrey when she came into her front garden. Or was it a leer?

She nodded. 'Hi, how're you settling in?'

'Good. Yeah, good. Looks like ya doin' some settlin' yeself.'

'Oh, just my old books from my parents' house.'

'Lotta books. It'll make ya brain explode.'

'Hah. That's funny. Anyway, I'm Audrey.'

'Right.'

'And you are…?'

'Who's asking?'

'Me. Audrey. I'm asking.'

The Little Clothes

'Greg. I'm Greg.'

'Nice to finally meet you, Greg.'

'Listen, if there are any books you don't want that you think some blokes might like to read…'

'Why?'

'Well, I look after a group of guys, some just out of prison, who might like a book or two.'

'I don't think they'd like my sort of books.'

'They might. You don't know what they like.'

'Just a guess.'

'That's the lot then,' said the man standing in front of her with a clipboard. 'Can you sign here that you got the boxes.'

By the time she'd finished seeing the delivery men off her property, Greg had gone inside.

The next time Audrey saw him was three hours later when she walked to the pub for trivia night.

'Oh, hello again. We'll have to stop meeting like this. Lovely night for a walk. Nice and balmy. My favourite time of the year.'

'Beg yours?'

'It's me, Audrey, I live next door. Twice in one day. We talked earlier. In the front garden.'

'Oh.'

'What's your dog's name?'

'Shit for Brains.'

'That's funny. How are you finding it round here?'

'Sokay.'

'Good. I'll have a think about books.'

'Sorry?'

'You said your group might like some books.'

'Sure. See ya, love.'

'Yep. Probably will since we live next door to each other. By the way, why do you muzzle Shit for Brains?'

'He's a killer.'

Audrey walked down the street, crossed the lane that bordered the pub and saw Shay-Lee sitting in the middle of the bitumen pressing a cat down hard in her lap with both hands. The little girl was otherwise alone. As she approached, Audrey could see that Shay-Lee's hair was matted and her clothes were streaked with tomato sauce. She was shoeless, her face dirty. The cat was patchy with mange.

'Hello Shay-Lee. Do you remember me?'

'I have kitty catty.'

'Yes, I can see that. Is it yours?'

'Yes.'

'What's your cat's name?'

'Kitty spitty poopy poo poo.'

'Wow. That's a long name.'

'And Mason. Mason is at kidney.'

'Is Mason a friend? At kindy?'

The little girl nodded her head solemnly.

'Shay-Lee, you need to get off the road. Cars come up here, and delivery bikes. You don't want the cat to get run over, do you?'

Shay-Lee tried to stand holding the cat by squeezing it around its front legs with its body dangling. It wriggled out of the child's grasp before running into the shade along a paling fence, then scrambling over a wall.

'You scare Kitty!'

'I'm walking down to see Mum and Dad. Do you want to come with me?'

Shay-Lee took Audrey's outstretched hand.

They walked into an almost deserted pub.

The Little Clothes

The mother was sitting at a tall table with the bar staff, who were all eating from tasting platters and drinking champagne. The obsequious pudding-faced chef stood nearby in his striped apron, explaining each offering and how it could be paired with wine.

'Hello! Missing something?'

'Excuse me? This area is still closed,' said the mother, turning sharply.

'I just found your daughter sitting in the middle of the road.'

'What! Oh my god. Shay-Lee, what do you think you're doing? You little idiot!' the mother screamed. 'You've got the brains of a mouse.'

'Hang on there,' said Audrey. 'She's a child.'

'Who are you? Do I know you?'

'I'm a neighbour. I come in for trivia. Lucky I came early tonight, because she was sitting in the laneway. In the middle. On the road.'

'Okay. Okay. I get it. Well, thank you. Thank you. She was supposed to be with her father while I was here working out next month's menu. Thank you so much. I'm just shocked. I didn't mean to be rude. But thank you. Seriously, thank you. Please, join us for a drink.'

'Oh, no. I'm meeting friends.'

'I have kitty cat.'

'Do you, darling?' The mother crouched down and kissed her daughter over and over on the face, hugging her tight, then berating her and spanking her hand hard.

'Owww! Take it off,' said Shay-Lee, crying, trying to wipe the sting away.

The mother kissed her child again and dabbed at Shay-Lee's tears with a sauce-streaked paper napkin.

'Nooo. Stop. Yucky. I don't like it.' The little girl pushed her crouching mother hard in the chest, making her fall back on her bottom, off her towering platforms.

'Mishy, can you keep an eye on Shay while I go and look for her dickhead father?'

Audrey left to join her table in the next room. She was first to arrive and circled back round to the bar to buy a drink. On the self-service table where the sauce bottles, napkins, condiments and cutlery were lined up ready for action, Audrey noticed familiar yellow pages and realised with a quick glance they were tonight's trivia questions. She could see Kevin the quiz master at the otherwise empty bar, talking to the barman with the tinkling bell on his beard. Audrey put the pages in her handbag and went and sat down near Kevin, who did not turn in her direction or acknowledge her presence. The father joined them from the beer garden.

'Anyway, mate, I better get myself sorted. They'll all be in soon,' said Kevin.

'No hurry. Have another one.' The father poured Kevin a beer, then looked to the other side at a newcomer and asked, 'What can I get for you, mate?'

Audrey had intended to hand the pages to Kevin but left the bar and went to the bathroom. In a locked cubicle she looked carefully at the answers she didn't know and then put the sheets at the base of her bag, under her junk.

•

'Hi guys. How are we? I'm feeling lucky tonight. Hi Tom, Elspeth. Lorraine, you look lovely. Marion, those earrings!'

'Hi Audrey. We were worried you weren't coming. Let me get you a drink,' said Sean. 'The usual?'

The Little Clothes

'Sure. Thanks. Why not? I'll come with you. Anyone else? Can you order me the special if they come round? I think it's the brisket burger.'

'Yeah. It's the burger again. I wish they'd do that red curry thing. That was great.'

At the bar Audrey could see Kevin heading out of the office area holding white pages to his chest.

'Thanks, mate,' he said to the father on the way through. 'Coulda sworn I'd brought them with me.'

'No worries. It's all good. I'll come out and introduce you in twenty. Gotta get upstairs. The bride is going off about something. Another beer?'

'Nah. Think I'll keep a clear head. I can't explain those missing pages. It's just weird.'

'Mate, don't worry about it. Ben here will look after you, won't you, Benny boy? Ben, look after Kevin. He's got thirsty work ahead.'

•

'Seven specials. One green salad without dressing, and a skirt steak with bearnaise,' said the mother, plonking the dishes down.

'The steak's here,' said Jeff.

'No, actually it's here. I'm looking at it,' said the mother, pointing in front of Elspeth. Tom hurriedly intervened and rearranged the dishes while his girlfriend gagged.

'Well, that's attitude for you,' said Lorraine. 'What's her problem?'

'God knows,' said Audrey. 'Still, it can't be easy working all day in a pub and raising a child at the same time.'

'You always see the best in people, Aud.'

Sean smiled in agreement. 'You do, Aud, you do.'

'Not always. Sometimes I see the worst.' Everyone laughed.

•

'Geez, Audrey, is there anything you don't know?' asked Marion while they waited on the result. 'The capital of the Ivory Coast? What was it? I didn't even know there was an Ivory Coast. Sounds pretty though. Like a resort.'

'Yamoussoukro.'

'I can't even say it.'

'I can't either, not really,' said Audrey. 'I only just learned it.'

'And then the French name for the extra point. What was it? Something about a coat.'

'I think that was a pretty easy question. Côte d'Ivoire. It was called the Ivory Coast because it was renowned for its export of ivory. So quite a sad history, really.'

'Sure,' said Marion. 'You would know. I have some ivory bangles from my great-aunt. I've never really thought about where the ivory came from.'

'That's the problem with the planet,' said Elspeth. 'We should know where things come from.'

Lorraine crossed her eyes and made a face behind Elspeth's back.

'Well, we have had a runaway success tonight!' Kevin announced. It's The East-Enders! First again!'

There was some polite clapping and some groaning. A bit of good-humoured booing and a hiss from another regular table, usually the runners-up.

Sean went to the podium to accept the prizes, insisting that Audrey accompany him. He clapped low near the

The Little Clothes

hem of her dress as if he was on stage acknowledging her contribution in an orchestra pit.

'Audrey, you're a genius.'

'I wouldn't go that far, Sean. We all did it.'

'Come on. You knew pretty well all of it.'

'I read a lot of things. Been reading a lot recently.'

'That's the best we've ever done. The team would be nothing without you.'

Audrey looked down into the room. Tom was bending Elspeth backwards over his arm and kissing her theatrically on the lips. Everyone cheered. Elspeth had answered a question about a K-pop band that Audrey had judged it would not be credible to answer herself.

The trivia teams started to drift from the room for the bar, and the piped music flooded in. Sean took Audrey's hand and helped her from the podium. Suddenly they were dancing. Some kick-ups and a nod to the Watusi. The rest of the team and some other onlookers were astonished and pleased by Audrey's rhythmic steps and joie de vivre.

The East-Enders ordered sparkling wine and high-fived.

'Well, I'm off then,' said Audrey after becoming breathless dancing with Sean and then joining in a rowdy round of self-congratulations. 'I'll see you all next week.'

As she was leaving the pub, the mother followed her onto the footpath. 'Hi. Just wanted to say thank you again. I'm sorry I took a bite out of you. Her father was supposed to be keeping an eye on her. It's easy to get distracted in there. We both feel terrible.'

'Sure. That's okay. I understand. I'm usually at work so it was lucky I happened to be here at the right time.'

'Oh. That's why I didn't recognise you. I thought that you might be a regular, but I couldn't place you. Well, come back again sometime.'

•

There was a fuzzy silhouette on Audrey's verandah when she walked down her path. She could see it was Greg, and stopped abruptly.

Stay calm, Audrey. Stay calm. Think.

'Third time's the charm,' she called out, trying to sound casual.

'What?'

'Third time we've met today.'

'Me dog's missing.'

Audrey exhaled. 'Shit for Brains?'

'What? What did you say to me?'

'You told me the dog's name is Shit for Brains.'

'Oh, okay. I see. Real name's Maximus. I just come round to see if you seen him and when you weren't here I thought I'd sit to wait for ya and figure out what to do next. You seem like a person who knows stuff. What to do n'all.'

Why hadn't the lights come on?

She stayed a good distance from Greg, as much as her short path would allow, and quite close to the gate. But what if the dog heard its owner and came into the garden? She'd be caught between the two of them. Then she thought of Joni.

'Oh god. My rabbit is in the backyard.'

'Rabbit? Why d'ya have a rabbit?'

'She's so sweet. Rabbits are lovely. Her name's Joni, after

The Little Clothes

the singer. You know, *The Hissing of Summer Lawns* and all that.' Audrey was gabbling. 'Oh my god. You don't think Maximus…'

'Think what?'

'That Maximus is in my backyard?'

'Nah. He can't get in. Anyway, you got that lock on your side gate.'

'What! How do you know about my gate?'

'Well, when ya didn't answer ya door just now I walked down the side passage. I also come here when the nice police lady come round and accused me of chuckin' bottles on ya roof.' Greg was standing now, getting closer, and seemed more animated.

'I helped her take a look. Offered her me ladder but she wasn't keen. Gotta be real steady to climb a ladder to a roof. A lotta accidents on ladders. Head smashes like an explodin' pumpkin when it hits the ground. Broken backs. Can fuck ya life in a second. Can go from eatin' pub steak one day with cuttelry to bein' fed porridge with a teaspoon through a head cage the next.'

'I have to go inside. My friends are coming up from the pub. We play trivia. They're on their way.'

'Sure. I'm just leavin'. An if you see Maxi boy don't go near him. Just give me a call. Here's me number. So now ya can call me direct at any time with any problems ya have with me or the lads. I don't give it to every Tom, Steve and Harry.' Greg handed Audrey a grubby Tally-Ho paper as he walked past her and into the night.

When Audrey had calmed down with a sculled glass of whisky from the bottle she had kept on hand for Alec, she crept into her back garden to bring Joni safely inside. She walked sideways and low to the fence and could see Greg lighting the drum. Maximus was in his usual place.

He knows everything about me, she thought. He's toying with me. He's got *my* number, too.

Chapter 7

In the morning Audrey woke from restless sleep and tested the movement-sensitive lights. They didn't switch on as she walked up and down the path and onto her porch. She opened the box on the verandah and found a fuse had flipped. She fixed it.

'Hi Papa, it's me.'

'Audrey, lovely to hear from you. Is everything all right?'

'Yes, it is. How are you?'

'All the same here. Did the boxes get there safely?'

'Yes. All here ready to unpack. Sorry it was such a palaver.'

'Not of your making.'

'Look, I'm just calling about the fuse box out the front. Is there a way of locking it?'

'Of course. Has there been trouble?'

'No. Not really. A fuse switched off and it meant my porch lights weren't working. I often come home in the dark. It made me think about how anyone can open the box. I just want to be sure.'

'I'll come and do it myself.'

'No, Papa. I can get someone in.'

'Yes, Audrey. I'll come this evening.'

'Okay. That would be great. I won't get home till seven.'
'I'll be there.'
'Stay for dinner.'
'We will already have eaten at five. Your mother keeps nursery hours these days.'
'Of course.' Audrey knew her mother would come too.

•

Eustace and Rita were sitting on the verandah when Audrey opened her gate. She had walked up the hill and was out of breath.

'Sorry. The bus wasn't there so I walked up. I hope you haven't been waiting long.'

'Only half an hour,' said Rita.

'Papa, I said seven.'

'I know. And I said seven. But your mother had other ideas.'

'Well, thanks for coming. Let's go inside.'

'I'll get started here. You go in, Rita. Audrey will make you some tea.'

'Or wine? Wine would be good. Have you got any wine, Audrey?'

'Yes, Mumma. I have wine. At least you've got light out here, Papa. Do you want something to drink?'

'I'm fine.'

'Your father has to watch how much he drinks before he goes to bed. Men's problems downstairs.'

'Rita. I am just here.'

'Well, it's the truth, Eusti.'

'And private, Rita.'

The Little Clothes

'We just met your lovely neighbour.'

'What!'

'Greg. He seems nice. Is he single?'

'Here, Mumma. Wine. What was Greg doing here?'

'He introduced himself and offered to help your father put the lock on. Said he had a few local friends who could help with little jobs. It could be useful for you, Audrey.'

'What did you say? I don't want him knowing my business. I don't want him on my property. I definitely don't want his friends on my property.'

'Your father said he didn't need help but thanked him and then Greg left. Really, Audrey, this is why you don't meet anyone. You're so defensive.'

'Mumma, you don't know anything about him. You don't know this neighbourhood. He's not a nice person.'

'He seemed nice. A little odd, but nice. Very tiny pale freckled hands, like trout. He has ladies' hands. Haven't you noticed? What does he do for a living? Obviously not men's work.'

'I have no idea.'

'Haven't you talked to him?'

'I don't even know his surname.'

'Anyway, what is that you're wearing, Audrey? Is that what you're wearing to work these days?'

'Yes. A suit.'

'I've never thought a jacket and pants is for you. And not many people can wear yellow. It makes your skin sallow. Yellow and black like a little round ladybird.' Rita laughed, pleased with her observation, before she took a startled step backwards.

'Oh god, Audrey, something just moved over there. It's a rat!'

Audrey realised she'd forgotten Joni. The rabbit had been inside all night and today.

'It's my rabbit.'

'Is that rabbit droppings I'm looking at?'

'Yes, Mumma.' Audrey spoke very quickly, trying to avert a barrage of criticism. 'I forgot I brought her inside last night because of disgusting Greg and his disgusting dog. I had to go to work so early this morning. I didn't get much sleep. I just forgot. I've been in a state.'

'Why you keep a rabbit, I don't know. But at least keep it outside. Animals belong outside.'

'I do keep her outside.'

'It doesn't look like that from where I'm sitting.'

Audrey picked Joni up and stepped over the droppings to go to the garden. In the middle of her lawn were three beer cans, a cigarette lighter and a McDonald's bag. She counselled herself not to react in front of her mother, and spread clean hay, fetched fresh water, probiotics and rabbit food, before settling Joni back into her cage. Then cleared up the scats in the house under Rita's guidance.

'There's some. And there. No, over there. And here.'

'They actually eat their faeces. It's a survival thing.'

'That's good to know, Audrey, in case I have an aneurysm and buy myself a rabbit.'

'Here, Mumma. Homemade taramasalata. And olives. Eat something.'

'Have you washed your hands?'

'Yes, Mumma.'

Rita hesitated and took an olive. Unfortunately, Ligurian. Audrey saw too late they were the size, colour and shape of Joni's droppings. Rita considered the olive, raised one eyebrow, and put it in the pit bowl.

The Little Clothes

'Audrey, that's a wonderful painting over the fireplace. It's Henry's. Why haven't I seen it before?'

'It's been there since I moved in, Mumma. You must have seen it.'

'I think I would remember seeing my only son's work.'

When the lock was installed and her parents had left in a burst of kisses and encouragements from her father and recriminations from her mother, Audrey put the cans and cigarette lighter inside the McDonald's bag and threw them back over the fence into Greg's yard. Maximus barked in a frenzy. Greg bellowed 'Shut up!' from his back verandah. Audrey went inside and turned up her music. Aretha. 'Respect'. And 'I Say a Little Prayer'.

After showering she put on fresh pyjamas. Then unwrapped the three-piece baby gift set she'd bought during her lunch break. Pale pink, banded with Gucci stripes. She thought of it as a celebration of Erin's daughter, Milla, born that morning. She placed the tiny bodysuit in a drawer she'd designated the pink drawer, then placed the beret and bib alongside the Burberry hat, the Tiffany comb and the knitted toys.

•

There was cake and champagne in the office the next day. Alec was clapped in when he arrived, everyone standing as he walked past their desks. He had his tie flipped over his shoulder, and flamboyantly pretended to smoke an already half-smoked Arturo Fuente. It's not like he did much, Audrey thought. Erin did all the work. Still, it was exciting to welcome a new baby. Nadine had organised the celebration in the Colton Room, where she stayed close to Alec and attended to his glass, while showily instructing Heidi about serving the partners first, cleaning up and answering the reception phone, which had been redirected to the Moisen Room next door. The gift, to which they'd all contributed, was presented along with a quite funny speech by Richard that frequently referenced Alec's virility. This was his seventh child. No mention of the mothers. There was something about Mick Jagger, and about how, simply by waving his underpants near them, Alec made women pregnant. 'I think I'll be in trouble if I don't take this home for Erin to open,' Alec said, as if Erin was difficult. Which she wasn't. Everyone laughed. Alec was such a wag.

•

'Audrey, it's Erin.'

'Erin. Congratulations. I was going to call but I thought I'd give you a couple of weeks to settle down at home. How are you? Did Alec give you the presents?'

'Yes, got all the presents. Thanks for the flowers. I love peonies. They were the best bunch we received. They're finished now but I really enjoyed them. And thanks for that little dress. I can't wait to put her in it. I'm sorry I haven't sent thankyous. It's been a terrible two weeks.'

Audrey could hear Milla squalling.

'So how are you?'

'A bit worse for wear. Pretty bad, actually. Literally torn to pieces to be honest. I had an episiotomy. Are you still in the office?' Erin was tamping down tears. There were silences and deep breaths.

'No. I just got home. Erin, talk to me. What's going on?'

The Little Clothes

'Mum's just left and taken Carter to her place for a sleepover. Alec's not here. I can't settle the baby. She won't attach. My nipples are so cracked and sore and she's hungry.'

'Can you tell your mum to come back? And where's Alec?'

'It's better that Mum has Carter. I caught him biting Milla on the arm. There's a deep mark.'

'What!'

'I went to grab a nappy in the next room. Alec's gone to a three-day conference on the Central Coast. Something to do with insurance and a golf tournament. I know this is a lot to ask, but can you come over?'

'Sure. Of course. On my way. I'll come, but is there a midwife or one of those lactation nurses? They'll be more help.'

'Not really. I want a friend.'

'Okay. I'm coming. Not sure how much help I'll be.'

'You always make me feel better and Hanna can't get here.'

Audrey immediately regretted that she was giving up her evening for yet another obligation to Erin and Alec. And that she was second pick after Hanna. Or maybe tenth pick, when she thought about the span of bridesmaids at the wedding. Still, it was better than not being picked at all, as it had been at school, when the teacher always concluded the agonising process with, 'Okay, Audrey and Maggie, just choose a side.' Whichever side they chose groaned and mimicked vomiting. At least the teacher didn't split them to make the teams even. Inevitably placed in the outfield in softball, they would hold their mitts up often enough to avoid complaint or discipline, gradually merging left outfield into centre outfield and finally sitting together in the clover to make daisy chains and talk about books.

Of course she'd said yes to Erin. How could she not? Before leaving she googled *episiotomy*, then *cracked nipples*, and finally *children who bite babies*. She packed a toothbrush, underwear, pyjamas and a change of clothes for work, then called an Uber.

Sue answered Erin's door.

'Sue, didn't expect to see *you* here! Erin asked me to come and help. Is everything okay?'

'Come in, Audrey. I couldn't settle Carter and had to bring him back. He was screaming and banging the walls. My neighbours complained. They're elderly and not very well. He needs his parents.' Sue gestured to her grandson, who was riding an electric Porsche in the foyer.

'Carter. Carter! Come and say hello to Audrey.'

'No.'

'Carter, don't be rude. Come here right now or you'll go straight to bed.'

'Hello Carter. I hear you have a new baby sister.'

Carter drove his car hard into Audrey's shins.

'Oh my god, Sue, that really hurt. Sorry but that really, really hurt.' Audrey retreated to the lounge room and sat down with tears pricking her eyes, bruises already appearing on both shins.

Erin came out of the kitchen holding Milla. 'Aud, you're here! What's going on? Are you okay?'

'Carter just got a bit road ragey with his Porsche.'

'Audrey, I'm so sorry. Alec bought it for him because of the baby. Carter! Come here right now and apologise!'

'Don't worry about it. It just took me by surprise. Let me see.'

The Little Clothes

Erin lowered Milla into Audrey's arms and sat down on a rubber ring on a dining chair that had been brought into the lounge room.

'She's perfect, Erin. So, so beautiful. Are you sure Alec had anything to do with this?'

'God, you're funny. I feel better already. I'm really, really sorry about Carter. I can't control him. And I'm sorry you had to come all this way when Mum's here now.'

'What can I do for you? She seems very peaceful.'

'Mum helped me position her and she finally attached. She's drunk on breast milk.'

'Then go to bed immediately. Go while you can. I'll hold her for a bit and put her down when you're asleep. Where does she sleep?'

'In with me. Bedroom upstairs. There's a crib.'

'Go, Erin. You need to sleep when you can. Sue can help me if I need anything.'

It was impossible for Audrey to be annoyed when Milla was lying in her arms, loosely swaddled in lavender and cream muslin, smelling of sweet plain cake, her long fingers reading a braille of milk pimples on her cheeks, jagged nails like mini bonito flakes rippling on the edges of a flat nose, black monkey hair. Audrey kept looking down at the baby, thinking about Milla's future, her life's story and what it would be on the warming planet in the world of angry men, especially her father, Alec, with his arrogance and disdain, and with Carter, who was already ascending the throne and would not be stopped except by his own limitations, his own actions, missteps, bluffs and expectations of what should come to him that might not now come, because the world was changing; but perhaps the lowly things he wanted could still be his, like a real Porsche, a trophy house, a meeting room in his name. But whatever it was he desired would never be enough to paper over the ruinous cracks beneath and what he would never have, without a garden, or a studio to paint in, a collection of books that he actually read, a wooden boat to build with his own hands, a copse or an orchard to plant and wander in at dusk, beehives, cooking to do and share, an inconsequential hobby, poetry, charitable endeavours and honest, giving relationships with friends. And yet here was his sister, a little girl who had been bitten hard and starved today, but who might have a fighting chance to forge a different path and an inner life.

'Audrey! You're still here. I thought you were dead. It was quite creepy. You were so still. It was like you were in a trance. I just got Carter to sleep. I had to bribe him with a toy for tomorrow. Anyway, finally he's gone. What are you doing?'

'I told Erin to go to bed. This one's asleep too. I said I'd take her up. To the crib. I don't know where it is.'

'I'll take her. Are you staying or going home? I can fold out this couch for you. It's quite comfortable. I've often slept on it. It's made up. There's even soap in the bathroom. That remains one of the many mysteries from the baby shower.'

'I'll call an Uber. Isn't she exquisite?'

'Yes. She's cute. Not sure about the name and it's upset Carter no end. He's furious. Not sure how that's going to go. Maybe they should have waited longer. Given the little boy some space. Listen, you know Alec, you've worked with him for years, right?'

'About twelve, maybe more. I knew him before that from around the traps. He recruited me before I was qualified.'

'Really?'

The Little Clothes

'Thanks, Sue, don't sound as if that's so unlikely.'

'I didn't mean that. Don't be so defensive. I just didn't know. Look, this is delicate, but what do you think about Alec?'

'Sorry, not sure what you mean?'

'I thought at first he was great for my daughter. I wasn't happy about the age gap, obviously, and the fact he was still married with a dependent child, but he seemed devoted, swept her off her feet, really, swept me off my feet too with holidays and dinners and flowers. He helped me pay off my mortgage. Sorted my finances. He provided Erin with things she's never had, a sort of father-figure for a start, then this.'

Sue flung her hands towards the walls of the lounge room as if to embrace the house and all it contained. All the things.

'But where is he now when she really needs him?'

Audrey didn't want to get involved. She had long worked for Alec and knew his character and behaviour, but she wanted to keep her job. She knew enough about the dance to not be indignant about every misstep. She herself had trespassed.

'I like the guy. He's charismatic and I get what Erin loves about him, but in the end he is all about Alec. You must understand it's always going to be all about Alec. If you're in a relationship with him, you'll both be in love with the same person. There is no more to know.'

'Just what I thought.'

'Okay, I'm going to get an Uber. And I think Erin needs to see a doctor about those nipples and maybe get some treatment. I've heard chilled cabbage leaves are good.'

'Audrey, you are funny. Cabbage leaves. I'll get her to Tone tomorrow. Get some proper advice. So how do you manage to be loved by everyone and make your own way in the world?'

'No one sees me, Sue. I'm not a challenge or a threat. I'm useful. And trust me, not everyone loves me. Which has never bothered me.'

'Well, even Alec seems to defer to you.'

'I just know too much.'

'Well, that sounds worrying!'

'No. God, no. Nothing like that!'

'Of course not! As if.'

'I just know my way around the law.'

Audrey cradled Milla into Sue's arms. 'You go, Sue. I'll close the door on my way out. I just need to use the loo.'

'Thanks for everything, Audrey. See you soon, I hope. I think you're good for my daughter and I'm grateful for that.'

Please, Audrey thought, don't do the praying hands.

'Namaste, Audrey.'

The bathroom was no longer lit with votives. Part of a breast pump lay on the limestone bench next to a maternity bra and a dirty damp handtowel. One of Carter's Crocs and a full potty were on the floor, an unspooling roll of toilet paper puddled in the corner. There were skid marks in the toilet.

Audrey wandered into what she thought must be Alec's office and saw in the desk diary that there had been a recent dinner with Hanna, Terrible Todd, Richard and his wife, Daniel and Nadine in the private room at Mr Wong. She poked around and unplugged a small Paul Smith Anglepoise colour-block lamp that she remembered the firm had given Alec for his sixtieth. She folded it and put it in her bag. She could hear Sue moving upstairs and took her time to

The Little Clothes

browse. Golf days frequently featured in the diary that was clearly kept by Erin in her looping hand. There had also been a recent boat trip on the harbour with what looked like half of the firm. Catered by Thyme and Plaice. The names Moisen and Salter were on the list for that jaunt. Audrey put a Montblanc pen from Alec's collection in her pocket.

'You can't be in Daddy's room!' said Carter from the door. 'You not loud.'

'What are you doing out of bed?'

'I feel sick.'

'Well, Granny Sue is just upstairs with Milla. Why don't you go and find her?'

'I hate stupid crying baby.'

'She's your sister, Carter. I wish I had a sister.'

'No, she is poo. You take her. Mummy doesn't want her.'

'That's not true, Carter.'

'You're not true. You poo-head liar!'

Out of the mouths of babes, Audrey thought.

'Carter! Carty! Where are you? Be quiet!' Sue hissed. 'You'll wake your mother. You're supposed to be in bed.'

Carter ran towards his grandmother as she came downstairs. Audrey followed him out and switched off the light.

'Oh, Audrey, thought you'd gone.'

'Just waiting on my Uber.'

'She in Daddy's room.'

'Don't be ridiculous, Carter.'

'She did,' said Carter, pointing.

'Sue, I'll wait on the porch. I was just peeking through the window in there to see if my driver was out the front.'

'Yes, maybe wait in the porte cochère. Carter's being very difficult, and we all need to go to sleep. We're terribly tired in this household. We don't need any more disruption.'

'Of course. Sorry I've disturbed you. I'll make myself scarce.'

•

'Out late,' called Greg from behind his front fence, where he stood with a friend, when Audrey arrived.

She pretended not to notice them, but overheard, 'The one I told ya 'bout' as she walked down her path, now flooded with light. 'I don't think she's Strayan. Talks fancy.'

'Like she's got a rod up her arse,' laughed his mate. 'Plenty of arse for it too.'

'Don't say that, mate.'

'Ya fancy her.'

'I don't fancy her but she's me nayba. And she's okay.'

'Ya fancy her.'

'Mate, she has a pet rabbit. I don't fancy her.'

•

Audrey dreamed about Milla at a Halloween party. The little girl was older, maybe three. Milla was in the guise of Shay-Lee, running around in a space under a house, between brick footings, wearing a nylon ladybird costume, carrying a lit candle in an old-fashioned brass candlestick like Wee Willie Winkie. Mr Johnson was there smoking his pipe. Rita, in a Pucci caftan, chatted to him, and offered empanadas and olives, except in the dream they became fairy bread and cocktail sausages.

The Little Clothes

Audrey woke up panicky, sweaty and thirsty. When she went to the kitchen for water, Joni was sitting on the rush mat. Audrey raised her blinds, opened the back door with a key rather than pressing the noisy electronic lock, and crept into the yard. At the fence she could see Greg standing alone near the flaming drum. Where was Maximus? She crept closer and could suddenly see the dog's face in the dark, against the fence, an inch away from her face. She gasped and reeled backwards. Maximus attacked, butting his head into the palings, jumping high and barking in a frenzy till Greg called him off.

'Maximus. Down.' A can hit the fence.

Audrey struggled to her feet and ran back into her house, followed by Greg's laughter. She bolted the door and lowered the blinds before gulping three fingers of Alec's whisky.

When she'd calmed down, Audrey went to the spare room and heaved boxes aside to find the one marked 'Diaries'. She slid one side of the scissors under the packing tape and rummaged through the books from her teenage years. She selected the lime-green plastic, the pink nylon fur with purple hearts, and the aqua satin with sequins, and took them into her lounge room. She used a pair of pliers that she'd shoplifted from the local hardware store to break the locks. It was especially easy to be unseen in the hardware store.

She began to read pages and pages of primary-school hurts and mundanities. A few forgotten triumphs. Annoyances with her parents and occasionally with Maggie and Henry. Parties she went to and more often those from which she had been excluded. Impossible crushes. Disappointment when she was cast as a swaying reed in green crepe paper instead of as a swan in a white tutu in the *Swan Lake* performance for parents. A list of who had their period and who didn't. An extensive entry on Miss Baldry, who left the toilets smelling of perfume, and whether that was because she covered the smell of her *rags* by spraying Shalimar.

Then she found it.

7 September
I went to Luca's house today after school. Luca and me walked there in the bush. Missers Johnson gave us orange cordigal and stale SAOs and stinky cheese. Mister Johnson took me in his study when Luca had his piano lesson and Missers Johnson was in the garden hanging out the washing and playing with Augie. Mister Johnson shut the door and sat in his big leather chair. He asked what colour underpants I was wearing. I couldn't remember so he pulled them down to check and put his finger in me for a bit to check everything was all right inside me. I think he's a doctor. It hurt because of his fingernail. He was very nice and stopped doing it when I said it hurt. He made me turn around and show him my bottom which was embarrassing because it's so big. He said I should hold up my uniform and look at the wall until he said to stop. He said he liked my bum and made me stand that way for a little bit. I think he touched it with his pipe because it was hot. I looked out the window and thought about how I should lose weight now I have a boyfriend. I could see Missers Johnson in the garden in her red dress hanging up washing. I think she is a gipsy. Mister Johnson cried out. I turned around to help him and he was wiping himself with his hanky. He smells like old shoes. He

said I make him very happy. I think I love him. He told me not to say anything or we would both be in trouble and that Missers Johnson would be jealous, so it is our secret forever. He is my one true love. He thinks I am special. I will never get him in trouble. I will go to live with him when I am older. Mumma came to get me to walk home and she was cross that I was sitting with Mister Johnson on the couch listening to Opera and not playing soccer with Luca and Augie in the garden. She doesn't understand I'm grown up. I am a woman now. I need to help Mister Johnson but she said I can't ever go there again. We'll see about that!!!!

It did happen, thought Audrey. It did happen. I wrote it down.

24 September
I hate Maggie. I told her about Mister Johnson and she promised to keep my secret and she went straight home and told her mother. Her mother came round to see my mother in the afternoon yesterday. I had to stay in my bedroom. Mumma yelled horrible things at me after. She called me a slut. I looked that up and it isn't true. I only have love for Mister Johnson. My heart is broken and I am going to go back and see him as soon as I can. He will want me to visit. He is probably waiting every day thinking where I am.

26 September
Luca and Augie Johnson left the school today. They're starting at St Francis. We all said goodbye and Miss Baldry brought marangs with sprinkles but Luca

walked away from me. I think he hates me because I am with his father. Henry gave me a chocolate when I was crying in my room. He said it would all be ok but I said it wouldn't be ok because I needed to see my one true love.

So Henry knew something.

9 October
I walked to the Johnsons after school. I couldn't stand it anymore. Mumma thinks I went to Sally Slarke's house which shows how much she knows because Sally would never invite me. Mumma wishes I was like Sally. I needed to see my love. I will die if I don't see him. Missers Johnson answered the door. She said I couldn't be there and should go straight home. I asked about Mister Johnson and she said he doesn't live there anymore. She's lying. She shut the door. She is just jealous. Maggie is jealous too. Missers Johnson had the red dress on and it was stained. She smells.

16 October
Maggie and me went to the swimming pool today on the bus and lay on our Disney princess towels on the concrete to get a tan. Mine is Ariel and hers is Jasmine. We got icecreams. Maggie is the best friend ever. She can move in with me and Mister Johnson. Two boys talked to us. The one who likes Maggie brought her some chicken chips and the one who likes me got me chocolate milk. We pashed them in the bush near the picnic place and Maggie got fingered. I didn't and that suits me because my one had a lot of pimples and I'm

saving myself for you know who. Plus it hurts. It hurt Maggie but I know she was pleased that I didn't get it too. As if I haven't already had it before her. Plus, with a real boyfriend.

29 October
Mister Johnson was outside school across the road today. He waved and I was worried someone would see me with him and stop me but no one did. I went across the crossing and he had his car there round the corner. He drove me to the oval with his hand on my knee and then under my uniform. No one was there so we could just be together. It was very romantic. He told me to get out of the car and we walked down a track in the bush. He held my hand which was exciting. I always wanted to hold a boyfriend's hand. He had a checked blanket and he spread it out and we lay down on it. He couldn't get down at first so I helped him. He straight away asked me what colour underpants I was wearing. I knew what colour but I think he likes that game. He pulled them down to check. He had a little bottle covered in leather. He called it improver. He told me to drink some and I nearly choked. Mister Johnson pulled up my uniform. He had a jar of Vaseline with curly hairs in it. He put some on me. He put his fingers in. Then he put his willy in. I was almost crushed. I didn't really know what a grown-up penis looked like before. Mister Johnson pushed a lot and it didn't really go in. It hurt but I didn't stop him. I want to be a good girlfriend, so I let him. I had to wipe myself after with a tissue from my pocket. I was sticky and there was blood. He said he had to leave me because Missers Johnson found

out about us. I started to cry. He kissed me with his tongue to say sorry. I didn't like that much because of his whiskers and he smells of fungus teeth. And I was worryed I had cheese breath from my sandwiches at lunchtime. He drank some more improver and made me have a sip to celebrate our love. I still nearly choked. Mister Johnson thought it was funny. I helped him get up. He dropped me back to the end of my street and Mumma was angry I was late, but I told her I'd gone to the library to work and pick up some books because Miss Baldry had put me to the top group in English. Mumma was pleased. I'm not going to tell her what I did with Mister Johnson because she will be angry with me again. No one understands. Most of all my mother doesn't understand. I am keeping the tissue with the blood next to Missers Johnson's camellia that I took from the party when it fell down in the limbo competition.

Audrey read on but couldn't find any more references to Mr Johnson in her diary over the next few weeks of entries. She wondered if the tissue carried his DNA.

It was as if nothing had ever happened, Audrey thought. She had no recollection of anything being said to her again by anyone about the Johnsons, except for Rita's urgent warning, after Maggie's mother called by, not to tell her father, and of course she hadn't told Eustace. What would she even say? She didn't tell anyone about the rape, and she didn't know back then that it was rape. Rita never spoke to her of Mr Johnson again, and now, more than twenty years later, Audrey sometimes wondered if any of it had even happened, and what exactly had happened. Yet she'd

The Little Clothes

always known it as a part of her, and if she ever thought of it she was ashamed and anxious and often woke frightened by nightmares where he appeared with his pipe and hanky, and once in a deerstalker hat. She knew that what he'd done had changed her in a profound way. She knew there were many dubious choices she'd made since. Terrible liaisons, awful men she'd fucked in alleys behind bars and in cars after too much wine. More recently she'd put those mistakes and transgressions in the Henry Dying box, when in fact they had seeded a long time before her brother's death, then grown and branched from a different dark place altogether. Perhaps, she thought, her common ground with her brother was that as children they had both been unseen and misunderstood by their mother.

Chapter 8

'Maggie, it's me.'
'Hello you.'
'Sorry to disturb you at work. Can we get a drink sometime?'
'Love to. Are you okay?'
'Mr Johnson.'
'Is that the guy next door? Has he been bothering you?'
'No. It's the guy who molested me when I was a kid.'
'Do I know about that?'
'Maggie! Mr Johnson.'
'Oh, okay. Was that the creepy father?'
'Yes.'
'Okay. You'll have to join the dots for me.'
'Can we meet tonight so I can do that? Join the dots.'
'Sorry, can't do. Tomorrow night?'
'Sure. Where? Anywhere for me except the place in Camperdown where we had that fish curry. I can never eat fish curry again, which is a shame because it was my favourite thing.'
'Let's go to Palisades? Let's go ritzy. My treat.'
'Not sure what I need to talk to you about is a Palisades moment.'

The Little Clothes

'Okay. Then you say.'

'What about I book at Golden Oak for seven?'

'Sure. I'll see you there. Sorry, Aud. I'm on call and I have to go.'

'Of course. See you then.'

Audrey was now adrift. She had cut the tight mooring lines and launched herself into the murky water. She didn't want it, but now it was here, rushing, splashing, flooding and submerging.

•

'Nadine. It's Audrey.'

'Yes.'

'I can't come in today. I'm sick.'

'Well, I think Alec's expecting you. He was looking for you. He's back from the conference and there's court today. You left it a bit late to call in, didn't you?'

'I just can't come. I'm really sick.' Audrey hung up and went to sleep. She had never felt so exhausted. Not even after Henry died. She couldn't move. For two days. She burrowed and hibernated.

'Audrey, it's me. Where are you? We were supposed to meet at Golden Oak.'

'Maggie, I'm fine. I have a terrible cold. I am so, so sorry. I fell asleep. Too much medication.'

'Audrey, where are you? It's Nadine. Alec's furious. You'd better call him.'

'Audrey, it's Mum. I realised Dad and I missed your birthday. I can't believe it. We're so sorry. We want to take you out. Maybe to that nice Austrian place in our shopping arcade? They do a delicious Hungarian goulash. And they have Chinese dishes too. And some Australian meals if you prefer. Your father always has the steak with peppercorn sauce. You watch. That's what he'll order. Medium rare. I prefer medium to well done. But I'll be having the goulash anyway. Call me back.'

'Audrey, it's Angus. Long time no see. I want you to meet Javier. You'll love him. I know I do. We want to take you to dinner. How does Friday week sound?'

Audrey slept on and on, except to tend to Joni.

She looked at herself in the mirror when she went to the bathroom. Her nightie was on inside out and backwards. She had a string of blue beads round her neck that she didn't remember putting on.

•

In the end Maggie came to the front door and didn't let up. Pressing the buzzer, ringing, texting, lightly throwing white pebbles at windows. Yelling.

Greg came around with one of his friends to see what was going on.

'Who are you? The sister?'

'Who are you?'

'The neighbour. And me mate, Tyrone. Say hello, Tyrone.'

'Oh, you're the neighbour.'

'S'what I said.'

'Everything is fine here. I'm her friend. She's unwell. You don't need to be here.'

Greg walked back up the garden path to the street, with Tyrone muttering, 'Lesos' and 'Don't think ya gonna see much action there, mate.'

The Little Clothes

Audrey came to the door. Limp, flat, oily hair matted at the back. Backwards nightie. Blue beads.

'Aud.' Maggie stepped forward and put her arms around her friend and hugged her.

'So, what's going on, Aud?' Maggie asked when she was sitting on the lounge chair opposite the sofa where Audrey had made a nest. Blankets and pillows, the diaries scattered around on the floor and the coffee table. Wine bottles, whisky bottle, remotes, a splitting bag of rabbit food, chocolate wrappers, reading glasses, legal files, notepads of scribblings.

Audrey wracked with sobs.

Maggie let her cry.

'Here. Tea. Please drink it. I'm going to make you some breakfast. You need to eat.'

'Maggie. Go to work. You have important stuff to do.'

'This is important stuff.'

'I can't eat.'

'Yeah, you can. And you will. You really need to have a shower, Aud. Just saying. Go now while I make some food. Not much in your fridge though. That will have to change.'

Audrey obeyed and came out in a clean T-shirt and pyjama bottoms, a towel turban.

They sat together at the dining table and ate scrambled eggs with chives and drank coffee bought from across the road.

'So Aud, what's going on?'

'What do you mean?'

'Aud, don't do this. What is going on? Don't make me fill in the blanks. I'm incredibly worried about you. You mentioned Mr Johnson?'

'You don't remember, do you?'

'Look, I do. A bit. I had to dredge it up. He was the creepy father who touched you, but I remember you thought he was your *true love* and asked me not to tell.'

'But you did tell.'

'Yeah, but I kind of knew it was wrong, what had happened. That's all. I was just a kid too. I was also a bit jealous that you'd transferred your love from me to him and I didn't have a boyfriend.'

'I know.'

'So, how's this all just come up?'

'He raped me. After.'

'No.'

'Yes.'

'You didn't tell me, all this time? Did you tell anyone?'

'No. At the start I was worried after you told your mother about the other bit and Rita went psycho. I knew all hell would break loose if she knew the next bit.'

'Okay. I didn't know that. Or remember that. But I'm sorry anyway.'

'Look, to be fair I didn't know I'd been raped till much later. Then I forgot. I thought it was romantic, except in my guts I knew it was wrong and even though I've tried to ignore it for so long and not give it any air it's been coming at me. It's been locked up forever and now it's here. It's caught me.'

'Aud, I want you to see this colleague of mine. She's pretty wonderful and very experienced in dealing with residual grief and anger after sexual assault. She works in the sexual assault unit at the hospital. I really want you to call her and go and talk.' Maggie gave Audrey her card with a name and number scribbled on the back. 'She's booked out for months, swamped actually, but I'll make sure she

The Little Clothes

fits you in straight away. You should go. Just tell her you're Maggie's friend when you call.'

'Don't you want to know what happened to me?'

'Only if you want to tell me.'

Audrey led Maggie back to the couch and riffled through the diaries. She handed the open page to Maggie, who read in silence. Audrey hid her face behind a pillow till Maggie was finished.

'Is he still alive?'

'Doubt it.'

'Could be. Did he stay with his family?'

'I don't think so.'

'What do you want to do?'

'Nothing.'

'Audrey. You must call my friend. And you need to think about pursuing him legally.'

'No bloody way. I know the legal side of things. That's what I do. It's historical anyway. He'd be dead by now for sure. I think he had emphysema way back then.'

'I'm so sorry, Aud. I let you down.'

'No, you didn't. We were kids. I was a fool. My mother let me down. I am so ashamed of how dumb I was. I thought he was my boyfriend. I thought I loved him. He totally saw who I was, looking for a little praise and attention. Low self-esteem. He picked me off. Rita was useless. It was hidden from my father. It was the business of women. If he had known what happened, Dad might have killed the cunning old pedo.'

'Yeah. I agree. Eustace would have been there for you, Aud. I do have to go in an hour but I'm going to clean up first. Why don't you ring Cathy now?'

'Cathy?'

'The counsellor.'

'Sorry?'

'The counsellor I just told you about. On the back of my card.'

'Yeah, maybe.'

'Audrey, you need some help. Please call her.'

'I will. Just not now. And don't wash up. I'll get going on this. You go back to work. I need something practical to do. I mean it. You've done enough.'

The two friends hugged at the door after Maggie washed up at the sink and changed the bed linen. In her bedroom Audrey fell back into a long sleep that lasted almost twelve hours.

•

'Audrey. It's Alec. You're in. Finally. You need to come up and see me now.'

'Sure. Give me five.'

'No. Now.'

Audrey went upstairs.

'So, Audrey. Where the fuck have you been?'

'Sick. I called in.'

'What's been wrong that you disappear for a week? Doctor's certificate, I suppose?'

'Yes, of course.'

'We're fucked in the Coulter case.'

'I left a message for Daniel to use my notes. My excellent notes.'

'We're fucked. You needed to be here.'

'Well, I'm sorry Alec but I was really sick. I've got literally hundreds of sick leave days. I've never used them.'

The Little Clothes

'What with? What were you sick with?'

'The flu.'

'Of course, the flu. The universal excuse. Do you know that hardly anyone ever gets the flu? It's a cold, not the flu. At least you spared Nadine the croaky voice. Even Carter can do that. Nadine said you sounded fine. You aren't out canvassing for other work, a new job, are you? Nadine seems to think you're upset about the recent partnership announcements.'

'Alec, I was sick. At least I didn't use the universal golf tournament excuse. Or the "It's something I ate, might have been the prawns" excuse.'

'Ha ha. You can be funny, Audrey. A sly wit. The thing I like about you. And I hear you went to see Erin?'

'Erin called me because she needed someone in the absence of her husband. It wasn't exactly what I had planned for my Thursday night.'

'Well, thank you for going.'

'That's okay. Milla is gorgeous.'

'Yeah. Doesn't stop crying. She seems very emotional.'

'She's a baby, Alec. That's how babies communicate.'

'I don't remember my other children crying so much. Anyway, I've had to move out for a few days just to get some sleep and try to recover this case. Are you ready to be briefed about where we're up to?'

'Sure. If I'm still on it.'

'Yes, you're still on it. Fucking Daniel is fucking useless.'

'And yet a junior partner.'

'Now is not the time.'

'Okay. I'll just grab a coffee and my files. I'll come back up.'

'Regular flat white, Dinah will have a latte.'

In the pub that evening Audrey was startled to see her neighbour sitting at the bar chatting with the bar fly. Greg nodded to her.

'Can I buy you a drink?'

'Thanks, but no. I'm late for my friends. We do trivia together.'

'So ya keep sayin'. Just want to be nayberlee. Won't be askin' twice.'

That's a relief, thought Audrey, noting his little speckled hands and pale feet in crusty black thongs, long jagged toenails.

'Ah, come on. Just one. This is me nayba,' Greg said, turning to the bar fly and gesturing towards Audrey, who had taken a stool.

'Just one then. A sav blanc.'

'I know what ya drink. Seen all those bottles in ya bin.'

'Cheers, then.'

'Cheers.'

'So what's this group you run? This group of men who seem to live in your backyard and want to read books.'

'It's for fathers who can't see their kids. Started as a Father's Day thing for dads who are separated from their kids. Court orders against them. I started it with the prison chaplain inside and kept it goin' when I come out. Just trying to do shit for other people. Trying to make up for me past.'

'I see.'

'Don't think you do see, Audrey.'

'Oh, I do. I work in the law and I see a lot of things. Battered wives and the like. Anyway, it was lovely having a drink. But I have to go and join my group for trivia.'

The Little Clothes

'Don't let me keep you from the important stuff.'
'Thanks for the drink.'
'Any time.'

•

Tom beckoned Audrey to sit next to him at the table.
'You're here. We missed you last week. You okay?'
'Just a bad cold. No Elspeth tonight?'
'No. She doesn't really enjoy it. Can't eat anything. Not really a drinker. Doesn't have a lot of general knowledge. I think it's boring for her.'
'Oh, that's a shame. I was just getting to know her.'
'Not really much to know.'
'That can't be true.'
'Trust me, Audrey.'
Tom whispered in Audrey's ear, bought her colourful drinks and laughed at everything she said, his face close to hers. Lorraine looked on, reproachful.
When the scores were being tallied, Tom followed Audrey into the bathroom.
'Tom! You can't be in here.'
'Well, I am. Who's stopping me?'
He spun Audrey into a cubicle, his arm stretching across her onto the wall, blocking escape. Then he pushed her lightly and shut the door. He put his hand down her top, squeezed her right breast. Kissed her hard on the mouth.
'You make me crazy,' he said, nuzzling her face. 'I've been wanting this.'
'Really?'
'Audrey. Really. You're so sexy.'
'Oh, come on, Tom. Neither of us believes that.'

'Audrey, shut up.'

They returned to the table after the break and did not conceal their frisson. The others murmured and furtively bumped knees with each other. Audrey was flushed with excitement. Sean seemed to be upset.

They missed out by two points on first prize.

'Well, if everyone had been concentrating,' said Lorraine.

'We can't expect to win every week, Lor,' said Sean.

'I'm just saying, if we'd all had our eyes on the prize and not elsewhere, we might be celebrating right now.'

'Well, we know who wouldn't have been buying the drinks if we'd won,' said Marion.

'What's that supposed to mean?'

'You know what it means.'

'Come back to mine for a drink, Aud. Let's get out of here,' Tom whispered in Audrey's ear.

Audrey followed him. 'Night, everyone. Maybe we'll win next week, hey?'

The women eyed her dubiously, the men with surprise, re-evaluating.

They were barely at the top of Tom's snaking stairs when he put a hand under her skirt and jiggled her bottom cheeks. From the verandah he pushed through the front door, with Audrey involuntarily straddling his shoving knee, then he manoeuvred her down the hallway and onto his bed.

•

When Audrey woke she shielded her face from the sun that was streaming through tiny stained-glass windowpanes. Her head ached on one side in intermittent bursts, and she remembered the cocktails. She gazed at Tom. She couldn't

The Little Clothes

believe her luck. She was here with him. She leaned on her elbow and stroked his hair.

Audrey was already late for work. Right then she didn't care. Tom was snoring softly. She got up, put on his silky gown and went to pee, tentatively pushing doors open till she found the bathroom.

'Oh, hi.'

'So sorry. Didn't know anyone was here. So sorry.'

'Don't be. There's another bathroom out the back. Follow your nose. Not that it smells or anything.'

Audrey backed away from the statuesque nude woman standing in front of the mirror applying her mascara, and found a toilet in the laundry. Tom came in when she was finishing.

'Sorry 'bout that. An old friend. Scarlet. Didn't know she was here. She comes and goes. Sleeps in the spare room.'

Where the spare blankets are kept, Audrey thought.

He leaned down, lifted Audrey's left breast and licked it. She pushed him back gently.

'Tom, I'm on the loo.'

'Can see that.'

'Maybe the bedroom?'

'Sure.'

Audrey followed Tom, who was wearing a towel around his waist, down the hall to the bedroom, where the curtain was now forgivingly drawn. While he laboured on top of her with his eyes closed, Audrey considered the ceiling and noted the rose cornices and a huntsman so large she fancied she could see its face. Tom kept going. He finally finished with a whinny.

After a while, as he dozed next to her, she spoke up. 'Tom. My phone. It keeps buzzing. I was supposed to be at work an hour ago. I'm going to have to leave.' Audrey stood, struggling to put her knickers on. She'd fished them from under the bed where they'd been flung, a tight elasticated roll in the dust drifts.

'Sure. Just let me have another little go. I love your tits. Real tits. Mammaries, great big bazookas. Fun bags. Jugs, pups, bunnies. Yours need a postcode. I'm a breast man, in case you haven't noticed.'

He reached up and grabbed her by one pendulous breast and put her nipple in his mouth, tweaking the other, as if milking her, and she obligingly hovered above him at an awkward angle, one knee on the edge of the bed, one foot on the floor, her hands gripping the iron bedhead to stay stable and not put her weight on him, conscious of how heavy she was and how her stomach flopped and bounced. She was able to glance down at her phone on the bedside table whenever he switched to her right breast.

'Tom, I really have to go now. Nice as this is, and it is nice, so nice, don't get me wrong, I've really enjoyed myself, but there's work and all. Lots of messages. I have to get dressed and listen to them. Hello, Tom? Tom, I really do have to go. You have to stop.'

'Sure. See you next Tuesday.' Tom released her abruptly and turned away to look at his phone. Something on his screen made him laugh.

'Oh, okay. Not before Tuesday? I thought maybe you could come round to mine and I'll cook dinner.'

'Aud, that's sweet. But not possible. I have an incredibly busy week of shoots for the pilot and a couple of upfronts,' he said over his shoulder.

'Sure. See you Tuesday then.' He didn't look up as she left.

The Little Clothes

Audrey descended the steep winding stairs onto the already scorched street as carefully as she could in bare feet, holding her shoes, her handbag and the railing. Once on the path she listened to her messages in a panic.

'Audrey! It's Alec. Where the fuck are you now? Not the flu again, I hope. What's going on with you? I think we need to talk. You better get yourself in here.'

'Audrey, it's Mum. We still haven't heard from you about your birthday outing. We'll have to make a booking. It's very popular. So we need a date.'

'Aud, I've been worrying about you. Have you called Cathy yet?'

'Aud, it's Erin. Thanks so much for coming over last week. You saved me. You won't believe it but I'm putting chilled cabbage leaves on my boobs. Turns out I have lactation mastitis. And just one other thing, and this sounds insane, but do you remember Alec's lamp? It's missing from his study. It's the one we all gave him on his sixtieth. We can't work it out. We think it might have been the cleaner or maybe Carter hid it, but Mum said you'd been in the study waiting for your Uber so I wonder if you noticed it so we can work out the timing of when it disappeared?'

'Maggie, it's me, Aud.'

'Aud, where have you been? I've been calling. Have you contacted Cathy yet?'

'Cathy?'

'The counsellor.'

'Oh yeah. No. Haven't had a chance. I'll do it as soon as I get over this hump at work. You're not going to believe this, but I have just spent the night with Tom at his.'

'Okay. That was sudden. The TV guy, right? Thought he had a girlfriend. How was it?'

'He is obsessed with my breasts. A little bit strange, to tell the truth. A bore in bed, to be honest. But he's fun the rest of the time, and we had a great night together. We met up at trivia and his girlfriend wasn't there, so he asked me home.'

'Okay. You sound a bit hectic. Are you okay? And what about the girlfriend?'

'I don't think they're together anymore. Not really. I'm okay. I'm just walking home. I'm out of breath.'

'Shouldn't you be at work?'

'Please don't spoil this for me.'

'No, of course. I'm really pleased for you if it's what you want. I promise not to ring my mother and dob you in.'

'That's not funny. I have to go, Maggie.'

Audrey hurried up the street. She had suddenly remembered Joni.

'Well, well, well,' said Greg from his front garden, where he was hosing. 'Look what the cat dragged in. Pulled an all-nighter! Respect!'

'Greg, I don't need your commentary every time I come and go from my own house. Please just leave me alone. Don't make me take out an AVO.'

'Well maybe *I'll* take out an AVO. Why do ya keep making my business your business, lookin' at me through me own fence an' callin' the cops?'

Audrey held her phone to her ear, as if taking a call from someone. She fumbled for her keys. Safely inside the door, she listened to a voicemail from Maggie.

'Audrey, it's Maggie. That was a terrible thing for me to say. Sorry. Call me so I don't worry.'

Audrey strode down the hall, composing an indignant reply, and found Joni lying very still on her side, stretched out on the rush mat in the kitchen. A Rabbitohs emblem.

The Little Clothes

'Oh, Joni, I'm so sorry.' She fled the room.

'Papa,' she said through sobs. 'My rabbit is dead. Joni's dead. I don't know what to do. I stayed the night at Maggie's and just came in and she's dead. I think I killed her. I can't look.'

'I'm coming over now. Don't touch her. I'll be there in thirty.'

'Don't bring Mum.'

'She's out with Nin buying sewing things. It will just be me.'

•

Audrey opened the door to Eustace and fell into his arms, crying hysterically. 'Oh my god, I'm an idiot. I went out and forgot about her. Again. I am so stupid. I don't deserve a rabbit. I don't deserve anything. I might have lost my job. I'm all over the place. I feel crazy.'

'Hang on, Audrey. Slow down. Where is your rabbit?'

'In the kitchen.' Audrey led Eustace down the hall and gestured without looking.

'Audrey, it's not dead.'

Joni was sitting up on the rush mat, twitching. Audrey screamed and dashed forward to scoop her up.

'Joni, Joni, Joni. I will never let you down again. Oh my god. You're alive. You're alive!'

She took Joni back to her cage and gave her a carrot and water and fresh hay.

'Now the rabbit is taken care of. What about you?' Eustace peered at his daughter and gave her a cup of tea. 'What's going on with you?'

'I'm not sure. My neighbour upsets me. He's spoilt

everything, poking his nose into everything I do. Actually, I'm terrified of him. He runs this sort of club for men who are estranged from their children. He started it in prison, for god's sake. I still miss Henry all the time. I hate work. I'm lonely. I've met someone, but I don't know if he likes me for me or bits of me. And I thought my rabbit was dead. How did that happen? I swear she was dead. How could I be that stupid?'

'Rabbits do sometimes lie down or flop when they're relaxed. I remember that from when I was a boy. I had a rabbit called Chester who did that. Maybe leaving it alone inside for a while made it happy and relaxed.'

'Oh god, do you think I make her nervous? She doesn't like me? I know people don't like me.'

'Audrey, darling. It's a rabbit. I don't know what it's thinking about you. But I like you. I'm sure lots of people do. Who cares what the rabbit thinks?'

They laughed.

'I have an idea, though. I could make you an indoor cage without a top but with higher sides. That way it's inside and you don't have to run in and out after work. On the weekend you can put her out on the grass for a bit of fresh air while you're out there. Would you like that?'

'Papa, you are so good to me. I love you so much. That would be perfect.'

'And now you can do something for me.'

'Anything.'

'Call your mother and give her a date for a birthday dinner before she drives me round the mountain.'

'The bend.'

'What?'

'Drives me round the bend.'

The Little Clothes

'Okay. The bend.'

'I'll call her when you leave.'

'I'm sorry we missed your birthday. I think about you every day.'

'I know, Papa.'

'And I wasn't here today. Okay? I don't want to worry your mother.'

'Sure.'

'So, Audrey, I think you might need to slow down. Stop giving so much time to other people. To that boss of yours and his wife. All that palaver for their wedding. They sound like frivolous people. They think their time is more important than yours. It isn't. Take stock. Your own stock. Live your own life. Don't be a prop for them. Start from itches.'

'Start from scratch, Papa.'

'Yes, from scratch. They really are superfluous to needs.'

'Surplus.'

'That too. You and your words. I can tell you're already feeling better.'

Before he left, Eustace sketched the plans for the new cage in thin ballpoint on an A4 page of printer paper. He drew separate spaces for sleeping on hay and hopping on astroturf. He added a water drip on the side and a feeding bowl. He drew three remarkably good rabbits in different postures in different areas of the cage with a few strokes.

'That's where Henry got it from.'

'Yes, maybe. My father could do it too. Draughtsmen all, we Mendes men.'

'I'm thinking of getting another rabbit to keep Joni company. So maybe a double feeder?'

Eustace raised his eyebrows, smiled and scribbled a note on his sheet of paper.

•

Audrey called Rita to set a date.

'I really should check with your father but he's not here. He sometimes goes to the library. Still, he's been gone a while so I'm getting worried. He knows how worried I get. He can be thoughtless.'

'He'll be home soon, Mumma. I'm sure of it. He's never thoughtless. Anyway, is that date okay for the dinner?'

'What dinner?'

'Mumma, you wanted to take me to dinner.'

'Oh, that. Yes. That's fine. Your father never really goes anywhere so it should be fine. Do you want to bring someone? A special someone. Like Maggie?'

'No, just me. We'll talk before then but let's agree next Wednesday at 7.30? I'll see you there.'

'Yes. You know where it is?'

'Yes, I know where it is.'

Rita always held family birthday dinners at the Schnitzel Snug in her local shopping arcade, but for each occasion it was presented as a 'discovery'.

'I bet your father will order the steak medium rare with peppercorn sauce. Just wait and see.'

'I won't take the bet, Mumma. I'm sure you're right.'

'Are you okay, Audrey? You sound a bit faraway.'

'Yes, I'm fine. I've been wanting to ask, do you remember Mr Johnson?'

'Of course. How could I forget that catastrophe! But we don't need to bring that up. It's all in the past, Audrey, and

The Little Clothes

there it should remain. In the mists of time. Let's talk only of fruit and flowers.'

'It's just that—'

'Audrey, I said I don't want to talk about it. Why on earth you're bringing it up now I don't know.'

'I've been remembering it and what happened and how it might be affecting me now. How it's affected my life.'

'Everything has to be examined and picked over these days. I blame Oprah. Or that Dr Phil, who had problems of his own. Not every upset leads to a terrible life, you know. Most of us wouldn't get out of bed if it did.'

'Well, a lot of people can't get out of bed. I hardly think being raped at the age of twelve was an upset. It was an outrage. A terrible crime.'

'But that's looking back. At the time you thought he was your boyfriend. And I presume you blame me?'

'I don't blame you, Mumma. He was a predator. I just want to talk about it. I was so young and don't remember it clearly. You were there. Why didn't you call the police?'

'We just didn't back then. We managed it ourselves. It was hushed up to protect you.'

'And to protect you.'

'I think he got his just deserts, Audrey. He moved away. He lost his family. I understand that he died a few years later.'

'I'm glad if he suffered. I hope he died a terrible death.'

'My advice is to leave it alone, Audrey. It's not like we all weren't molested. Nin and me that time by the youth leader at the church.'

'What? You were molested? What time?'

'And Nin. Not just me. Ninnie was there too.'

'Tell me what happened.'

'There's nothing to tell, really.'
'Mumma, you have to tell me now. You said it.'
'It's nothing.'
'Mumma! Tell me or I'll think the worst.'
'In a way, it was the worst.'
'Now you definitely have to tell me.'
'Okay, Audrey. Keep your hair on. We went to a youth group meeting one night at his house.'
'Whose house?'
'The youth group leader. Audrey, if you're going to butt in every five seconds…'
'Sorry. Go on.'
'My father was very strict even by the standards of his day. We were allowed to go because it was a church thing. He chased us with all the other kids.'
'Your father chased you?'
'Audrey, I'm going to hang up.'
'Sorry, Mumma. Keep going.'
'The youth leader, I think his name was Rod, chased us in and out of the rooms in his bungalow that was next door to the church. I don't know if the church let him stay there for free – anyway, it was as if it was a big funny game, and we all romped to the couch and fell on each other, and his hands found Nin and me. He took us into his walk-in wardrobe with his torch and left it with us, saying we were the prize. I think we felt special. He said we were playing hide-and-seek. He was the adult, so we did what we were told to do. We could hear him telling the others to go away into the garden and count to one hundred out loud and then come and find us. He came back into the wardrobe and fumbled in our underwear with the time counting down. We could hear it counting down. Nin copped the

The Little Clothes

worst of it. Tried to get to her mouth, if you know what I mean. He was very worked up. She clamped her teeth. Typical Nin. So it went on her face. I should have protected her. I think I knew what was happening but she didn't know at all. Maybe I was jealous he'd chosen my little sister over me. Isn't that terrible? I think he was quite a sad young man, looking back. An oddball.'

'That's so awful, Mumma. I can't bear it. It wasn't your fault.'

Rita continued in a hurry to get ahead of her daughter's despair.

'I told Nin he'd brought a salty drink into the wardrobe and accidentally sprayed it after it had been shaken. Nin and I slept in one bed together that night. The only time. I can't remember if it was hers or mine. Nin clung to me. I felt guilty. Our room was tiny, with just two single beds and a shared bedside table and our wardrobe. That night the room felt like a very big terrifying place. We were alert, if you know what I mean. We kept watch.'

'Mumma, you did try to protect her. I can't stand it. Lovely young Nin.'

'Don't cry, Audrey. It was a long, long time ago. Like you and Mr Johnson.'

'Did you tell Grandma? Did Nin? Did Grandma call the police?'

'God, no. Our mother didn't even mention periods until I got one and thought I was bleeding to death. Even then she was embarrassed, threw a homemade pad and a belt at me and told me to clean myself up. Grandma Joan was tough. She sort of lost interest in being a mother and a wife. As you might remember, she turned to the sherry in the end. All that claptrap about tea leaves and visions. She couldn't speak to our father unless he asked it of her. Of course, when I was quite young, my father would round up all the local hobos in town during winter and let them stay in our shed. There were quite a few who exposed themselves to me.'

'Of course. Did Grandpa know?'

'No. He would have been furious with me for going into the shed. He was always busy doing God's work, but not for us. He did the showy work. For the church hierarchy.'

'Why did you go into the shed?'

'I don't know, Audrey. I was curious. I wanted the attention. I don't know. Stop asking questions.'

'It's all so sad.'

'No, it's just life, Audrey.'

'I want to go and shoot that church guy. Does Dad know?'

'Don't be so outraged, Audrey. You're always outraged. It's tiring. And no, your father doesn't know.'

'I am outraged with good reason.'

'But for what? What are you going to do all these years later?'

'I just think we all put up with too much.'

'Of course. It continued long after that.'

'The church guy?'

'No, of course not. We never went back to youth group again. We were terrified our parents would find out what had happened and we'd be in trouble. No, it was at work. Mr Baston used to put his hand on our bottoms when I first started in the typing pool. He was always at the back of the lift or lurking in the tearoom. Then the sleazy sales guy. Now, what was his name? Let me think. I can still see him. My memory! It's on the tip of my tongue.

The Little Clothes

Mr Smithers! It was Mr Smithers. He was always touching me. We just put up with it. Thinking about it now, that was a bit strange, because I once stayed back to do some work for Mr Baston and I went to Mr Smithers' office for carbon paper and found him sitting there dressed as a woman.'

'What?'

'Full pancake make-up, a wig, a hat with a half veil across the eye, woollen boucle suit, stockings bunching round his ankles and lace-up women's leather shoes. Granny shoes. He was just sitting there relaxing.'

'What did he say?'

'Nothing.'

'What did you say?'

'Nothing.'

'Seriously? You didn't say anything?'

'Oh, no, Audrey, that's right, I actually said, "Nice hat, Mr Smithers. Where did you get the suit?" Of course I didn't say anything. I was an office junior. I was stunned. I had no idea about those sorts of things.'

Audrey couldn't help giggling. Rita joined in.

'I'm so sorry that happened to you and Aunty Nin, though.'

'I think your father's just arrived home. I have to go. See you at dinner next week. And never tell Nin I told you.'

'Do you ever talk to Nin about it?'

'No. And I won't. I have to go.'

•

Audrey called Alec and left a message.

'Alec, it's me, Audrey. You're right. We do need to talk.

I'm sorry I've let you down lately. I'll explain when I see you. I'll be at work tomorrow.'

Then: 'Maggie, I'm fine and I'll call Cathy ASAP. Sorry for everything.'

'Hi Erin, it's Aud. Hope those cabbage leaves are helping. Sorry I can't enlighten you about the lamp. Pardon the pun. Talk soon.'

'Hi Tom. It's me, Audrey. Sorry I left in such a hurry. I know you're busy, but I just wanted to say what a great night I had and thank you for having me. Would love to catch up before Tuesday, but if not, that's okay too.'

Audrey spent the rest of the day taking stock. She shopped for groceries, tidied her entire house, rearranged and smelled the growing collection of little clothes, weeded around her pebbles and sat on her back verandah reading a cosy crime novel while Joni jumped, hopped and sometimes stopped to quiver and listen. She drank a glass of wine in the sun, had a nap on the couch and packed a healthy lunch for the office the next day. She ordered lacy underwear online, cooked a Nigella chicken pasta and enjoyed looking at her full fruit bowl on the sideboard even though she rarely ate fruit, just the occasional nectarine in summer. She imagined a future with Tom.

Chapter 9

Alec was brusque with the young woman at the front desk in the restaurant, pointing out that he was there every week and sometimes twice, and had been dining there for fifteen years. He wanted to speak to her boss, whom he now claimed as a *close personal friend*, and he wanted his usual table. Had they opened his wine? They hadn't. And his table was taken. The young woman was impassive.

'I'm sorry, sir, but you only booked twenty minutes ago, and that table was already occupied. I can offer you one of our booths, which are also very comfortable and private. And I'll get our sommelier to speak to you as soon as you're seated.'

'I guess that will have to do. But I will be talking to Michael about this. The table is usually kept for me. What's your name?'

'Grace.'

Audrey loathed eating in restaurants with Alec because he was punishing to the waitstaff, which made her become obsequious and panicked in her attempts to soothe both sides. Eustace had taught his children that it was a sign of low character to be rude to people who are serving you. She smiled apologetically at Grace as they were handed over to a waiter.

'No, no. I've changed my mind, not a booth. Is there a table? I'd like a table for grown-ups.'

They were shown to a table in the middle of the floor that Alec approached with an extravagant display of eye-rolling exasperation, making Audrey's gut clench, wondering what was coming next.

'So, Audrey, I have an hour. What's going on?' Alec shook out his napkin.

'I first want to say how sorry I am that I've let you down lately.'

'So you're leaving?'

'No.'

'What then?'

'I'm trying to tell you. Give me a minute.'

'I'll have the snapper pie. Audrey?'

'Same.'

'Two snapper pies. A green salad, dressing on the side, a bottle of the Giaconda Chardonnay and some of that flatbread with the olives and Swiss chard while we're waiting. But I only have an hour, so we don't want to be waiting long.' Alec flicked the menu at the waiter without looking at him.

'So, Audrey. Get going.'

'I am burnt out. I need some time off. I'm struggling with some personal stuff. I want to take some leave.'

'Cancer?'

'No! I think I've earned it. The time off.'

'You think you've earned it.'

'Yes, I do.'

'Tell me about that.'

'Well, I work very long hours, I mentor lots of the younger people, they all come to me from all departments. I did both trials in the Aziz case almost single-handedly, I

The Little Clothes

have been there for more than ten years and still don't have an office even though I was promised one over a year ago, I think I have served the company well, I rarely take time off, I do most of the pro bono work, and I fly economy on company business.'

'Really? You fly economy?'

'Yes. That's what Sally in Accounts always books for me. I assume she's been told to.'

'What's it like? Economy.'

'It's fine. It just seems that others in the firm don't fly economy.'

'You know what your problem is, Audrey?'

'Tell me, Alec.'

'No stamina.'

'That's not true.'

'No, we already ordered wine ten minutes ago. It would be good to drink it before Christmas.'

'Thanks so much,' said Audrey, smiling at the sommelier.

'Then what do you want, Audrey? Acknowledgement?'

'Yes, I would like a little acknowledgement, as a matter of fact. I would like to be a partner.'

'Audrey, you're a brilliant technician but you're not a rainmaker or a team player.'

'Well, I don't agree with that, but I'll take brilliant technician for now, and because of that ability I believe I bring work to the firm indirectly, and I haven't had a pay rise in years.'

'So this is about money? And travel? Nadine warned me.'

'No, it's about mental health. I need to take a couple of months. I need to take stock. And why have you already spoken to Nads about this before we talked, for god's sake?'

'So, two months' unpaid leave?'

'Paid leave.'

'Well, how can that happen? Be reasonable. If we do it for you, we have to do it for everyone.'

'I'm not everyone. I have been there the longest of anyone who hasn't been offered a partnership or gone elsewhere because they weren't offered one. I know I have long-service leave coming in a matter of weeks but I want to save that. Or I can take everything that's owed to me now in a lump sum and I'll go for good and find something else when I'm ready. I do get approached from time to time.'

Audrey had never been approached. No one noticed her flying under Alec's banner. Or under his *brand*, as he now thought of it. The brand, an amalgamation of his family name, his OAM, his business and his media coverage. The profile pieces in financial pages, glossy magazine spreads at his beach house with glamorous friends gathered at the table of plenty, his family dressed in white for a magazine shoot for Father's Day, then, more recently, his philanthropic activities.

Alec stabbed his fork at the pie, breaking the crust, allowing the heat to rise and fog his seldom-worn but necessary readers. 'Bloody pie. Too hot. Fucking glasses. Fucking pie. Can't see a thing. Now you're threatening me. I always thought I could rely on you, of all people.'

They ate in silence, except for Alec, who was in a sulk that bordered on rage, barking orders and complaints that the wine was over-chilled and being poured too quickly, that he needed more water and another napkin, his butter knife was dirty and his chair was rickety. And no, he didn't want the chair chocked with a piece of folded paper, he wanted another bloody chair!

The Little Clothes

'Is that too much to ask in a restaurant? A stable chair!' He appealed to Audrey in a caricature of astonishment. She looked down at her plate.

Audrey left with indigestion, an agreement that she could take leave in a week after she'd briefed Daniel, a month's paid leave and a month's unpaid leave, and a bottle of wine from Michael that Grace gave to Alec as they were leaving.

'Thank you so much, Grace,' said Audrey on Alec's behalf.

'Carry that for me, Aud. I don't want to be wandering down the street carrying a bottle of wine at lunchtime.'

'And I do?'

'No one will notice you. In fact, keep it. I'm never going back to that fucking restaurant. Ever again. Even if they beg me.'

'Well, I thought the pie was delicious. Thank you, Alec. So what if you can't have your usual table? The food and service are wonderful. By the way, I doubt they'll beg you. They seem to have plenty of customers.'

He was already on his phone. 'I'll be there by seven tonight. Can't your mother come over? I'm working, Erin. Remember working? It pays for things. I have to go.'

•

On the way up the hill from the ferry, Audrey thought about Tom and wondered what he was doing. Had he been thinking about her? She wished she had a good reason to call him other than that she wanted to see him.

After her excruciating lunch with Alec, Audrey shopped in David Jones to calm herself and now she detoured with her bags and bottle of wine down the lane on Tom's side, in the shadows below the houses. When she craned her neck and stood on tiptoes, she was startled to see him sitting at the top of his serpentine stairs in the sun on the verandah with Scarlet. She had her long bare legs across his lap and was throwing her head back, laughing throatily. They were comfortable together. So much for his busy life. Audrey dawdled down the lane on the same side and thought how she didn't want to be an Erin waiting on an Alec. Waiting for a man like Alec who would never be there. Still, her heart yearned for someone.

'Maggie, it's me.'

'Thank god, Aud. I've been worried about you. Is there anything I can do to help?'

'No need. I've arranged to take two months off work from the start of the week after next because I'm tired and I'm going to look after myself for a bit. I'm going to have my place painted inside and out. I'm going to go to movies in the mornings, cook and eat healthily, walk, try to lose some weight, visit my parents. They're getting old. They won't be here forever. I'm thinking of taking a week up the coast. Just rent a little cottage somewhere. I'll take Joni and read. Swim in the ocean. I need to get away from you-know-who next door. In fact, I'm thinking of selling and moving. I also want to get away from Alec and Maleficent.'

'Who?'

'Nadine.'

'Well, that all sounds very good. I can't tell you how pleased I am.'

'How are you?'

'Same old, same old.'

'Maggie, I'd like to take you out for dinner. Palisades?

The Little Clothes

Not next week but the week after? I'll be on leave by then. I really need to do this, so say yes.'

'I'd love that. I could do... let me see, Friday twenty-fifth?'

'Perfect.'

'Great. See you then. But call me if you need me before.'

'Jo. I'm fine.'

'I know, Amy.'

•

'So, leaving all the heavy lifting to us, Audrey? How did you swing that? Do you have photos somewhere of Alec with a goat?'

'I'm sure you'll be fine without me, Daniel, especially if you pay attention right now. I've organised all my files here. I'm going to walk you through them. I've arranged for you to meet the Carmodys at three o'clock on Wednesday – I spoke to Vanessa about your availability. It's in your diary. It will be in the Salter Room; I've booked it with Nadine. I've reassured them they are better off with you, in the hands of a partner, than with me, a non-partner. They were pleased with that. They think they've been promoted, so don't let them down. Just arrange to have some tea and coffee and biscuits set up. They like that. They think it's what they're paying for.'

'Good old Salty, hey? Why he had a meeting room named after him is anyone's guess. Have you ever met him? Complete tosser. I heard he had to leave the firm after some unsavoury dealings. Yet Marketing have seen fit to honour him. You must have worked here with Salty. How did you find him?'

'I've also arranged a meeting with the Bardwells, who were less pleased about my temporary departure, but it's a straightforward case so you'll do it on your ear, and that's what I told them. We've already got their first tranche and we haven't fully absorbed it yet. Here are my time sheets for that, so keep track. I've also shared them online. They ring a lot for advice disguised as a request for updates, so take notes. Just keep them in the holding bay. Hang on to the money but look after them. I will be surprised if it ever gets to court. It might end in mediation. But don't say that to them. They're champing at the bit for their day in court.'

'So seriously, Aud, how did you swing it?'

'Meet me back here tomorrow, Daniel, and I'll walk you through the rest. It would be great if you could read what I've already sent you before then.'

'Seriously though, Aud.'

'I have a lot to do, Daniel.'

'Okay, Miss. I consider myself dismissed.' Daniel spanked his own bottom on his way out of the Fabien Room.

•

The quiz had already started when Audrey arrived at the pub on Tuesday night. She'd been anticipating seeing Tom all week, having rationalised that Scarlet was an old friend and TV people were effusive and demonstrative. She wore her new cream satin shirt under her black suit. He wasn't there.

'No Tom?'

'No. Might be late like you. We thought you were probably together.'

The Little Clothes

'No, Lorraine, we aren't. I'm going to get a drink. Anything, anyone?'

Shay-Lee was sitting at a table near the bar with her toy doctor's bag in front of her, plastic stethoscope hanging from her ears. A long line of dolls and soft toys sat in the 'waiting room'.

'Hello Shay-Lee. What are you doing?'

'Blue Bear is very sicky.'

'Oh no, what happened to him?' Audrey cuddled the child's bedraggled bear, patting it on her shoulder, away from her nose.

'He doyed from a kaboom in the house.'

'But he's not dead. He's just resting. You must be a very good doctor.'

'And Peg-Peg is sicky too.' Shay-Lee offered up her naked, half-bald doll after pressing a plastic needle onto its forehead.

'What happened to her? Poor Peg.'

'Peg-Peg.'

'What happened to Peg-Peg?'

'Her eyeballs exploded.'

'That sounds nasty. Can you help her, Doctor?'

'I not real docta. You do it.'

Audrey extracted herself from the game by suggesting bed rest for all the patients, under napkins that she took from the self-service table, and went to the bar to order a salad and a glass of wine before rejoining the group.

'Sit here, Audrey,' said Sean. 'I've been saving the chair for you.'

'Thanks, Sean.'

Sean was attentive to Audrey for the remainder of the quiz, and complimented her appearance more than once.

His knee brushed fleetingly but clearly intentionally against hers. Audrey had never really considered Sean anything more than a quiz friend. After all, he tucked his T-shirt into jeans that were belted in faux lizard and rhinestones. He wore a sateen Rolling Stones souvenir jacket from 1995. His hair was absent at the front but hung in strands on the sides and at the back, like a shower curtain pulled open on a round loop. He wore embroidered cowboy boots.

On her way out of the pub Audrey passed the mother scolding Shay-Lee for using the napkins and making a mess.

'She said I can.' Shay-Lee pointed at Audrey.

'Shay-Lee, don't lie. And don't blame other people. And don't point. You did this.' The mother looked at Audrey, apologetic.

'It's okay,' said Audrey. 'I did suggest the napkins as bed covers. It was a game. I'm so sorry. I can pay for the napkins. She's such an imaginative child. Very bright.'

'Oh. You think so? Thank you.'

Hurrying to Tom's, Audrey stuffed her jacket into her bag and undid another button on her shirt. She fluffed her hair with her fingers.

'Audrey! Hello. Didn't expect to see you on my doorstep.'

'You weren't at the pub. We won. Thought I'd bring you a share of the spoils.' She handed him a bottle of cheap sparkling.

'That's kind. But not necessary when I didn't help.'

'Oh, well, you're part of the team.'

Audrey stood awkwardly.

'So, I just thought I'd call by on my way home.'

'That's kind.'

'Not really. As I said, you're part of the team.'

Audrey held her ground.

The Little Clothes

'I'm learning lines, Audrey. But come in if you like. Not for long, though. You mustn't distract me.'

'Sure. Just for a minute. I have work to do too.'

Tom led Audrey down the hall to his kitchen with the ease of a practised Lothario. How many women had followed him here? Walked this hall? Audrey knew he was doing the bare minimum. He had, after all, bedded her just a week ago. Yet something made her follow. He had told her she was sexy and she wanted that affirmation again. She fluffed her hair up and quickly smelled her breath.

'Glass of wine?'

'Sure. Thanks.'

'Sorry it's from a box.'

'That's fine.'

'Not fussy then? Anything will do?'

'I'm not a wine snob, if that's what you mean.'

'I know how you ladies are. Getting blotto by night then standing up straight as a pin the next day and going to work.'

'Sure, you've nailed me. So how are you, Tom? You've been so busy no doubt with the audition for the quiz show. The pilot.'

'Not really. I'm not doing anything much at the moment.'

They drank their wine at the kitchen table, Audrey at the head and Tom on the side next to her, quite close given the length of the table and the availability of space. Their legs were touching with no way out, Audrey's feet tucked under her chair and Tom's legs sprawled in front. Audrey thought about how she might adjust her legs without seeming to court intimacy or make it obvious how she felt. More obvious than it already was from her coming to Tom's late in the evening. Her feet were cramping. If she pushed her legs forward, they would inevitably run under his. Or worse, over his. Or she could push her chair backwards, but she was anxious about scratching the floor.

'So how was trivia? Sorry I couldn't make it. Still, you've got it all covered, haven't you? Listen, I must get this work done by tomorrow. So maybe just this one glass?'

'You can always text me. You know, so we're not saving a chair.' Dumb, Audrey thought. Why would she talk about chairs? She scrambled to think of something sharper.

'I'm sorry. Didn't think anyone would miss me.'

'You know how it is with the chairs.'

'Sure.'

'How have you been?'

'Yeah, good.'

'How's Elspeth?'

'We're not seeing each other anymore.'

'That's a shame.'

'Not really. It wasn't working for either of us. We'll still be friends.'

'I thought you seemed lovely together.'

'And yet you fucked me.'

'Well! I think it might have been the other way round. That wasn't what I planned. That just sort of happened. You came after me. All the way into the bathroom, if I remember correctly.' Audrey's face burnt with indignation and anger.

'But you did it. And here's what I think: you didn't give Elspeth a second thought.'

'Hang on. You did it too. She wasn't *my* girlfriend.' Audrey was enraged by Tom's attack but was also cowed. All of her fury repressed in shame and fear. She thought of Elspeth and was consumed with dread that Tom might

The Little Clothes

think she was a nasty person because she hadn't considered Elspeth.

'Take your top off.'

'What? No! No, I won't. Come on, Tom.'

'Take it off. Let me see them now. That's why you're here, isn't it?'

'I thought we could just chat and get to know each other better.'

'I don't have time. Take your top off.'

Audrey gulped her wine. She knew she had something he wanted and yet he somehow had the upper hand. She undid her buttons and put her blouse in her handbag as bidden. She sat obediently for inspection.

'There they are.'

Tom stood up and walked behind Audrey. He unhooked her bra and pushed his hands inside the loose lacy cups, flopping her breasts out. He massaged them with olive oil from the salad-dressing dispenser on the table. She was ashamed that they hung so low and were now dotted with flecks of parsley and mustard seeds. Her bra dangled loose, like a ghastly geriatric medical dressing. Beige. Why had she worn beige and not black? Or even red. Still, under a cream shirt? She made a mental note to buy a red bra trimmed with black lace and vice versa, or maybe black with chocolate lace, and a darker shirt. She thought about Scott's wedding, where the bridesmaids had been dressed in red and black lace over taffeta, saloon-girl style. Feathers in their hair, bustles on their bums. Someone's silly idea taken up without pause in a wedding-planning frenzy. Rita had made her distaste abundantly clear by widening her eyes at Nin as the bridesmaids walked up the aisle. It had been a surprise to both sisters. Nin shook her head in a panic to shush her sister in front of the almost-in-laws. On the church steps, Audrey refused to meet her brother's eyes where he stood in the photo line-up with the head saloon girl, her bustle nearly obliterating Henry's slender body when they were told to half-turn to the camera. 'Everyone say "chucky cheese chunks".'

Tom dipped his finger in his glass and circled Audrey's nipples with wine, staining her marbled skin crimson.

He pulled her chair out to face him. An ugly scrape on the wooden floor under her weight, just as she had feared. He crouched down surprisingly nimbly, then moved onto his knees to push her skirt up around her waist, revealing more beige, and then he sucked her breasts before going to work on his penis poking from his fly. She tried to join in but he slapped her hand down. She sat on the hard narrow bentwood chair like a schoolgirl being held back at recess. She was conscious of her thighs spilling on each side. He kept going and going and going, working on each breast in turn, kneading them the way she made her yoghurt bread. Over his shoulder she could see a small Bakelite clock. Already almost ten, and she had to get up for work the next day.

'Steady on, Tom, that hurts a bit. They are attached, you know. Let's go to the bedroom.'

'Don't talk.'

'Tom, I have to get going to prepare for work tomorrow.'

He stopped and stood up, masturbating defiantly and baldly, directly in front of her face. She didn't move. It felt like violence. Finally, at 10.18, he whinnied.

Audrey turned her head in shame. Tom handed her a sheet of kitchen paper. She wiped her chest and chin. She couldn't look at him. She was almost naked, and he was standing over her. He zipped his fly. He was finished.

The Little Clothes

'Audrey, what's your problem? You came here. You came to me. You interrupted my work. You undressed. Here's what I think. You wanted that. And now you're blaming me because you feel guilty about Elspeth.'

'Who would want that? What *was* that?'

'Well, don't come here and take your clothes off, because that just feels like a mixed message. A tease. You have to go now. I've got to prepare.'

'You told me to. To take my top off.' She momentarily thought about Shay-Lee accusing her over the napkins.

'You didn't have to. I was here doing my work, minding my own business, and you knocked on my door quite late with a bottle of booze and your tits half out.'

Audrey found her bra and her shirt in her handbag under the table. She dressed hurriedly, fumbling and shell-shocked, while Tom waited on his enclosed back verandah beyond the kitchen, sipping wine and surveying the city skyline.

'I'm off, then.'

'Bye Audrey. Don't save a chair for me next week.'

Hurrying back up the street, Audrey crossed paths with the rest of the trivia team, who were spilling out of the pub at closing time. Her shirt, stained with olive oil and wine, was sticking to her bra and skin. Mascara streamed down her face. A heel had broken off her shoe as she'd slipped on Tom's last three unlit sandstone stairs, hitting her chin hard, grazing her hand and face. There was blood on her cuff and collar. She held her right foot at an angle to make her gait even. She hadn't thought to take the good shoe off.

'Geez, Aud, what happened to you?'

'Aud, are you okay?'

'What happened, Aud?'

She kept walking. Sean ran after her. 'Audrey, stop. Are you okay?'

'Yep. I'm fine. Please leave me alone.'

'Audrey, let me help you. Please.'

'I said I'm fine!' She flung Sean's hand off her arm and kept walking.

In the shower Audrey wept for her stupidity and her sad heart. For her humiliation. For her lumpen body and ruined cream satin shirt that she had loved. For the loss of the possibility of Tom. She wept for her twelve-year-old self.

After showering and drying her hair, Audrey inspected her wounds and thought about how she might explain them at work tomorrow. She opened the herringbone shopping bag to savour her latest purchase. A navy sailor suit for a baby boy. Size 000. After snipping off the labels she put the suit in an empty drawer in the spare-room wardrobe. She didn't love the room as much as before. It was now cluttered with boxes and the diaries. The fresh smell was wearing off. She checked on Joni, paid little attention to the neighbour's drum fire and barking dog, and went to bed.

•

'Audrey Paudrey, pudding and—' Daniel walked into the Fabien Room, where Audrey had set up camp.

'Shut up, Daniel.'

'God, Aud, what happened to you?'

'Fell down sandstone stairs.'

'That actually looks pretty bad. Did you see a doctor?'

'Not yet.'

'Were you pissed?'

The Little Clothes

'What's that supposed to mean?'

'Were you pissed?'

'A little bit.'

'You should be more careful, Aud. You're not taking time off to go to rehab, are you?'

'No, Daniel. Let's start.'

'No coffee?'

'Yes, I have my coffee.' Audrey raised her cup in cheers.

'Give me a minute. Where's Heidi?' Daniel went in search of a willing female. Any of them would do. He didn't return.

The day wore on for Audrey. Everyone greeted her with 'God, Aud, what happened to you?'

She wanted to say, 'I have no idea what happened to me, except that at the end I slipped down some stairs.'

She was acutely aware of the handover of the Carmodys to Daniel in the Salter Room that afternoon. When she made her third trip to the bathroom an hour before the meeting, the side of her face and her chin had begun to scab into one dark crust broken by two tiny islands of pus. It couldn't be plausibly covered with make-up. She decided to brazen it out.

'Hello, thank you so much for coming in.' She offered her hand to Stan and Barbara Carmody and their son, Byron. Stan and Barbara were riveted by the scab. Byron, as always, by her breasts.

'Daniel! I went looking for you.'

'I was right here. On time. We waited for you but had to get going. Everyone's busy.'

'Audrey, what happened to you?' said Stan.

'I know it sounds made-up, but I slipped on some stairs last night and face planted.'

Everyone laughed, including Audrey. What could be funnier than a bit of slapstick at someone else's expense?

'Well, we've all been there, haven't we, Byron?' said Stan to his son.

'You poor thing. Have you seen a doctor?' said Barbara. 'It might need stitches.'

'No, I haven't seen a doctor yet. Probably will later this afternoon. I just wanted to be here to introduce Daniel, but I can see you've all already been talking. Daniel will be more than able to take over from me for the time being. I'll be back soon and I'm always on the phone if anyone needs anything. But I'm sure you won't, because Daniel is very accomplished and experienced in this area and we still have a few months before the trial date. I've run through our proposed defence with him, including the asthma attack and the fact that Byron voluntarily handed himself in. How's the trolling going, Byron?'

'Not much since I shut everything down. The husband has been on the radio. People seem to be taking his side.'

'Well, it was his wife and unborn child. But we will have our say in court. And we'll do our very best to limit the sentence. Have you been offered coffee or tea?' Audrey looked at Daniel pointedly.

'Not necessary. We've just come from lunch,' said Stan.

'A glass of water?'

'Yes, I wouldn't mind some water. It's quite warm out there today.' Barbara rearranged her scarf to indicate her discomfort.

Again, Audrey looked at Daniel, who smiled back. 'Yes, water would be lovely, Aud. Barbara is right. It is warm. Thanks.'

The Little Clothes

Audrey went to the kitchenette.

'That's a nasty cut on her face,' she heard Barbara saying.

'Well, alcohol and high heels can be a lethal combination. You just need to look at the wash-up from the Melbourne Cup,' Daniel said. They all agreed.

After the meeting, Daniel led the Carmodys through the foyer and into the lift lobby, jocular and amused at their every thought and quip while they waited together for a door to open. He took Byron's hand between his two hands and shook it paternally, then patted him robustly on the shoulder. He complimented Barbara on her scarf and bantered with Stan about golf handicaps and the Wallabies. Audrey trailed after them, at one stage standing behind a wall of backs: Daniel, Stan and Byron. She circled around and inserted herself next to Barbara.

'Daniel's right. That is a lovely scarf, Barbara.'

Audrey knew she was being judged by Barbara. Had Audrey ever believed in her Byron? Had she ever been on his side? At least now they had a proper lawyer and a partner.

'Do go and get that seen to as soon as you can, Audrey. I used to be a nurse and I think it needs a stitch or two.'

•

'Well, that was a shitshow,' Daniel said to Audrey as soon as the lift doors closed.

'What do you mean?'

'I wasn't properly briefed. You were late, and your face. Fuck's sake, Audrey.'

'You were fully briefed, Daniel. You have copious notes. I've shared everything with you online. You didn't pay any attention when I was briefing you and you disappeared from the second briefing. And you know it! I wasn't late. I was right on time. You hijacked the clients. And if you ever pull that stunt again about water—'

'Calm down, Audrey. I think it might have been up to you to make sure of all the little details, like tea and coffee. I am, after all, a partner. Alec called me in when I went looking for coffee this morning. I didn't say anything because you're not exactly his favourite person at the moment, so in a way I was protecting you.'

'Fuck off, Daniel. You're a very junior partner. Even Hanna has an office. And I won't be available to you on the end of the phone when I'm away.'

Audrey turned and fled to the bathroom. Nadine was preening in front of the mirror.

'Slumming it, Nads?'

'Audrey, what happened to you?'

'I was raped. That's what happened.'

'Aud, what's going on? I just never understand your humour. That's a pretty heavy thing to say. You frighten me.'

'Oh, I don't think you're that easily scared, Nads. In fact, I think you're one of the toughest people I've ever met.'

'That's not a nice thing to say either. Or is that meant to be funny too?'

'I think if I threw a rock at your face, I'd get gravel.'

'Did someone throw a rock at you?'

'No, Nads. I fell down some stairs and face planted.'

Nadine suppressed a smile.

'Thanks for your empathy. You can be so mean.'

'Audrey, have you been drinking?'

'Yeah. I have. I always drink in the middle of the day

The Little Clothes

in the office, just like you, because I have nothing else of importance to do. I have a little bottle in my drawer, and I put vodka in my teacup, just like you do.'

'I do nothing of the sort! What a thing to say!'

'Sorry. I meant coffee mug.'

'Audrey, I am going to walk out of here and pretend we never had this conversation. I haven't heard anything you just said.'

'Business as usual then.'

Nadine left the bathroom, rattled. Audrey returned to her desk and continued to sort files, sign her leave forms and send briefing emails to Daniel.

Alec sent Dinah down at the end of the day to whisper in Audrey's ear that he wanted to see her in his office straight away. Dinah was strained and apologetic.

'Audrey, that looks nasty. What happened?'

'Oh this? Just a flesh wound. It doesn't even hurt. Looks way worse than it is. Did Alec say what this is about?'

'Not to me.'

'I'll be up in a minute.'

'Richard's there too.'

'Thanks for the intel, Dinah.'

'You didn't get it from me.'

'Of course. Not. Of course not.'

After a final trip to the bathroom to fluff her hair, apply lipstick and gently pat and dry her wound, Audrey took the lift to the executive floor and announced herself to Dinah.

'Well, here I am, as summoned.'

'I'll just let him know. Won't be a minute.' Dinah disappeared into the inner sanctum while Audrey hovered nervously.

'He's ready for you now, Aud.'

Audrey smoothed her skirt, quickly fluffed her hair again and walked past Dinah into Alec's office.

Alec pushed back into his leather power chair. Richard, another senior partner who was never quite on a level with Alec, hovered behind him. Framed photos of Alec's many children lined the shelves.

'Come in, Audrey. Close the door. Take a seat.'

Audrey noticed them recoil at her injured face.

'Would you like a drink? We're having one.'

'Are you going to sack me?'

'No. I don't think so. We just need to talk to you about a few things. Here, have this. You look like you could use it.'

Richard poured whisky from a decanter. The men remained behind the desk and handed Audrey one of the heavy Waterford glasses.

'Aud, what happened to you?'

'I fell over.'

'Okay. It looks nasty.'

'So I've been told at least forty-seven times today. I hope you didn't get me up here to deliver that news, 'cause it's old. Things move very quickly in the news cycle these days. You need to keep up.'

'Have you had it checked?'

'Not yet.'

'Don't you think you should?'

'Let's get on with this.'

Richard sat down on a chair to the side of and slightly behind Alec. Like a security guard. A minder.

'So, Audrey, I am, well, we are' – Alec tilted his head to Richard – 'concerned by some complaints, and some… concerns we've heard today and over previous days from some of our colleagues about your actions and concerning

The Little Clothes

behaviour in the office that seem to fall outside of our code of conduct and are generally not what we would consider acceptable interactions with other staff members and, therefore, as part of that, our obligations to our clients. And these communications we've had with various employees concern us greatly.'

'What are you actually saying, Alec?'

'Well, I'm saying what I just said.'

'Just tell me, Alec. Then I'll know. Who's been in your ear?'

'We can't divulge who has approached us but it has been more than one senior person, so we're concerned, and we wanted to talk to you and see if there's anything we can do to help, apart from the two months' leave that you're about to take.'

'No. I'm fine. If I don't know who it was or what was said, I can't answer to anything. I can't defend myself. Is this about the mouldy salad I left in the fridge? Because if it is I'll clean that up before I go on leave. Is that what this inquisition is about?'

'Well, okay. Look, apparently you have been slow to brief Daniel. He feels you are purposely withholding important material that he needs to be able to take on the extra workload in your absence.'

'You're kidding, right?'

'Why would I be kidding?'

'Okay, what else?'

'Nadine is worried about... how should we describe this? She is worried about your state of mind. She says she felt threatened by you in the bathroom on the third floor, although why she was in there I don't know, since she's one of the only females on the upper floors, so more or less has her own bathroom. She says you've been drinking in the office. Out of a coffee mug.'

Audrey threw her head back and laughed heartily. She laughed so much she snorted. She nearly wet her pants. She couldn't stop.

'Audrey, this is exactly the sort of thing that's concerning. This is not the way to behave at work. We need to be thoughtful of each other and adhere to our clearly set-out code of conduct.'

'Really, Alec? The code of conduct. Do you want to invoke the code of conduct? Let's go for it, shall we? Let's talk about what that pesky old code entails. And where many others before me may have transgressed. Why don't we talk about that?'

'Okay, that is enough, Audrey. We think you should take your leave immediately. From this afternoon. You should pack up your personal things, including the salad, and we wish you well and we'll be in touch.'

'You can't be serious! I've done everything you've asked of me. I know you know that Daniel has been the one not taking my briefing seriously. He's attended only some of it even though I've been well prepared and practically spoonfed him, and he hasn't paid any attention and hasn't read anything. He was hopelessly underprepared for the Carmody meeting. It was embarrassing. And that's no fault of mine. He was full of trickery but without knowledge.'

'Well, he said the same about you.'

'But Alec, you know me. You know Daniel. Who do you believe?'

'I think the truth is somewhere in between. Nadine says you were pissed off about the new partner appointments.'

'Oh, Nadine. The oracle. Nadine, seriously? Do you

The Little Clothes

really think she felt threatened by me? Come off it. You must know she keeps vodka in her drawer and can barely conduct any meeting or social interaction unaided by her tipple. Since you want me out right now, I want to see the money in my account before I leave the office or I will take this argument elsewhere. So I'm going back downstairs to my desk, where I will start to pack up, but I won't leave until I see the payment for my month's paid leave hit my account. I'll keep checking. If it's not there in the next two hours, I'll come back in here tomorrow as originally agreed and scare some more of the children. And I'll stay till Friday as also agreed. And I will bring my scabby face with me.'

Audrey stood up, smiled at Alec and Richard, thanked them for the drink and calmly walked out of the office, winking at Dinah as she passed, then took the lift downstairs. In the bathroom she sat in a cubicle, her heart beating fast, feeling faint and nauseous, and certain that at any minute security would storm through the door and accompany her out of the building. That she'd have to walk out in front of everyone carrying a box containing her pot plant, lunch box, coffee mug and battery-powered lucky cat stiffly waving goodbye with its arm. She sat for fifteen minutes. No one came in.

Back at her desk, and after a vigilant hour constantly refreshing her bank app, Audrey could see her monthly salary and the extra month's pay in her account. She could see Dinah whispering in Daniel's ear and then Daniel walking hurriedly to the lift, nervously straightening his tie, without glancing in Audrey's direction.

She took her time methodically and thoroughly cleaning the fridge. *Please keep the firdge clean*, someone had mistakenly written on an index card and sticky-taped on the door. First she binned her salad, then other people's forgotten yoghurt tubs, claimed in permanent markers. 'Don't touch!' 'Hands off.' She binned lunch boxes with leftovers from a month ago, curdling milk, desiccated slices of birthday cake on paper plates, uncovered pizza slices, furry strawberries. Audrey wiped all the shelves as best she could with limited cleaning equipment. She felt not only virtuous but satisfied she had done the right thing, as Eustace so often advised her to do. She had cleaned up the mess.

There were few items to put in her tote bag, gym bag and a small box. The lucky cat, the often commented on photo of Henry, the paddle plant, her framed degree certificate, her *New Yorker* desk calendar, six beige lipsticks and glosses, two novels, an umbrella, her keep cup, a Cressida Campbell birthday card from Maggie, and Daniel's wallet, keys and Zippo lighter, which he'd jettisoned in his drawer as Dinah spoke to him.

Audrey remembered from an insurance-claim case she'd researched several years ago that the type of sprinkler system in most modern buildings would not be triggered by heat from a small lighter, as it so often is in crime and action films. Nor could she hit and break the glass on the little boxes near the lifts to make it rain. She also knew, as she had discovered back then, when she briefly took a special interest in sprinkler systems, that in the women's bathroom near her desk the original deluge technology was still in place. Now she stood under the spigot on a small metal stepladder from the cleaners' closet, held Daniel's lighter as high as she could above her head, flicked it open and waited. Soon enough she was soaked. She put the stepladder back in the closet, slung the gym bag over her shoulder,

The Little Clothes

picked up the box and her tote and left the building via the stairs.

'Who's the rainmaker now?' she thought as she staggered through the Wynyard bypass to the ferry wharf, her clothes sticking to her skin, her face scabbed and her heart light. Audrey knew no one was looking.

Chapter 10

There were several missed-call notifications and messages on Audrey's phone the next morning when she woke from a sound and restorative sleep.

Aud, you left without saying goodbye! Thought you weren't going till Friday. Are we still on 4 drinks tnight? Hanxx

Aud, I know you're mad with me but I need to talk to you about whether you saw anything yesterday evening.

Hi Aud, WTF! Alec says you've left the Company. Please call. Erin xxx

Hi Aud. How are you going? Cathy says she hasn't heard from you or booked you in. Joxx

'Audrey. Alec here. Please call.'

Scrolling through holiday-house websites while she watched Joni hop on the grass occupied most of Audrey's morning. She found a little cottage, Ocean Dreaming, at Pearl Beach and booked it for the week starting the day after her birthday dinner at the Schnitzel Snug. She washed her floaty Indian woodblock-print muu-muus and white linen beach cover-ups to take with her for leisurely strolls along the shore. She made a list of food to buy at Harris Farm and put in her thermal bag. Gravlax, cutlets, Manchego cheese, olives stuffed with anchovies, eggs, fresh herbs, basmati rice, chicken thighs on the bone, spices for curry,

The Little Clothes

shell pasta and fettucine, crackers, chocolate, wine, tomato paste and passata, Lurpak, olive oil, etc. It was as if she was catering for a large family in celebration mode. Then she made a list for Joni, including her hay and recently prescribed eye drops. There was another ambitious list: the books to take. *The Goldfinch, Eggshell Skull, Rebecca*. Audrey started to make a playlist on Spotify. It was just a week. A week inflated by the promise of something she couldn't quite see or grasp; but it beckoned. It would be relaxing, meaningful, restorative, warm and sunny, and a chance to take a stand for herself. To take stock. *A fresh start*, as Rita would have said.

'Hanna, it's Audrey. Unfortunately, I'm calling to cancel. I have to see the doctor about getting my face stitched and will no doubt be on antibiotics. I can't drink. I'm so sorry. We'll catch up soon.'

'Daniel. Sorry we've missed each other. Never mind. I'll see you in a couple of months.'

'Alec. It's Audrey. You wanted me to call.'

'Hi Maggie. I'm busy packing up at work. Cathy is definitely on my list but as you know I'm going away. I promise to do it when I get back. Hope you're well. Looking forward to our catch-up. Love you.'

'Erin, hi.'

'Oh my god, Audrey, what's going on? Why are you leaving? You can't leave. You run the joint.'

'Erin, I do not run the joint. What are you talking about?' Audrey was pleased at the thought.

'I mean you keep it all going in the right direction.'

'Look, I wasn't aware I was leaving. Not really. I'm just taking a couple of months off. Why do you think I'm leaving? How are the kids?'

'Yeah, all good here. Milla's more settled. Carter's a nightmare. I was told you're leaving by Alec and Hanna.'

'Well, they know more than I do.'

'Did you hear about the flooding on the third floor?'

'What do you mean, flooding?'

'Somehow the sprinkler system faulted in the women's bathroom and it flooded out onto the carpet and soaked most of the floor before the cleaner saw it. They arrived at about ten and raised the alarm. Alec was called around midnight by security.'

'What? That sounds crazy.'

'Apparently it was an old system that hadn't been maintained. Alec's already suing because there was so much damage. The carpet, some furniture, files, everything. People's stuff. They've got insurance assessors going in right now. Everyone on the third floor has been accommodated higher up in a shared office space. Better views, I guess.'

'Really? That's nuts. I was there till 7.30. Went into the bathroom before I left. Glad I missed the drama.'

'Oh, and Daniel couldn't find his wallet and keys. He was all over the place after drinking with Alec. He couldn't drive, so Nadine volunteered to take him home and call a locksmith. Thank god for Nads.'

'Nadine was there?'

'Yeah, she was in a meeting with Alec and Daniel.'

'The three musketeers.'

'Sorry?'

'Alexandre Dumas.'

'Oh, I haven't met him. Haven't been in the office for ages. Is he nice? I don't think he was in the meeting.'

'He was a writer.'

'Sorry, I can't quite hear you, Aud. The cleaner's here

The Little Clothes

doing the vacuuming. Hang on, I'll move. Can you hear me now? Hello Aud, can you hear me now?'

'Yes, I can hear you. Listen, Erin, I really have to go. I had a bit of a tumble a few nights ago and cut my chin open. I'm seeing my doctor in fifteen minutes. Might need a stitch.'

'Alec told me. He said you look terrible.'

'Did he really? It's a cut and a scab. Hardly terrible. But thanks for passing that on.'

'Come on, Aud. He sounded quite concerned. He was concerned, I'm sure.'

'That's all okay, Erin. Go back to your gorgeous baby, give her a cuddle for me. I'll be in touch.'

'Bye, Aud. Don't leave. They need you. And before you go, I just wanted to ask, would you consider being Milla's godmother? I mean, you don't have any children of your own and I think it would be good for both of you.'

'Have you discussed this with Alec?'

'Not yet.'

'I think you should. And think about Hanna.'

'But she'll have her own kids, and I know how sweet you are with children.'

'Erin, I'm only thirty-nine. I might have my own kids too.'

'Well, yes you could. But not likely, right?'

'I still like to hope, Erin.'

'Aud, I'm sure there's someone for you. But still think about being Milla's godmother.'

'I will.'

•

'Well, well, well,' said Greg from his front garden as Audrey arrived home, stitched and clutching a script for antibiotics. 'Look what the cat dragged in.'

'Repetitive.'

'What?'

'Just saying you've already said that to me.'

'What happened to you?'

'Just took a fall and face planted.'

Greg smiled. Even chuckled. He plucked one of the climbing roses that Eustace had planted along the boundary when Audrey first moved in.

'For you.'

'Well, it was always for me because it is mine. Please don't pick them.'

'They're on my side of the fence.'

'But I planted them in the first place.'

'Your father told me he planted them. I'll only pick them on my side.'

'Don't. I don't want them touched. They're beautiful growing. Just as they are.'

'I thought you might enjoy one in a vase.'

'Please, just don't pick my roses!'

'What *is* your problem, woman?'

'You. You're my problem.' Audrey didn't catch what he said next as she strode away and shut her front door.

Safe inside, she packed for her holiday. The clothes she'd washed, a jumper and trackpants because it was turning cold, sunscreen, a beach towel, a beach chair, and bathers because she was hopeful. She packed all the diaries into a shopping bag to take with her. She was relieved to be leaving for somewhere else. Anywhere, really. Away from Greg and the office.

The Little Clothes

'Audrey. It's Alec.'

'Alec. Hi. I tried to call you.'

'I know. I just wanted to clear up any misunderstanding.'

'Okay. I don't think I've misunderstood anything.'

'Just listen, will you?'

'Listening.'

'I don't want you to leave the company. You're an integral part of who we are and what we do.'

'I know.'

'Things got a bit heated. I should have done better.'

'Alec, I am offended that Daniel's opinions are given more weight than mine. I work way harder and know way more.'

'You're right. So, that's sorted.'

'If I come back I want to be a partner. Not a junior partner. A full partner. I cannot tolerate kowtowing to such a twit.'

'Hang on, Aud.'

'No, you hang on.'

'No, you hang on.'

'No, you.'

They laughed. 'We'll sort it out when you come back.'

'Sort it before. Or I won't be back. Send me an offer. A decent offer. And I'll consider it.'

'When did you become so tough? By the way, did you hear about the flooding? I wish you were here to work out the insurance. With all your experience on that case. What was that case again?'

'Oh well. I'm sure Daniel can do it. Or Hanna. You promoted them to be useful, after all. Goodbye, Alec.'

Audrey arrived ten minutes late to meet her parents at the Schnitzel Snug. They were expectant, bordering on agitated and, in Rita's case, annoyed. They both stood, alarmed at the sight of their daughter.

'What did you do to yourself?' Rita said.

Eustace reached out. 'Are you all right, darling?'

'Fine. I'm fine. Took a tumble.'

Eustace pulled Audrey's chair out for her. 'Here we sit in the charmless suburban shopping arcade for a six o'clock dinner,' he muttered close to his daughter's ear.

'Eustace, I heard that. Someone has to do all of the booking and arranging.'

'I know, Rita. And we're grateful. Aren't we, Aud?'

'So, what on earth has happened to you?' Rita leaned forward and peered at her daughter's face. 'Drinking, I suppose?'

'Rita! Leave it alone.'

'It's all right, Papa. I had drunk a little wine. I was distracted and missed a step. Fell down a few stairs. I saw the doctor today. It's all okay.'

'Okay, what are we all having, then?' Eustace said, suddenly fixated by the menu.

'I'll have the goulash.'

'Me too. I'll have the goulash but with the extra dumplings.'

'Do you think you need the extra dumplings?'

'I do. That's why I'm going to order them.'

'I'll have the peppercorn steak, medium rare.'

'What did I tell you, Audrey?'

'So, darling, here's a little gift for you. And we're sorry we missed your birthday. We really are. We've had so many appointments with my doctor.'

'Are you okay, Papa?'

'If you don't like it, I've got the receipt.'

The Little Clothes

'I'm sure I'll love it, Mumma.'

'But if you don't, you can exchange it. Can't she, Eusti? You were there. You heard what they said.'

'Rita, let her open it before we start returning it.'

Audrey did like the delicate gold and emerald bracelet. She was surprised by it. It wasn't the sort of thing they usually gave her. Last year it was a teapot. The year before, a high-end vacuum cleaner.

'It's a tennis bracelet. Not that you play tennis, although perhaps you should. It's a style of bracelet.'

'Well, I love it. Thank you both so much.'

'So you don't want the receipt?'

'No, Mumma. I love it and I'm grateful you bought it for me. I will not be returning it.'

'I wouldn't mind showing you the receipt so you can see how crazy your father went in the shop.'

'Rita! Don't be vulgar.'

'Eusti, she needs to know the value.'

'Mumma, I will look after it. Thank you again.'

'Happy birthday, Audrey.' They clinked glasses and ate their meals mostly in silence in the draughty arcade with its Rotary wishing well and worn Christmas tree, already erected in November.

'So, let's talk about Christmas. What will we do this year?'

'Mumma, let's not.'

'I agree with Audrey. Let's talk about it in a few weeks. Let's just have Audrey's birthday first. Anyway, we do the same thing every year.'

'No, we do not. Nin is thinking she'll have it at hers, and Scott and Sierra might come. That would be nice. It will be different.'

'Sienna, Mumma.'

'Well, that's what Nin thinks.'

'You two are obviously in cahoots.'

'Just trying to plan, Eusti. Someone has to do it. I don't think sisters talking to each other is being *in cahoots*.'

'Well, that was delicious, and I feel very spoilt. But I need to get going because tomorrow I'm leaving on a little holiday.'

'Good for you, darling,' said Eustace, putting his hand over his daughter's.

'What? What do you mean you're going on a holiday? When were you going to tell us?'

'I'm telling you now. It's just a week on the Central Coast, Mumma. It's not Positano. Definitely not Positano. I have some time off work and I'm going to go up to a little cottage with Joni and read and take stock.'

'Do I know Joni? Is she one of your work friends? A special friend, maybe?'

'She's my rabbit. You met her.'

'You're going on holiday with a rabbit?'

'Yes.'

'Well, now I've heard it all. Do send us a postcard and tell us how it's going and whether we need to announce the engagement.'

'Just call me if you need to talk to me, Mumma. It's literally six days.'

•

Audrey arrived home to a bundle of her climbing roses on the front doorstep. They were cut at different lengths and squashed inside torn pages from the free local magazine, with gaffer tape wound around and around, holding the bouquet together. Some buds and blooms peeping out; some upside down, their thorny stems among the buds and flowers. A madman's bouquet. She walked back to the fence and saw that not a single rose was left on the previously abundant twisting branches. Was he flirting or threatening? Either way she was distressed about the denuded vine. Audrey arranged the offering as best she could in Grandma Joan's rose bowl that she'd been given grudgingly by Rita because The Will said so. She crept outside to see Greg, through the fence, slumped on his white plastic chair near the unlit drum, alone. She wondered if he was okay.

•

Before light, Audrey loaded her car as quietly as she could. The food packed in thermal bags. The diaries. Her books. Her beach gear and suitcase. Her chargers and laptop. Backwards and forwards from the door to the car on the street. Last, Joni's hay and food, and then Joni in a cat cage. Audrey had booked and paid for the night before so she could arrive when it suited her. She kept glancing at her neighbour's house to see if he, too, was up and doing. She didn't think so.

By the time she arrived at the beach house the day had slid within minutes from vaguely promising and just a little bit dull to threatening and dark. So much for Ocean Dreaming, she thought, turning into the driveway.

'Maggie, it's me.'

'I know. You okay?'

'Yep. As I told you, I've come away to Pearl Beach for a week, so I have to postpone our dinner. I feel very guilty because I suggested we go out. I got the dates muddled. Can we do it when I get back?'

'Of course. You sound nervy.'

'It's just a bit strange here. More Cape Fear than sunny holiday spot. There's no one around. The houses seem empty. The smell of the bush makes me feel ill. The smell of you know what.'

'Audrey, I beg you to go and see Cathy when you get back. Also, it feels empty because most people are at work. There are plenty of permanent residents there. I'm sure you're not alone.'

'True. Still, this house that was described as a luxury escape is barely clean. I put the kettle on to make a cup of tea and a dead cockroach was jiggling up and down in the clear panel on the side. Plus, the sheets are at least 70 per cent synthetic and I can't get the TV to work.'

'Well, none of that seems like the end of the world. Just go for a walk on the beach and grab a takeaway.'

'The shop is closed too. It's closed because no one is here. Can't blame them. I'd have to drive for takeaway. I've brought food with me.'

'Go for a walk and cook something. Read a book. Sorry, Aud, I have to go. I'm on call.'

Audrey was further unnerved by an ibis spreading the contents of the previous occupant's garbage across the back garden. A rotisserie chicken carcass half in a foil bag, dog poo bags, and salad leaves turning to soup. She thought about the strangeness of the ibis eating the dead chicken and tried to shoo the bird away, but it persisted. Defeated, she went inside, leaving the door ajar to allow some fresh air into the stale rooms. Thunder rumbled and some of the lights in the lounge room flickered. She tried to connect

The Little Clothes

to the wi-fi and finally resorted to her dongle but couldn't work the TV remote. She thought it needed a new battery. A brush turkey came in through the door and started to poke around. She chased it with a broom for half an hour until she was finally able to shut it outside. She put on her warmer clothes and lay on the bed to read. When she woke, it was dark. She used her phone to navigate to the light switch, then checked for messages.

I am Greg. Your nayba. Ware r you?

Greg has my number? How?

Audrey looked into all the rooms. She checked the bathroom, where Joni sat quivering under the basin. In the lounge room she knelt on the stained cream carpet to survey the bookshelf. Harold Robbins, Danielle Steel, Nicholas Sparks, Dale Carnegie, half a dozen Agatha Christies, Minette Walters, and several more self-help writers she didn't recognise. *Reader's Digest*s. Some twenty-year-old *National Geographic*s. She drank neat whisky and read the decades-old *Woman's Day*s. Bert and Don. As it became light, she slept again.

'Audrey, it's me. Your mother. Call me.'

'Mumma, it's just me. Returning your call.'

'Just you. I know it's you. Who else do you think would call me Mumma now that Henry has passed?'

It will always be now for Rita, Audrey thought.

'I was calling to let you know that neighbour of yours called me looking for you. You didn't tell me you had become friends. He's lost your number.'

'Mumma, we are not friends. How did he get hold of you?'

'I don't know. We're still in the book. Did you tell him your surname?'

'You obviously gave him my number.'

'Well, what was I supposed to do? He made out you two are friends.'

'We're not. I'm terrified of him.'

'I think that's going too far. You always go too far. He seems harmless enough.'

'You didn't tell him where I am, I hope.'

'Oh Audrey, what difference does it make?'

'You told him, didn't you! I gave you the address for emergencies only. You may have compromised my safety.'

'Don't be silly. You're always so dramatic, Audrey. You need to calm down.'

'Mumma, listen, I am genuinely frightened of him. He cut up all my climbing roses that Papa planted and left them on my doorstep.'

'That's quite sweet. I think he's a bit simple. Anyway, I'm sorry if I've upset you but that does seem to be inevitable. You're always upset.'

'That's not true.'

'Okay. I beg to differ. I also wanted to let you know that Nin and I have been discussing Christmas and she says Scott will definitely be there. And there is some news that I'm not supposed to tell, so don't say anything to anyone, but Sierra is pregnant. Nin is over the moon. I am too. I'll be a great-aunt. Also, you left your tennis bracelet in the restaurant, and I think that was a bit hurtful to your father.'

'Rita! Give me the phone. I am not hurt, Audrey. I also left my glasses at the restaurant and your mother left her handbag hanger that she puts on the edge of the table. We have the bracelet, the hanger and the glasses, and you can collect the bracelet at the next Sunday lunch in a couple of weeks or I'll bring it to you if I finish the new rabbit cage before then. Have a nice holiday. I'll put your mother back on.'

'I'm sick of hearing about the bloody rabbit from both of you. For goodness' sake, you'd think it was an Icelandic unicorn.'

'Mumma, I have to go. My phone is about to run out of battery. Please do not speak to my neighbour about me ever again.'

'Part of your problem is that you are—'

Audrey hung up.

Rita rang back.

Audrey didn't answer. She looked through the kitchen cupboards and drawers and wondered about the owners and why there were two egg cups from Fernie and why an egg cup would be a souvenir from a ski resort and who would buy them. She noted there were three whisks but no platters, an assortment of thick, heavy mugs that didn't invite tea drinking. The wine glasses were enormous bowls on tall, thin stems, her least favourite style, and there were twelve rattan placemats but only enough cutlery for six, if you mixed and matched large and small. She made a mental note to take the Lake Pontchartrain corkscrew with her when she left. She'd once stayed in the Garden District in New Orleans with Maggie in their pursuit of all things Anne Rice.

Through the flyscreen door Audrey could see the brush turkey busily adding to its incubation mound, which was almost as big as a Volkswagen Beetle, in the back garden. Piling it up and piling it up. Plotting to catch a female. The kitchen still felt grimy, so Audrey poured more whisky and took it with a plate of cold cuts back to bed.

She trawled through her diaries in detail, carefully reading everything from 29 October, the day she was raped.

And there it was. Some part of her knew it was lurking in the pages.

18 January
Today Mumma and Aunty Nin took me to see a special Doctor. Mumma said I needed to be checked.

Checked. There's that word, Audrey thought. So comforting, so concealing. Just checking. I'm just checking in. I'm checking on you. Let me check you. Just lie there and let me check you. Hold the line please, I'll check.

'Audrey,' Rita had said, 'I think you need to be checked. When was your last period?'

'Mumma! Don't say that! Why are you saying that? Yuk!'

'I usually know when you get your period, Audrey.'

'I don't want to talk about this. How do you know?'

'I do the washing.'

I was checked and then Mumma and Nin and the Doctor left the room to talk and a lady came in and asked me questions about who I had sex with. Yuk! I didn't tell her anything. Did I have sex? I didn't give her his name. She described a curette procedure and gave me a pamphlet. She asked me if I could read and understand it. Durr. Of course I could read it. I'm in Miss Baldry's class in the top group with Sally Slarke and Maggie. The Doctor came back in. Nin held my hand while he did more checking and the curette procedure. He put his hand up under a towel so Nin couldn't see my privates. Mumma didn't come back into the room. Then we went home and Mumma said to never mention what happened today to anyone or no one will ever want to marry me. I know

The Little Clothes

Mister Johnson will marry me. My mother is crazy. She said to specially not tell Papa or Henry. I won't. It's too embarrassing and I don't really know what happened. She brought in a hot water bottle and a tablet and made me go to bed.

Audrey lay in bed for the rest of the morning thinking about the enormity and mundanity of what had happened to her when she was twelve and why she didn't know what had happened. She marvelled about how it was never spoken of again and how quickly she herself had forgotten the whole episode. She had found others to replace Mr Johnson. There had sometimes been a surreptitious queue outside the sports-equipment shed at school, where Audrey lay on the gym mats at lunchtime and let boys pull her pants down to look at her sprouting pubic hair. The show-offs touched her and pulled their hands away as if burnt, shouting, 'Slag germs!' They'd call her a slag in the playground. Maggie had tried to dissuade her friend, but Audrey believed Maggie was jealous of her popularity. She knew now that she had been desperately seeking the attention Mr Johnson had shown her and that she felt worthy of nothing much. Without Mr Johnson, what would she have? She knew as she lay in the depressing holiday cottage that life had not continued as it was before she met Mr Johnson at the birthday party. It had been horribly derailed.

•

'Hello. My name is Audrey Mendes. I am renting 6 Ruby Court for the week. The television isn't working. The remote seems to need a new battery. At least I think that's what it is. And there's not much cutlery.'

'Can't you buy a new battery?'

'Well, I could. But I've paid in advance through your agency for this property and I was led to believe there would be a working television.'

'Most people use their laptops now.'

'Please come and fix the TV.'

'I don't know when we can get someone there. We're very short-staffed.'

'Okay. Maybe call me back? And the cutlery?'

'How much do you need?'

'You know what? Forget about the cutlery, but I do want the TV fixed. And you should know the house is dirty.'

'We've never had a complaint before. Quite the opposite.'

'Okay. Please call about the TV.'

Audrey showered and drove to Patonga for lunch. She had planned to buy fish and chips and sit at one of the picnic tables to read, but the sun was weak and there was intermittent sprinkling rain, so she ordered a counter lunch at the pub next door. She took out her book, *The Goldfinch*, and drank her wine while she read and waited for her number to be called.

'G'day. Mind if I join you?'

Audrey looked up to see a portly, ruddy-faced man looking down at her. He was wearing an orange T-shirt that barely covered his girth, emblazoned with a cartoon of a fisherman hooking a shapely 1950s-style woman in a bikini on his fishing line. The rod protruded from the fisherman's fly. A logo, *Reelin' Them In Since 1955*, in raised green letters above the image. She swept her eyes across the large dining area, which was almost empty.

The Little Clothes

'Ah, I'm just waiting for someone. So, sorry, no. I do mind. Sorry.'

'I'll buy you a drink. By the way, what happened to you?'

'Oh, no, thanks. I have a drink. But thank you.'

'I'll buy you another one. You look like you could use it.'

'No, really. I only want one and my friend will be here in a minute. But thank you.'

'Well, if you change your mind.'

'I won't.'

'S'pose you come from Sydney. Think you're better than us. That's a big book. We call you lot the blow-ins. I thought you looked like you could use some company.'

'Sorry. Wrong impression.'

The man waddle-swaggered to the bar that bordered the dining room and hoisted himself onto a swivel stool, from where he stared at Audrey until two women sat three stools down. He sent glasses of champagne with a half strawberry on the rim to the women, and they beckoned him to join them. He did. Audrey ate her meal in peace. As she left, the man said something about *imaginary friends* that made them all turn to look at Audrey and laugh.

•

'Hello. Bill Barnes here. TV repair guy. I'm on my way to yours. About six minutes away.'

'Hi Bill. I'm on my way back there now from Patonga. They said they'd give me an hour's notice but they haven't.'

'I'll go and do another call and I'll be at yours within the hour.'

'Okay. Thanks. See you then.'

Soon Audrey was halted by a road crew in hi-vis, one holding a lollipop STOP sign. Witches' hats were being placed to block one side of the narrow road. She judged she was perhaps nine cars back in the queue of traffic leaving Patonga.

Audrey took the opportunity to glance at her messages.

Its ya nayba. I put ya parcel on ya back veranda.

Audrey, Alec here. I've sent you an email. Please ignore it. Call me.

Cars began to pass on the descent into Patonga. Audrey clutched the steering wheel so tightly she thought her fingers might snap. She felt sorry for herself. Her holiday wasn't unfolding as she had hoped it would and hadn't provided any respite from her neighbour. How had he managed to get over the side gate into her back garden? Maybe he'd climbed over the paling fence? She thought about the bouquet of roses, the backyard drum, the dog… Her anger with the roadworkers, whom she judged to be doing nothing much, was suddenly so overwhelming she started to cry.

Eventually the lollipop sign was swivelled to SLOW and the cars in front began to move. As she approached the head of the queue, the sign was turned again to tell her to STOP. Now, at least, she was first in the queue, but what if she couldn't start from the steep slope promptly enough? What if she slipped into the car behind her? She wondered if she was losing her nerve. Possibly her mind. Audrey was aware of an unravelling. An unspooling at her core. She momentarily thought she might dissolve.

She listened to her voice messages as she waited.

'Bill Barnes here. I'm out the front of the residence now. Can you come out.'

The Little Clothes

'Hi Bill. Audrey Mendes from 6 Ruby Court. I am stopped in traffic. Behind roadworks. I should be there in fifteen.'

'Sorry, love. I have a full list this afternoon. I've been here twice.'

'Well, it wasn't my fault. They were supposed to give me notice. I would have stayed in.'

'Look, just call the real estate agency back and set up a time for tomorrow. Also, a courier came by and left a parcel on your back doorstep just now. Seemed very keen you got it.'

'Oh, okay. I wasn't expecting a parcel. So that's weird.'
SLOW.

Audrey drove to the holiday house in trepidation. Surely Greg wouldn't have driven up to Pearl Beach? She decided not to look at Alec's email straight away. He could wait, for a change. After Henry died she had seen a counsellor a few times, who had suggested she sit with her grief and her difficult feelings rather than trying to block or resolve them. This is what she now invoked for dealing with Alec. He could wait.

As she descended into Pearl Beach, Audrey called to make another appointment with Bill Barnes.

'He's booked out tomorrow. There's been a storm here recently and a lot of the antennas were knocked out. Some of the houses were flooded and we're trying to determine the extent of the circuit damage in quite a few properties.'

'I am sorry. I'm trying to be patient but I rented this house with the understanding that I would have a television and various platforms on which to watch shows. If I don't get this fixed today or tomorrow I only have a few more days left. The weather is terrible, so I would like to have the TV.'

'We can't help the weather, Mrs Mendes. We're in Lay Neena. We sent Bill over. He says he's been there twice.'

'That's true, but you didn't give me any notice he was coming. Or I would have been here. No one called me.'

'You didn't say you were going out.'

'I don't have to tell you what I'm doing. You were supposed to give me an hour's notice. This is hopeless.'

'You don't have to be rude. We'll see what we can do.'

'Thank you, Maria. I'll wait to hear. By the way, I'm a lawyer.'

'I don't care if you're Genghis Khan's wife. You need to calm down.'

'You don't need to be rude either.'

'Well, don't threaten me.'

Pulling up cautiously next to the driveway, Audrey looked around for Greg or his car. She waved through the open window to a woman standing across the street at her letterbox. Audrey wanted to make sure someone noted her arrival in case anything happened. If her stalker attacked, for example. The woman turned, startled, and walked hurriedly down the path back to her house without acknowledging the friendly gesture. The towering gums, the leaf litter, the silence, except for bird calls before rain, felt oppressive.

When Audrey was a teenager, Rita had advised her to look for a middle-aged woman or a group of women and ask for help if she was ever lost or in trouble. If she was being harassed or followed.

'Stand with a woman or women about my age. Signal to them you need their help.'

Yet now, as she watched the woman across the road disappear into her house, Audrey thought she had not

The Little Clothes

been protected by her own middle-aged mother and aunt. The very people she had relied upon. Rita had wanted to present well to an imagined panel of judges, and Nin had always followed her sister's lead. There had been no other path to tread. That was the family contract. Audrey secretly thought Nin was much smarter and better organised than her older sister, but Rita prevailed. Even dominated. Still today she dominated. Audrey knew she herself belonged to the dominant family and once told Scott, after reading Mario Puzo, that Rita was the matriarch. As if they were Calabrian. 'Sure,' Scott had said. 'I don't know what that is, but I agree if that's what you say. You're smarter than me.'

Rita never seemed to doubt she was the matriarch, even when Grandma Joan was alive. As the wife of the only son, she also assumed her place in Eustace's family when Grandma Valentina died. She wrote bossy letters on aerogrammes brimming with her opinions about a world of which she knew nothing. The sisters-in-law mostly didn't read them because her words made no sense, she had no authority, and they were wary of Rita given Valentina's commentary over the years, although they welcomed Audrey and Maggie with open arms when the young women travelled to Europe and then South America in their gap year. The aunties told Audrey that Grandma Valentina felt she had lost her only son to the other side of the world because of *that woman*, and surreptitiously educated her daughters in the disdain of Rita.

Audrey didn't park in the driveway but left her car outside for a fast getaway and crept around the side of the house to the back garden with her keys gripped between her fingers below her knuckles, just as Nadine had instructed. The brush turkey was tending his mound in the corner of the garden, waiting for a female to come and mate with him or lay an egg. Any egg would do. When she'd done her bit, the male, wobbling his golden wattle, would drive her off and she would go in search of another mate and another mound. And so on.

On the back step there was a small brown box addressed to her. The parcel. So Greg had been here. Lace underwear spread from the box down the step and onto the lawn. The ibis was beaking a red lace thong. The sun, just spilled through clouds, made the day instantly searing. A large gum tree branch separated from its trunk with a crack and fell springy across the grass, startling the brush turkey from its mound and even giving the resolute ibis a momentary hurry-up.

'Shoo, shoo,' Audrey said to both birds, flinging her arms in warning. She tentatively picked up the opened box and gathered the strewn underwear. She imagined a small snake nestled between the layers of lace.

Her dream of a tranquil bush setting fringed by the cooling ocean was now beset with wild birds, reptiles and insects, the deafening din of cicadas, cockatoos and falling eucalypt branches. Eustace called the gum branches *widow makers*. Why, Audrey thought, was she so nervous in the landscape of the country in which she had been born? It didn't seem a part of her or she of it. She preferred the containment of fireplace and hearth, barbecue and swimming pool, to the pin-pricked black skies and inestimable darkness beyond the campfire where creatures of spine, scale, feather and fur rustled in scrub, and bumped on the roof during their nightly migratory patterns.

A folded sheet of paper was sticky-taped to the top of the box. Audrey circled round to the front of the house, let herself in and called out, 'Hi Greg. You still here? Really kind of you to come all this way to deliver my parcel. You really didn't have to.'

She checked all the rooms, behind the doors and in the wardrobes, under the beds. She had been checking under the bed since she was two. She checked behind the shower curtain screening the bath and was startled by a fat lizard scuttling near the waste with no way out. She looked for feet sticking out below the floor-length curtains in the lounge room. Nothing. She opened the curtains. Still nothing. She opened the blinds in other rooms to let the fleeting sunshine flood across the laminate furniture-scape. She opened the kitchen window but locked the front door. She didn't want to be trapped in a closed house and she didn't want to leave it open for an intruder. A stalker. Or a brush turkey.

Finally settled with a glass of wine and Joni on her lap, Audrey opened the note from the top of the box. It had been written with a permanent marker on the back of the last page of a receipt for a Ryobi leaf blower from Bunnings. Great, she thought, now he's bought a leaf blower, so I will definitely have to sell and move.

I opend the box coz I thort it mite be inportent. I sined for it so I was responsible. Nice undies. Woulda staid til you got here but Maxi is at home alone. Just like you. Your nayba Greg.

Audrey looked at the underwear. The underwear she'd ordered for Tom. That seemed a very long time ago. She gathered it all up and took it to the washing machine. She knew the ibis had had its way with some of it and she was squeamish about bird germs. Plus, Greg had handled it. Maybe he'd worn some? He'd definitely touched it with his little hands. She finally threw it all in the bin. It wasn't the life-changing perfection she'd imagined it would be. She could never wear it now because of Tom, Greg and the ibis.

Did she need to acknowledge Greg's delivery? Audrey wondered. Was he genuine? A simple person with some mental health issues who was possibly also nice in a weird way? Or was he threatening her? Was he trying to improve himself and make amends for past transgressions? Maybe losing his child or children had unhinged him? If Audrey contacted him, would he be encouraged? If she didn't, would he be aggrieved? Vengeful? Was he still roaming around Pearl Beach waiting to creep in during the night?

By eleven, Audrey had made the decision to leave as soon as it was light. To go home to the comfort of the little clothes. She didn't want to drive in the dark. Having woken suddenly from jagged sleep, she filled the time wiping down the bathroom sink, scrubbing the toilet and mopping the floor. She would leave Ocean Dreaming cleaner than she had found it. Take that, Maria! She packed the Pontchartrain corkscrew, the unchipped Fernie egg cup and a Minette Walters paperback, *The Scold's Bridle*.

Audrey stayed awake until it was light, then moved purposefully, loading her car, relieved and exhausted. She would go home to safety.

Chapter 11

Dreading that her arrival home would be noted by her neighbour, Audrey circled the block twice, checking to see if he was in his front yard. He was not. There was what Eustace called a *rock n' roll carpark* in front of her gate. She pulled up and quickly took Joni inside. Then the food in the thermal bags with ice bricks, and next her computer and chargers. The rest could wait. She didn't want to risk being seen or, worse, engage in a conversation with Greg. Yet there he was when she came out to lock her car door.

'How'd the underwear work out for ya, sweetheart? Hot date up there?'

'It's none of your business.' Audrey aimed for a neutral tone.

'Last time I do you a fava.'

'Look, Greg, I didn't ask you to do it. I don't know why you did it. I could call the police about you stalking me all the way to the Central Coast and opening a box that was addressed to me.' Her voice cracked as she finished.

'So ya didn't have a good time, eh? Too bad.'

'What's wrong with you?'

'Nothin' I know of.'

'Just please stay away from me. Don't talk to me when I enter and leave my house. Don't cut my flowers. Don't accept parcels on my behalf. I'm going inside now.'

'Took a lotta stuff for a few nights.'

'I would have stayed longer if you hadn't spooked me by coming up there.'

'So now it's all my fault.'

'For god's sake! Do you ever stop?'

'Goin' inside. Goin' inside, sweetie.' Greg held up his palms in mock surrender. As if Audrey was being unreasonable.

'Me too.'

Audrey turned abruptly and slammed her front door behind her.

Inside, she braced for Alec's email.

Re: Partnership consideration
CONFIDENTIAL
Dear Audrey,
I regret to inform you that we are unable to offer you a partnership at this time. Unfortunately, the choice and decision are not mine alone or you would definitely be a partner. I have reached out to my fellow board members and we agree, as one, that we want you to stay. We agree we can offer you an office when one becomes available, although recent flooding in our building has delayed our immediate plans and limited our flexibility vis-à-vis floor space. We will review the partnership issue in six months. We can also offer a modest increase of 7% of your salary and a one-off bonus of $10,000.00 payable at the close of the financial year.

You are a most valued and important part of our business moving forward and I, personally, would be very sad to lose you from the team. You have been a very generous member of the team with your time, knowledge and accommodation of our needs. You are, in short, a great team player.

If you agree to these terms, please sign the attached agreement below and return it promptly to Ms Nadine Drexler in Human Resources as soon as possible so we all know how we will move forward. Please call me directly with any further concerns.
Sincerely,
Alexander P. Aycock

Immediately below Alec's email to her was another email.

Re: Audrey Mendes and possible partnership
CONFIDENTIAL
Dear partners and board members,
One of our colleagues is pressing for an offer of partnership. You all know Audrey so you'll know she means business. She can be tricky and difficult.

I do not want to offer another partnership at this time when we have just taken on two new junior partners, but equally I do not want to lose Audrey to another firm.

Please get back to me with any thoughts on how we can entice her to stay without offering a partnership. I will meet with all of you in the Colton Room at 10.00 a.m. on Tuesday to discuss. Please advise Dinah if you will be there and email her your coffee order by 5.00 p.m. the day before. If you can't attend, send your thoughts to me by email before then, so they can be shared in the meeting. If you do not respond you will not get your bespoke coffee that morning.
Alec

Audrey went to her kitchen and returned with a narrow metal skewer from a set that she used for kebabs on the barbecue. Or, she thought, it could be shoved into the ear and brain of a lying bastard. She stabbed at her work laptop and carved into it. A rainbow corona spread across the screen. She slipped and the skewer gashed her arm, the blood spreading on her white throw rug like a miniature tie-dye or ikat. Rorschach, even.

She lay down on the couch and slept heavily, waking in the early dark to the sounds of the harbour hosting booze cruises for high-school formals, and the *doof doof doof* of her neighbour's music. Audrey checked her phone.

Alec: *Auds, I know how that email might have looked but I really want you to call me so I can explain. Please give me a chance. Obviously you weren't meant to receive the email to the partners. Dinah has been disciplined over that and she apologises profusely for any hurt she's caused. I'll wait to hear.*

Daniel: *Audrey, please call me. I have a problem with the Carmody case. I need your help.*

Maggie: *Audrey, I just want to know how your holiday is going. I'm sorry I haven't been around enough. This job is so much bigger than I thought it would be.*

Tom: *Audrey. I was pained to hear from Sean and Jeff that you were injured the other evening after leaving my place. They don't know you were here and I'd like to keep it that way. What happened here is just between us.*

Rita: *Audrey, your father and I thought we might pop up and visit you at Pearly Beach. Just for the day. It sounds so pretty. Like a fairy grotto. Would you like that? I think your father needs to get out more.*

Eustace: *Audrey my love, ignore your mother's message. We have no intention of coming up and disturbing you. I do not need to*

The Little Clothes

get out more. If anything, I need to spend more time in the garden and less time running senseless errands for your mother. Today I went to Spotlight for 100 centimetres of yellow brick braid for cushions for Scott and Sienna. See you when you get back.

This is a courtesy call from Telstra. You have an outstanding account. To avoid immediate disconnection, please call to pay now.

Audrey cooked tagliatelle with prawns she'd bought in Patonga, and mushrooms, chilli, garlic and chicken stock.

'Smells good over there!' Greg called out cheerfully as she visited her herb garden to pick a garnish of coriander. She wondered if he had a camera set up to see what she was up to.

'Don't mind sharin'!' He had a remarkable ability, a talent even, Audrey thought, for putting one foot in front of the other.

She hurried back in with her leaves without responding and locked the door. After eating, she called home.

'Hello Papa. I just wanted to tell you I'm back.'

'Already?'

'Yes. It was all gloomy up at the beach and I thought, why not come back and be comfortable in my own home? By the way, it's ric rac braid that Mumma sent you out to get, not yellow brick braid. I just wanted you to know where I am. That I'm home.'

'Well, I'm glad you're safe. Also, I've almost finished the rabbit cage. I'll call you in a couple of days and bring it over. I can bring the bracelet with me.'

'Eustace! You will not take that bracelet. I will give it to Audrey. It was my idea to buy it.'

'Okay, Audrey. I'll call you.'

Audrey started to fully unpack and found Daniel's wallet, keys and lighter in one of her food bags, where she had tossed them.

She pocketed the $87.70 in his wallet before sorting through his receipts, business cards and credit cards. She was demoralised to find he had a company credit card when she still had to use her own money for company business and provide receipts at the end of each month for often-queried expenditure, even though there was so little of it. There was a card for Madame Layla at The Dungeon and receipts from the Toolshed, BWS, Coles, Bunnings, Rockpool Bar & Grill, Franca Brasserie and Flower Drum.

'Hi Daniel, Audrey here returning your call. Give me a ring. Happy to help on the Carmody case now I've had a few days' break. By the way, I had a strange call from a PI making some enquiries about you. Not really sure what it was about or why they came to me. Something about a Madame Layla? Whoever that is. Thought I'd give you the heads-up. I haven't called him back yet. Anyway, call me so I know what to say if he calls again. Is this about one of our clients?'

Next, Audrey arranged to meet Nin in Leichhardt for coffee on Thursday morning.

'Please don't tell Mumma. I need to speak to you about something from the past and I don't want a fuss. But it's really important.'

'Are you all right, Aud?'

'Yes, but you have to promise not to tell anyone. I just need to talk to you.'

'I won't tell Rita. I'll see you there at 10.30 a.m. I'll tell Gary I'm going to… the dentist. No, that won't work. He

The Little Clothes

always takes me. I'll tell him I'm going to... where could I be going on my own?'

'The movies?'

'I never do that.'

'A manicure?'

'I've never done that. I do my own nails.'

'Well, tell him you're meeting an old friend.'

'I've never done that. We do everything together. With our friends. There's only the bowling group: Snoopy and Ross, Hazel and Doug. You've met them. Hazel's ill with shingles so I can't invite her.'

'Aunty Nin, don't invite anyone. Come alone. I'd come to you, but Uncle Gary will be there and what I need to talk about is between us. How about you tell him you're meeting me but he can't tell Mum because it's about a Christmas surprise.'

'Yes. Perfect.'

'Okay. That's sorted. Make sure Uncle Gary's very clear about not telling Mumma. I'll see you there, Aunty Nin.'

'Sounds very mysterious. I'm excited.'

•

Audrey waited nervously at a corner table. She was pleased it was noisy and her chosen spot was far enough from others for a discreet conversation, even though it was just a step to the bathroom. She opened her book, still *The Goldfinch*, and kept an eye on the door. Nin arrived with Gary.

'Don't worry, Aud. Gary will sit over there with his coffee and betting guide. Won't you, Gary?' Gary nodded and went to another table. Audrey noticed he was wearing slippers. Nin noticed Audrey noticing his slippers. She shooed her husband to a more distant table.

'He's just had a nasty case of gout. Can't wear proper shoes yet. Don't mention it to anyone. He doesn't want people to know. Don't tell Rita.'

'Would you like coffee, Aunty Ninnie?'

'Oh. If that's okay. Are you going to have coffee?'

'What would you like?'

'A cappuccino, if that's all right.'

'Of course.'

'With extra chocolate. If that's okay.'

Audrey went to the counter to order, trying to hasten to an end the now regretted meeting with her aunt.

'Uncle Gary, I'm ordering for us. What would you like?'

'Oh, I don't know. What do they have?'

Audrey swept her hand at the floor-to-ceiling blackboard menu in front of him.

'I'll have bacon and two well-done poached eggs with breakfast potato wedges and a cappuccino.'

'Okay. I'll just place the order.'

'Did you know you're my favourite niece?' Gary squeezed Audrey's hand as she stood next to his chair.

'Only niece,' she said, stepping through her paces.

'What did he order?' Nin asked when Audrey returned to the table.

'Breakfast.'

'He's already had breakfast. No wonder he gets gout. Here, let me pay. You don't have to pay for us. You young ones should hang on to your money. You're going to need it. Have you seen the property prices? We're all sitting on a goldmine.'

'My shout, no argument. I've dragged you out. And thanks to Henry I already have my house.'

The Little Clothes

'No. It's great to be out.'

'Also, we'd each have to buy another house if we sold ours, so we're not really sitting on a goldmine. We're just living in our homes.'

'True.'

'So, Aunty Nin. This isn't an easy conversation, but I want to talk to you about—'

'Cappuccino, extra chocolate?'

Audrey pointed at Nin.

'What's that, Audrey?'

'Just a flat white.'

'No chocolate?'

'No.'

'What a treat. This looks delicious. And what are these?'

'They're ricciarelli, a sort of Italian almond biscuit.'

'Yummo. This is lovely. Did Gary get Italian shortbread?'

'No. He's having breakfast.'

'I'll take one in a napkin for his afternoon tea. So, go on. What were you saying?'

'I was saying that this isn't an easy conversation.'

'Poached eggs well done, and—'

'Just for that table there. The man with the newspaper. Thank you.'

'Please don't tell me you're not coming to Christmas.'

'No, no. This is something else. I will come to Christmas, of course. I haven't seen Scott for so long and I'm very excited about the baby. You'll be a grandma.'

'Who told you about the baby?'

'Mumma, of course. Don't tell her I told you that she told me.'

'I won't. I think it's wonderful. Gary isn't so happy because they're not married, but who cares.'

'That's right. It's only their business. A baby will be wonderful. Have you met Sienna yet?'

'We have. She's a tiny slip of a thing but they seem happy together.'

'Okay, now here's the thing that I want to talk about.'

'So, we're doing presents this Christmas? Yes?'

'Yes, let's do presents.'

'Oh, good. I hate all those bossy rules about no presents. It seems dull. I like to give a present.'

'Okay. Presents it is.'

'I'll tell Rita.'

'Now here's the thing, Aunty Nin. I've been thinking about the past and I remember that you came with Mumma and me to a doctor when I was twelve and I had a curette.'

'Yes. That's right. But I promised your mother I would never discuss it. And I've kept my promise.'

'But it was my body, my pregnancy.'

'You were twelve. You should talk to Rita about it.'

'She won't talk.'

'Do you know if they have any hot sauce here?'

'For god's sake, Gary! Go to the counter and ask! I told you to stay away. Sorry, Aud.'

Audrey had never heard Nin be sharp with anyone before.

'Aunty Nin, I just want to know what you thought was going on back then. Why no one called the police. I was twelve.'

'Well, Rita worked out you were pregnant. Or at least she thought you might be. It was shocking. She was horrified. She blamed herself. She didn't want anyone to know. She thought she was protecting you, but, looking back, she was also protecting herself. I can't blame her. I love my sister,

The Little Clothes

but she was always keeping up appearances. She thought it might have been that creepy father, or maybe an older boy from the high school down in the bush. We had no idea what to do. You wouldn't talk. In any case it was all sorted after Rita met with your GP, who put her in touch with the right people.'

'It was the creepy father.'

'Yes. That's what I thought from the beginning, but at one stage Rita was even looking at Scottie.'

'What!?'

'Yep. Nearly tore us apart.'

'Nin, I'm so sorry.'

'No! I'm sorry that all happened to you. As I said, I love my sister but I felt she should have paid you far more attention. It was always about Henry. And that suited Henry, to have you there as the black sheep. Left him to do what he wanted without anyone looking. I loved Henry, but he had the rails run. Wasn't good for him. He lacked resilience. Rita always backed him and excused him no matter what. You're the strong one. You had to be.'

'The only one, now.'

'I know. I love you and I'm here for you. Your mother loves you in her own peculiar way. She never saw anyone much after Henry was born. We were all sidelined. I think it was hard for him too. So much pressure.' Audrey didn't want, in that moment, for Henry to be excused. She knew he had accepted her as the black sheep to his own advantage when they were growing up and now it had been spoken out loud by Rita's confidante, Nin.

'And as for your father! You have him tied around your little finger.'

'Thank you, Nin. What you've just said means the world

to me. I've always felt all of those things and I thought I was a terrible person because of them. It's sort of like I absorbed all the bad stuff. I was the black sheep *and* the scapegoat!'

Aunt and niece laughed together.

'And Rita was the cow,' said Nin, taking it way too far.

'What are you going to do now?'

'Nothing. There's nothing I can do.'

'I think that's best. Things happen. But you have a good life now. The job, the house. Try to finish with the past.' Nin covered Audrey's hand with hers. 'I have to get going. Get Gary out of here before he orders a third breakfast or stinks up the toilet.' Nin rolled her eyes towards the bathroom door behind their table. 'We'll see you for Christmas.'

'What do you want me to bring?'

'I'm just planning the menu with Rita. We'll let you know.'

•

'Audrey! It's me. Where are you?'

'At home, Mumma.'

'So you and Nin decided we're doing presents this year? Was anyone going to ask me what I thought?'

'Hang on. What did Nin say?' It had been barely an hour since Audrey farewelled her aunt and uncle from the café. Her mood was light when her mother called. Yet now she was defending herself.

Audrey had never been able to be as close to her mother as Nin was. It was a closed shop for two. They had settled on each other a long time ago when they shared a childhood bedroom, even though Rita's ceaseless rearranging of the furniture had bothered Nin. They were each other's confidante.

The Little Clothes

'I never knew where my bed would be.'

Well, that can't be true, Audrey thought when she was older. Just four pieces of furniture, two of them beds, a shared table between and a small freestanding wardrobe in a tiny room. Still, the family script was trotted out. 'I never knew where my bed would be!' Rita and Nin would collapse with laughter. Rita especially enjoyed being outed as a spontaneous person with a decorator's eye in the face of Nin's plainness. Her younger sister's lack of spark.

'Ninnie just said that you met at a café and we're doing Christmas presents. So now it looks like you two are in cahoots.'

'No, Mumma. We're not in cahoots.'

'But you went to a café together.'

'We did. I wanted to talk to her about the Mr Johnson thing.'

'Why? I told you to leave it alone. For goodness' sake, Audrey. Stop picking at that scab. Why did you go to Nin?'

'Because she was there when it all happened and you won't really talk to me about it.'

'You have to leave it in the past, Audrey. What can be done now?'

'That's sort of what Nin said.'

'Well, at least we're in agreement on that. And did she tell you Gary's had gout?'

'Yes.'

'So why don't you and I go to the café next week and discuss Christmas? Just the two of us.'

'Sure. Can we talk on Monday about that?'

'You call me. Eustace might need to bring me, but he'll sit at a separate table. He'll be wearing shoes. I'd like to try some of the Italian shortbread.'

'Yes, Mumma. We'll do all of that.'

After speaking with her mother, Audrey drove to Little Darlings on Parramatta Road. She'd had an idea when she was driving home from Pearl Beach towards translucent clouds on the horizon. A christening gown. She had resisted the urge until now. Until now, when Rita had quelled her elation from the intimacy with Nin.

'Can I help you with anything?'

'You can. I'm looking for a christening gown.'

'For your baby?'

'For my sister's baby, actually. My sister died so I'm helping the family. Her husband is grieving and looking after the other little ones.'

'That's sad. I'm sorry. How old is the baby?'

'A tiny newborn. Premmie.'

'*Che tragico!* A girl?'

'Yes.'

'What's her name?'

'Pippa,' said Audrey, feeling the weight of *The Goldfinch* in her handbag.

'*Meraviglioso!* How many other children, did you say?'

'I really don't want to talk about it. I'm sorry. I just want a christening gown, and a party dress for the three-and-a-half-year-old as well.'

'Of course. And what's her name?'

'Audrey. After me.'

'Ah. *Roman Holiday. Vacanza. Bellissima!* And I'm Gianna. Follow me and we'll find something perfect for the bambinos,' the woman said, putting on the cat's-eye reading glasses that dangled from a diamanté chain around her neck.

Audrey followed her to the back of the shop, where white dresses in plastic sleeves billowed, cocooned and ready for

The Little Clothes

the day of celebration, when they would be brought into the light for all to see.

'Newborn, you say?'

'Yes.'

'What size the bambina is now?'

'Triple zero at the most.'

'*Piccola, piccola,*' Gianna repeated to herself as she used a hook to bring the cocoons down before laying their contents on a viewing table. It reminded Audrey of Eustace and his avocado hook. She momentarily felt ashamed of her behaviour but was too far into the exchange to back out. She dismissed her saintly father from her thoughts.

'I love this one.' Audrey chose the most expensive of six gowns. French lace and organza with ribbon embroidery and Swarovski crystals.

'Very good choice. Quality. Can use again. Keep in family. *Cimelio di famiglia.*'

Gianna peered at Audrey as if she sensed something was awry but couldn't quite put her finger on it.

'Very small,' she cooed, stroking the gown. '*Piccola.* Need to fatten up. Like us.' Gianna laughed, making the wrinkled flesh of her upper arms wobble and swing.

Audrey watched Gianna wrap the christening gown and a hastily chosen party dress in cream tissue paper before placing them in a suit bag. She felt a discomforting mixture of relish and an urgency to leave the shop as quickly as possible. The rooms, a trove of gaudy and extravagant children's wear, patent shoes, dolls, floral headbands, miniature bow ties, and silver christening gifts adorned with blue and pink ribbons, now felt claustrophobic and no longer offered the release she had anticipated when she first entered Little Darlings. She remembered a holiday moment at Fiumicino Airport, where she observed English tourists telling their children to stand away from the moving luggage conveyor while the bags were being unloaded, for collection, when a Roman couple, fresh from a holiday that had left them deeply tanned and happy, urged their children to jump onto the belt. The beautiful parents held their children's hands while the little boy and girl danced in merry steps just ahead of the first bags before leaping into their father's arms. Their pretty mother clapped and smiled and kissed them all.

•

After a shower Audrey unfurled the christening gown and swirled it on the hanger. She imagined the baby in it. She imagined holding the baby at the baptismal font, next to a faceless father. An absent father. The spare-room wardrobe was purpose-built for short clothes, so she reluctantly placed the long christening gown in the hanging space of her own wardrobe. She now thought of it as Pippa's dress. The dress for a three-and-a-half-year-old fitted, just, into the hanging space of the spare-room wardrobe. It was a size five. The little girl was pudgy, she had told Gianna.

"'Tis good. Flesh very important for growing strong to have baby. And more for him to hold on to.' Gianna had made a sly thrusting movement that finished in a hula, and she laughed and spluttered, wiping her glasses and tears.

'You know what I'm saying. Men like flesh. You make own bambino, no? You growing bambino?' Gianna placed her palm on Audrey's stomach. Audrey flinched and sucked in. 'But you are shy. You should be proud. You have the

The Little Clothes

flesh. Your husband, he like to hold on to you. *Maniglie d'amore*.' Gianna did her hula dance again.

'I am not pregnant or married.'

'Ah, sorry. Sorry. You will be. You big strong girl. Good for making bambino.'

Gianna had thankfully been diverted by incoming customers and Audrey was able to escape with her suit bag while the shopkeeper went to fish in the back room again. She had heard Gianna say, 'Very sad story. *Tragedia*.' Audrey wondered if she herself or the imaginary dead mother was the tragedy. On her way out of the shop she plucked a silver apple candy dish from the counter and a plush rabbit with a pink ribbon collar from the shelf.

Chapter 12

Late on Saturday morning Audrey walked to the pub to buy wine. Maggie and Colin were coming for dinner and the beef shin was already in the slow cooker for the ragout. She'd had misgivings about cooking something so hearty in the heat, but she planned to balance it with a large green salad and homemade lemon sorbet and raspberries.

'Shay-Lee, what are you doing here? I told you not to play on the road. You'll get run over. Where are Mum and Dad?'

'Fighting. I wait for kitty cat. I spank kitty cat.'

'You don't want to hurt the pussycat, Shay-Lee. Why would you hurt the cat?'

'Very naughty. He runned away.'

'Come with me and find Mum and Dad. I do like your Cinderella dress.'

'No. I hurt kitty cat. I will hit him hard on his bum bum. And on his face.'

'Shay-Lee, you don't want to hit anyone.'

'I will smack him on the wall.'

'Shay-Lee, would you like to come and see my rabbit?'

'Yes. I love it,' the little girl said, touching her palm to her heart.

'But you must be gentle. No hitting.'

The Little Clothes

Without thinking, Audrey walked back to her house holding Shay-Lee's hand. The lunch crowd was beginning to gather outside the pub and daytrippers were driving around and around the surrounding blocks looking for non-existent parking spaces. A car came rushing around a corner and Audrey yelled, 'Watch out! There's a kid here.' A woman yelled back through the window, 'You just need to calm down!'

Later it was said on the early-evening news that Shay-Lee had *disappeared into thin air*. And that police had *few clues and are calling on those in the area to report anything they might have seen, no matter how small or seemingly insignificant.*

By then, the father, in his backwards cap, and the frightened mother were pleading with the public for help.

'Shay-Lee, I want you to wash your hands here.' Audrey placed a footstool at the kitchen sink and gave the little girl the pump soap she'd taken from Erin's bathroom.

'Push it down. Like this. And here's a lovely soft towel for you to dry your hands on. That's the way. Now hop down and come and meet Joni the rabbit.'

Shay-Lee hopped with her hands flopped over like paws in front of her face.

'You sit here on the couch and I'll put her on a towel on your lap. You have to be very gentle if you want her to like you.'

Shay-Lee squealed with excitement and grabbed at the rabbit. 'Remember what I said, Shay-Lee. Gentle. Like this. Just stroke her like this.'

'Soft. Liddle bit squiggy.'

'Yes, she is a little bit squiggy. I hadn't thought of that but you're right. Do you like her?'

'Yes.' Shay-Lee nodded solemnly. 'She loves me.'

'She does. But now we have to leave her and go back to Mummy.'

'Noooo! I stay. I hungry.'

'What would you like to eat?'

'Chips.'

'Well, what about an egg and salad sandwich?'

'No. Chips.'

'Okay. Hot chips?'

'Yes.'

'I'll just have to go out for a minute to get the chips, Shay-Lee, and I want you to stay here on the couch. Joni has to go outside now for her lunch. You can see her again later.'

'What she eat?'

'Carrot. Would you like a carrot?'

'No. I not wabbit.'

'Of course you're not. I'm going to put the television on for you. What do you like to watch?'

Peppa Pig.

'Okay. But don't move from the couch while I'm gone.'

Audrey found *Peppa Pig* and took Joni back to her cage. She locked the back door and lowered the blinds.

'I'll be back, Shay-Lee. Here are some biscuits.'

'Chips.'

'Please.'

'Chips.'

'Please. You need to say please.'

'Please.'

'That's better. I'll be back. I'll know if you move from the couch.'

What the hell are you doing? Audrey thought to herself as she hurried to the pub, worrying about leaving a little child in her house unminded. She thought about sharp knives, the slow cooker on the counter, a possible fire, Greg next door, Greg's friends. At the pub, as she went to order a takeaway serve of hot chips, she noted the father behind the bar placing bets, and the mother talking gossip to the kitchen staff. It was apparent no one had yet missed Shay-Lee. She was giving the child a break from the negligence, she told herself. Someone had to look after her. She resolved to give Shay-Lee a lovely lunch, even though it was usual fare, then bring her back to her undeserving parents.

'Thanks for that.' Audrey smiled at the mother as she paid. The mother smiled back without a flicker of recognition. I am doing the right thing, Audrey thought.

She hurried back to her house to find Shay-Lee transfixed by *Peppa Pig*. She put the chips into a bowl on kitchen paper and gave the child two tea towels. One for her lap and one to cover the bodice of her grimy costume.

'I should make you wash your hands after touching Joni.'

'No. No more wash.' Shay-Lee did not make eye contact.

There was a Crunchie wrapper on the coffee table and a sticky brown smear around the child's mouth. Audrey looked in her fridge and found signs of rummaging on the lower shelf. Then she saw the cheese for her dinner with Maggie and Colin. It jolted her. What are you doing? You have guests coming for dinner. You have someone else's child sitting on your couch without the parents' knowledge.

She texted, *Maggie, I seem to be doing this to you all the time right now and I am so sorry but I have to cancel tonight. I am so sorry. Eustace isn't well. I'll call you later. Tomorrow. With an update. Let me know you got this.*

Audrey was able to stir the slow-cooker pot on her counter and watch Shay-Lee from the kitchen. It pleased her. Would the little girl like ragout for dinner? No, Audrey thought, she's not staying for dinner. She's eating lunch and going straight home. Shay-Lee had been with Audrey for more than an hour and still no knock on the door. No harm done…

'Did you like your chips?'

'Icecream now.'

'No icecream. You had biscuits. And you had chocolate.'

'Yes icecream.'

'No. No icecream. How about I cut up an apple?'

'I want Mummy.'

Of course she wanted her mother.

'She can't come now. She's busy. Do you want to hold Joni again?'

'No.'

'Well, how would you like to try on a real fairy dress?'

'Yes. Fairy dress.'

'Then come and wash your face and hands back here in the kitchen.'

Shay-Lee obediently stepped onto the stool and washed her hands with Erin's soap. Audrey brought a warm flannel and gently plumped the little girl's face just as Eustace had done for her when she was young. The chocolate, snot, salt, sleep and grease all wiped away in the steamy warmth.

Audrey took the party dress from the spare-room wardrobe while Shay-Lee looked on in wonder.

'I bought this just for you. You'll have to take your other dress off.' Audrey had bought the dress mostly for herself but with Shay-Lee in mind. She wanted to make the child happy.

Audrey noted the child's dull underwear, as if it had been washed with workwear, black T-shirts and dirty tea

The Little Clothes

towels. Why didn't they cherish this child as she would? Audrey wondered. She wanted Shay-Lee to be clean and comforted. This would have to do, she thought. Hopefully there were enough layers in the dress to conceal what was going on underneath.

'Do you need to use the bathroom?'

'No.'

'I think you should. It's just in here. I'll bring the stool.' Audrey saw a puddle of urine near the toilet bowl.

'I'm sorry, Shay-Lee, I should have thought.'

'I want Mummy.'

'No, no. Don't cry. You're not in trouble. Let's just pop this over your head and we'll see how it looks. You'll be like Cinderella at the ball.'

The dress just fitted. That'll be the chips, Audrey thought.

'Shay-Lee, you look beautiful. Perfect.'

'Liddle fatty.'

'No. Who told you that?'

'Mason at kidney.'

'You're gorgeous. Strong.'

'You fat too.'

'Maybe a little.'

'I show Mummy dress.'

'No. Not yet. She's still busy. I thought I could read you a book about Cinderella.'

'Yes. TV.'

'No. I'll read it. The Brothers Grimm version. The original.'

'No. TV. Barbie TV.'

Audrey found *Cinderella* on Disney and settled Shay-Lee on the couch, the white frock spreading pleasingly to cover the child's puce Crocs decorated with SpongeBob and

Hello Kitty shoe charms. She cleaned the bathroom floor and checked her phone.

Auds, I hope you and Eustace are ok. I'll wait till you contact me and we can talk properly. I'm worried that you haven't contacted Cathy yet. I'm disappointed about tonight, too. Take care, Maggie X

Audrey wondered with shame what Maggie might say if she knew Shay-Lee was sitting on her couch. Only a goody-two-shoes would condemn her behaviour, she reassured herself.

Audrey, Alec. I have been trying to contact you to no avail. Just wanted to say again how sorry I am about Dinah sending that email. So thoughtless. But I also wanted to let you know you've been nominated for the company's inaugural Moisen Prize for outstanding contribution to the company's culture, community and growth. It comes with a cash amount for future education of your choice and an overseas exchange with our sister companies in Basel and Glasgow. I think it's exciting and I want you to think seriously about this instead of putting all your ambition into a partnership, which can be more punishment than prize. Trust me on that. Also, Erin and I want to ask if you would be Milla's godmother. Daniel's agreed to be godfather. I promised Erin I'd call you about it. Call me.

So she would be standing at the font with a baby, but she would be next to Daniel. She almost laughed, except she teared up in despair.

'Hello Audrey. It's Mum. I am looking forward to catching up next week. I keep thinking about the shortbread biscuits you bought for Nin. She hasn't stopped talking about them. Anyway, now we're doing presents, I wondered what you think about a mini spice blender and a set of write-on spice jars for Nin? I also need ideas for you. Obviously your father

The Little Clothes

is socks and a gardening book, which we could choose together after our coffee next week. Then there's Scott...'

For god's sake, thought Audrey, doesn't she know what sort of pressure I'm under right now?

Audrey, can we get together for another drink at mine soon? I feel terrible about the distance between us. BTW I'm getting a bit of heat from Sean.

Good on Sean.

Audrey turned the slow cooker off, poured a glass of wine from a half-drunk bottle, and joined Shay-Lee on the couch.

'Can I have?'

'Certainly not. You don't drink wine. You're too young.'

Together they watched Cinderella rush from the ball in her pumpkin carriage and return to her life of drudgery and her bed on the hearth. When Audrey woke to darkness, Shay-Lee was asleep on the other end of the couch and someone was knocking on her front door. Shay-Lee had painted her face with Audrey's lipstick. The grotesque smile of a clown.

'Shay-Lee, get up. Quickly! Get up. I'm going to let you sit in a special cubbyhouse.'

Shay-Lee drowsily followed Audrey to the pantry.

'I tired. I want Mummy.' The little girl sat on the cushions Audrey had placed on the floor.

Audrey closed the pantry and locked it. The lock had been installed by Eustace when she'd rented her house as an Airbnb one New Year's Eve. She'd gone to stay with Maggie and they'd split the absurdly large proceeds from the two nights.

Another knock on the front door.

'Hello. Oh my goodness, what's going on?' Two

uniformed police officers filled the doorway. 'Sorry, I was having a nap.'

Over the officers' shoulders, the street hummed: police cars, flashing lights and people milling on the footpath.

'Are we being evacuated? Is it the gas mains?'

'It's not about gas. Do you live at this address?'

'I do. I own it.'

'Is there anyone else at these premises?'

'I live alone.'

'Your name?'

'Audrey Mendes. What's happening?'

'A missing child. Do you know her?' The silent partner held up a photo of Shay-Lee attached to a clipboard.

'I wouldn't say I know her but I know who she is. She lives at the pub down there.' Audrey pointed helpfully towards the pub and the cafés.

'Have you seen her today?' said the speaking partner.

'You know, I might have because I went to buy take-away at lunchtime. But she's often around on the street. I can't definitely say I saw her today down there – though I can't rule it out either. She's sometimes in the lane next to the pub or running around inside. I've rescued her off the road a few times. Oh my goodness, how terrible. She's very sweet. How long has she been missing?'

'Since early this afternoon. It's been about seven hours. We're just going door to door.'

'What's everyone doing over there?'

'Volunteers. Neighbourhood search. They're being briefed. Police and SES.'

'I should go and join. Is that all? Is there anything else I can do? I don't really know the family. I see them when I go to trivia nights.'

The Little Clothes

'Just take this card and call if you think of anything. Anything at all. Also, please look in your backyard or in any sheds.'

'My side gate's locked and the fence is too high.'

'We're asking all the neighbours to check.'

'I will. Of course.'

'And if you're joining them, take a torch. They've run out.'

Audrey walked to her front gate in time to see Greg being escorted to a police car. Was he suspected in Shay-Lee's disappearance? She could see Tom, Lorraine, Sean and Scarlet standing with a group of locals on the other side of the road. Audrey waved.

Sean waved back. Tom beckoned her. Audrey, conscious of Shay-Lee trapped alone in the cupboard, was about to run across to quickly say hello but held back when she saw Scarlet lean into Tom and drape her arms around his neck. Tom kissed her on the forehead. He gave her his jumper. He tied the sleeves like a scarf around her neck. It reminded Audrey of a perfume advertisement. Such was Scarlet's beauty and Tom's apparent devotion.

I am an idiot, Audrey thought. A complete fucking idiot. And she didn't just mean Tom.

She turned abruptly and walked back towards her house, away from the madding crowd, but not before she noticed locals and strangers being stopped by the media, no doubt being asked the standard questions. 'Do you know the little girl?' 'Do you have any thoughts about her disappearance?' There would be the usual platitudes and cliches. 'She's an angel.' 'The perfect little girl.' 'We all love her.' 'This sort of thing doesn't happen around here.' And 'We don't live here. Just came to the pub for lunch. But it's terrible. We'll be praying for her and her family.' Helicopters irritated overhead. DoorDash drivers puttered down the other side of the road. The side where Audrey had seen Tom and Scarlet embracing.

When Audrey opened the pantry door she found Shay-Lee eating Maltesers, dry spaghetti and caster sugar. Shay-Lee smiled at Audrey and lifted the bag of sugar above her head like a sacrifice.

'More chips?'

'Soon,' Audrey promised. 'Perhaps you'd like a bath? Get all that chocolate and lipstick off you?'

Audrey ran a luxurious bath with Shay-Lee's help. Lots of bubbles.

While Shay-Lee played in the tub, blowing the soapy foam from her hands onto the wall, Audrey washed the child's grey clothes on the quick cycle and then dried them in the dryer.

'So, Shay-Lee, do you think we should go back to see Mummy for some chips?'

'With wabbit.'

'No, Joni has to stay here for now. But we could go and look for your cat.'

'Yes!'

'So, we'll go out the back way to where the cat lives. Let's get you dressed.'

'Fairy dress?'

'No. But I'll dry your hair curly.'

•

Audrey held Shay-Lee's hand and together they crossed the back garden. Audrey wondered if Greg was already being

The Little Clothes

cautioned by the police and whether he needed a solicitor. Whether the police were suspicious of him or of one of his brigade of fathers. She unlocked the gate that led to the dunny lane, peeked out, and saw no one was there.

'Let's be really quiet, Shay-Lee. We need to sneak up on the cat if we want to catch it.'

'It dark. Scary.'

'You'll be fine. I'm here. Just hold my hand.'

At the intersection of the dunny lane and the wider lane that ran down to the pub they were backstage to the drama unfolding on the main street. Audrey could sense movement, see the police lights and, inexplicably, a fire engine blocking the end of the lane.

'Keep coming this way,' she urged Shay-Lee as they walked across the intersection, back on the course of the dunny lane. Past the back gate of the pub and two more blocks down.

'Kitty cat live there.' Shay-Lee pointed behind her. 'Go back.'

'Cats live everywhere. They move around. They're clever. The cat will be frightened by all that noise. Let's keep creeping quietly this way. Your job is to watch out and tell me if you see the cat. Then we can try to catch it.'

'And spank.'

'We won't spank. We'll be kind and gentle.'

'This a liddle road. For fairies.'

Audrey wanted to promise fairies but was suddenly aware of the enormity of what she had done. Perhaps she too would soon need a lawyer.

'It's the old dunny lane,' Audrey said, drawing on her knowledge from a case when she'd defended an occupant who had built a community vegetable garden beyond his title deed and into a neighbour's allocation of the dunny lane. 'A long time ago, once a week, a man came and collected all the poo in buckets from the houses and took it away through these little lanes. They called the poo the night soil. Now we have inside toilets.'

'Poo. You say poo.' Shay-Lee dissolved in giggles. 'Poo-pooey-poo-poo. You're a poo.' Audrey tried to subdue the little girl's glee.

Well past the back of the pub, Audrey could see the spire of the pretty stone church that fronted the main road. Although she had never been inside, St David's might be the sanctuary they needed. She had sometimes seen the Sunday-afternoon soup kitchen set up at the front.

Shay-Lee began to complain about being a long way from the cat and from her mother. She whined about a stone in her shoe. Audrey bent down, allowing the child to lean on her shoulder while she removed the Croc and emptied it of gravel.

'It still hurts.'

'The stone isn't there now. Why does it still hurt?'

'It do. Ouchy. I want Mummy,' Shay-Lee wailed.

'Keep looking for the cat. I think it's very close by,' Audrey said, trying to bring the worn-out game back into play.

'There's the storch.'

'Sorry?'

'The storch.' Shay-Lee pointed to the spire.

'Ah. The church. Let's go in for a minute and sit down. Then we'll find the cat and take it to Mummy.'

'Mummy hates cat.'

The gate to the churchyard from the dunny lane opened easily. They walked across the barren yard to the curved

The Little Clothes

oak door. Audrey pushed it open and took the child inside. They sat on a pew.

'Kitty cat not here.'

'It is if you think it is. Let's use our imaginations, Shay-Lee. This is a place of imagining. Where could he be hiding?'

'Hiding in a box.'

'Hello!'

'Shhh! You scare kitty.'

'I just want to see if anyone else is here. Like the pastor.'

'I like pasta. I hungry.'

No one answered. The church was lit softly with fake candles. Shay-Lee lay down on the hard bench and put her head on Audrey's lap.

Audrey thought about Rita and Nin and the man who had molested them. She thought about her grandfather, who had done what Rita called *the showy work* for the church. She thought about her mother's need to hide mess. She thought about what she was doing to Shay-Lee and how terrible it was. She knew she needed to reunite Shay-Lee with her parents. She briefly thought about her own current mess but pushed it away.

The church was as sweet as a child's naive drawing. A tiny relic that had recently found new life in Instagram weddings, with its quaint stone exterior and what wedding planners called *proximity* to Hemmes restaurants. Polished wood and velvet. Stained glass. One cracked panel held crookedly with silver duct tape. The light from a street-lamp slanting in. Tapestry cushions made decades ago by the local devout women. Each bearing a biblical quotation and the maker's initials.

Let the little children come to me. AC

Let your heart take courage. VP
Children are a gift from the Lord. MM
Our faith can move mountains. SW

Audrey thought about Henry and wished she had lit a candle, but now she couldn't budge the child without awakening more complaint. She needed a plan. She thought about the school chapel and her brother's funeral. That, she thought, was the last time she'd been in a church. There were flowers in urns on either side of the altar in front of her. Wedding flowers? Or flowers for a christening? A funeral? Perhaps all three. The big three. She remembered her mother saying they'd paid for the flowers at Grandma Joan's funeral that had been left over from the funeral before, even though they'd spent time carefully choosing blooms from the funeral director's catalogue and paid for them. Rita had called it *trickery* and *deceit*. *The business of death*.

Audrey stroked Shay-Lee's brow and closed her own eyes for a moment, then opened them to see a cat spring from the closed piano lid onto the altar. The rough-furred tabby looked down at the strange wayfarers in the second row with slight curiosity, then proceeded to lick its paws.

'There you go, Shay-Lee. We found a cat. A little miracle.' The child slept on. 'And now I know what to do.'

I found the child, she thought. I found the child. It felt like an epiphany.

Audrey knew she wasn't strong enough to carry Shay-Lee all the way up the hill to the pub, so she slid the child's head onto a kneeling cushion and edged out into the aisle. She found a chorister's robe hanging in the vestibule next to two left-behind coats and a discarded umbrella with tangled spokes. She spread the robe over Shay-Lee, then

The Little Clothes

walked out the front door of the deserted church. It was darker now. The terrace houses were lit with porch lights and streetlights. Some of the overhanging frangipanis were traced in fairy lights. There were people inside the houses going about their Saturday-evening pursuits that did not involve mayhem or kidnapping. Presently she came to the terrace with a stroller folded beside the door. She'd seen it before. She'd spoken to the mother of the little boy whose carriage it was and she'd watched the boy's mother fold or unfold it while they exchanged neighbourly courtesies about weather and traffic and noise. She took the stroller and went back to the church.

Audrey slumped Shay-Lee into the chair and left the church to start her perilous pilgrimage to the pub. The path to her redemption.

At the terrace house where the little boy and the slim mother with strawberry curls lived, she laid the sleeping child on the footpath with her cardigan as a pillow while she put the stroller back on the porch, then, with a mighty effort, she heaved Shay-Lee onto her shoulder and staggered up the last part of the hill. Up the Ape Run. No one stopped her as she ducked around the police line and called out, 'I've found her!'

No one turned as Audrey walked into the pub, where a police briefing was in train in the trivia-night room with SES volunteers and media. An officer stood on the little stage where Kevin usually prevailed with his yellow pages on Tuesday nights. There was a lively party atmosphere. There was purpose, camaraderie and common engagement.

'I've got the child. I found her!' Audrey called from the back. At first she wasn't noticed or heard so she pushed through to the front. Gradually, and then in a deluge, the word spread. Cameras flashed, police officers rushed forward and took Shay-Lee from Audrey, the mother and father were summoned. The child woke up.

'She was in the church down the road,' Audrey said.

'I was looking for kitty cat,' Shay-Lee added helpfully now, and several times over the next few days, whenever she was asked why she went to the church.

'My grandmother sometimes takes her to St David's,' said the mother. 'Shay knows that church. We sometimes take leftover bread and vegetables from here for the food bank.'

Audrey was asked the same. Why had she been in the church? The pastor unhelpfully said she had never been there before. He'd never seen her before. 'I went there for solace,' she told the detectives. They looked confused. 'I wanted to light a candle for my dead brother. I was seeking comfort. I didn't light the candle because I became aware of the child. I called out but no one answered. No one was there. I think you'll find there's not always someone in attendance. Anyone can walk in and out unseen.'

'Everyone is seen in the church,' said the pastor when questioned at the police station.

Chapter 13

'So ya had me arrested?' Greg was hosing his front garden when Audrey walked up her path on Sunday evening with a takeaway pizza.

'And why would I do that, Greg? How *could* I do that?'

'Dunno. But I know you did somethink. Seen you on the news.'

'Why were you arrested?'

'Not really arrested. Just taken in for a chat.'

'Why?'

'Dunno.'

'Well, there has to be a reason.'

'Well, there has to be a reason.' Greg imitated Audrey in a surprisingly accurate high-pitched voice.

Audrey stifled a laugh. 'Look. I don't run the police. Maybe it's because you've got form.'

'Not for kidnapping.'

'Good to know.'

'Hey, wanna come in for a drink later? After all that's gone on.'

'Sure. Why not? But can we make it next weekend? I have so much to catch up on; my phone's been running hot since yesterday.'

'Serious? You'll come?'

'Yeah. Why not? We *are* neighbours and you came all that way with my parcel. One drink won't hurt. Next Saturday. Okay?'

'Ya windin' me up.'

'Do you want me to come or not?'

'Definitely want ya to come.'

'Okay. About four on Saturday, okay?'

'Yep. I'll tie Maxi up.'

'Thanks. Have a good week. Sorry you were arrested.'

'Taken in for a chat.'

•

Audrey agreed to an interview with *A Current Affair*. There was to be an on-set reunion with Shay-Lee and her parents. She didn't weigh the possible consequences but worried a little about what she might wear. Rita worried too.

'I'm worried, Audrey. What are you going to say about me? Don't get started on what a terrible mother I am.'

'Why would I do that?'

'I know what you're like.'

'Mumma, it's about me finding the child. That's all. You won't come into it. By the way, I wouldn't say anything mean about you. Plus, it will all be over in a couple of days. Everyone will move on.'

'Well, I hope you're not going to bring the rabbit into it. You don't want people thinking you're crazy. I had no idea you light a candle for Henry in your local church. You never light the candle at home. Just makes me wonder how well I know you.'

'How's Papa?'

The Little Clothes

'He's obsessed with the rabbit cage.'

'Okay, Mumma. How's that Christmas pudding going? I really have to go now.'

'I'm soaking the fruit. I thought you might like to come over to make the florentines with me? I promised Nin florentines on Christmas Day. And mince pies. I could do with some help. It can't always be about helping other people, you know. Family comes first. Blood is thicker than water.'

'I would love that, Mumma. I'll call you.'

'Audrey, it's Alec. I've seen all the media hoopla. I'm very proud of you. You're trending everywhere. Please be mindful of what you say about us to the media. Call me when you can. I want you back here as soon as possible. We are family after all. And you're a story. It's all about our story. Over at Jake and Jackobsen they don't have a cohesive story, they don't know their story. Let alone how to sell it. We're ready to offer a full partnership.'

Tom: *Aud, just saying hi. Also, just a thought, please don't mention me on the media stuff. I have a public profile that I need to protect. I know you'll understand.*

And on it went.

Maggie: *What a heroine. I've seen you all over the media. But I'm still concerned about you. Please call.*

Angus: *Wow, wow, wow. Call me because I'm working on* Speak Easy *now and we want to book you for your first interview. By the way, I'm not with Javier anymore because I just met the love of my life, Steve, and I'd like you to meet him too. Please don't say anything to the media about Henry and me. Steve wouldn't be happy with that. And don't say anything to Steve about Javier when we all finally catch up. Please call me.*

'Hello Audrey Mendes. It's Sharnie from *A Current*

Affair. I just want to talk hair, make-up and wardrobe, arrival times et cetera. Please call as soon as possible.'

Erin: *Give me a call when you're ready. You might need a shoulder or a break from your neighbourhood and I'm here if you need me.*

Nin: *We're so excited for you. Maybe brush your hair. And wear darker colours on the telly. Scottie called. He's excited too.*

Amy: *Hi Audrey. You might not remember me from high school. It's Amy. Amy Bales. Long time no speak hey? But I just saw you on the TV and remembered how much I miss you. Call me. I might get the band back together. Not that we had a band. You know what I mean. I'd love you to meet Realm and Tame. My boys. Call me.*

Angus: *Audrey, we need to come out and see you as soon as possible tomorrow. We'd like some local colour shots in the church. Maybe you lighting a candle for Henry.*

Sean: *Give me a call. About anything. Specifically, thought we might have lunch today. Thought we could just go up the road for a sandwich?*

'Hello Audrey, It's Shay-Lee's mother here. I feel that we really need to talk. I haven't had a chance to thank you properly. It's been a bit mad. But I want you to know that *A Current Affair* only want to speak to us. I hope you don't mind. It's a big opportunity for us. We'd also like you to come to a party we're holding in the private room upstairs at the pub. To thank everyone, like the SES guys, some neighbours, some regulars and the police. We've been asked to try and get a crowd together for the cameras. Most importantly, you. Tonight, starting at 6.00 p.m.'

•

The Little Clothes

'Audrey!' Shay-Lee's mother welcomed her child's saviour with a warm hug. There were cameras filming for the Tuesday-night special on *A Current Affair*. Shay-Lee hung behind her mother when she saw Audrey.

'Go on, Shay-Lee. Give Audrey a kiss and a hug.'

'No. She lose kitty cat. She take fairy dress.'

'Shay-Lee!'

'She's just shy, love,' said the father. 'There's been a lot of coming and going. She's tired.'

'Shay-Lee, I've brought you a special present.' Audrey had wrapped the silver Tiffany comb with the pink tassel and the toy rabbit from Little Darlings.

'Where fairy dress?'

'Shay-Lee! Now you're being rude,' said the mother. 'I have no idea what she's talking about!'

'Oh no. That's all right. She's obviously tired. Been through a lot.'

'You're so thoughtful and kind,' said Sean, gazing at Audrey. Marion, Jeff and Lorraine nodded in vigorous agreement. Tom had been cornered by Wanda and nervously made eye contact with Audrey and waved, looking for intervention or forgiveness. Or did he simply want to be on camera? Audrey couldn't tell and realised she didn't care.

'Can you grab me a drink, Sean? I just need to go to the loo.'

Audrey practically fell into a cubicle and bolted the door. She knew she had done something terrible and would have to live forever with the lie and the toll of the deceit. She knew it would bother her in the days to come when she sat in her office and told her clients to prune their truths. It would probably niggle her in thirty years' time. Would

Shay-Lee remember what had happened and be credible in her remembering? It was a stain Audrey would never outrun. She would never be able to trust anyone with her secret. Not even Maggie. Maybe Eustace? No. Especially not Eustace, who thought she was perfect and whom she couldn't bear to let down. Audrey looked into the mirror and tried to see herself and understand her behaviour. She had no explanation.

Everyone has a dark secret, she reassured herself. We all hide something, even if we don't acknowledge it to ourselves. Daniel, for example. Nadine. Greg. Alec. Henry. The mother. The father. Rita and Nin. Even glorious Maggie wanted to mow down her father's trees. Audrey would put this catastrophe behind her. She would shut it away. In an instant she decided to sell her house and leave the neighbourhood. Make what Rita would call *a fresh start*. She resolved to take the little clothes to a charity bin and burn the diaries. The trivia group had had its glory days. Audrey had almost encountered a life-destroying disaster and now she was jolted to make the most of what was ahead. She would no longer live in the past, except to talk to Cathy and try to sort herself out.

Audrey fluffed her hair, swished her cardigan and wrote in the lower right corner of the cubicle door with the Montblanc pen she'd stolen from Alec's study: *A was here*.

'Audrey. I was worried about you. The speeches are starting. They want you there.' Sean handed Audrey a glass of champagne and guided her with a gentle palm on her middle back towards the brightly lit inner circle around a podium.

As Audrey approached there were cries of 'Speech! Speech!'

The Little Clothes

'That's very kind,' she said into the microphone. 'But I am not a hero. I am just glad Shay-Lee's been reunited with her family. It's all I ever wanted.'

Chapter 14

'Audrey, it's Angus. Call me. Urgently.'

'Hi Angus. I'm sorry I missed your call. I was asleep. Feeling very tired after all the kerfuffle.'

'Audrey, we're seeing promos with you in them for tonight's *A Current Affair*! Adam is furious. He's organised the crew for later today and hair and make-up and now he wants to cancel. You owe me an explanation. A lot of hard work has gone in here.'

'Look Angus, I went to the thank-you party with the parents at their pub. Half the neighbourhood was there. I didn't do an interview. They filmed everyone at the party. I can't help that. I don't mind if you cancel. I'm genuinely sorry.'

'Audrey! You've put me in a terrible position. I mind! I care! You have been played. Worse, we have been played.'

'Angus, it's fine. It was their story to tell. Not my story. I can't control who they speak to.'

'But you shouldn't have gone to the party!'

'Angus, I'm sorry but the story couldn't stretch much further. It's a little story with a happy ending. And who cares about me? I'm no one. I made a mistake.'

'You've totally blown your chance to be on TV. I've tried to do the right thing for you and give you an opportunity

The Little Clothes

and you just throw it in my face. Henry would have been horrified by the way you've treated me.'

'I am sorry for this inconvenience, Angus. I meant no harm. But please don't invoke my dead brother's name in your pursuit of TV ratings. And please don't ever call me again.'

Audrey hung up and enjoyed being calm, firm and sure.

The next afternoon she called several real estate agents and began the process of unshackling herself from Henry. From the past. From Greg. She needed a house with a lawn for Joni, maybe a car space, and somewhere closer to her parents. She knew that was a role soon to become more pressing. And she wanted a change. First, she had to sell.

On Christmas morning Audrey knocked on Greg's front door and delivered a box of wrapped books and beribboned jars of homemade mandarin jam for his guests, who were arriving to help at St David's Christmas food-bank lunch.

'Ya won't join us? Could do with a bit of chick company. And an extra pair of hands. The blokes can be dud. All the fellas loved ya when ya came for the catch-up.' Audrey hoped her face did not betray her thoughts about the hour she'd spent in Greg's backyard drinking a home-brewed beer and being menaced by Maximus. She'd even nibbled a tinned smoked oyster on Jatz to be polite. 'There's cabanossi and Cheezels too,' Greg had said, hovering with a flyblown platter.

'No. I'm going to my aunty's house for Christmas lunch with my parents and my cousin. His partner's expecting a baby.'

'I'm going to my aunty's house,' Greg mimicked. Audrey tried to suppress her giggle with pursed lips.

'So, these are the books I promised. And some of my excellent jam. I also wanted to let you know I'm selling my house in the new year. I need to move closer to my parents.'

'Yeah. Thought so when I seen all those creeps coming and going with their fancy cars and tight suits last week. Why aren't they wearing socks? They're like sharks. They don't even hide their money anymore. I might try to get into real estate.'

'Well, I'll keep you updated. Are you seeing your children today?'

'Nah. There's just the one. That I know of.' Greg winked at Audrey. She ignored him. 'It's just the little fella. Not so little now, come to think of it. Me ex doesn't want it. Can't blame her.'

Audrey thought Greg was going to cry. Christmas was a difficult holiday.

'So, anyway, Merry Christmas, Greg. And here's a present for Maxi.' Audrey whipped an absurdly large plastic-wrapped marrow bone tied with a flamboyant red bow from her handbag and gave it to Greg.

'Ya breakin' me heart here, sweetheart. I didn't get ya nothin'. Hang on, I'll pick a rose. Whoops, they're all gone.'

When Audrey arrived at Nin and Gary's the oppressive heat had already seeped into every part of the fibro house. Nin was struggling under Rita's tutelage with a turkey that didn't fit into the tiny oven. The thrusting breast had been sliced off to reduce it to a more amenable size.

'Audrey, there you are! You need to help Nin. Someone needs to help Nin. Everyone knows she won't listen to me. The story of my life. It's hard being the eldest.'

The Little Clothes

'Merry Christmas, Mumma. Papa! Scottie! How long has it been? And this must be Sienna. I'm Audrey. Okay, Aunty Nin, let's get that bird back out and we'll butterfly it and cut it in halves. One can go on the barbecue and the other half in the oven. Uncle Gary, is the barbecue fired up? Is there an apron, Aunty Nin?'

Presents were exchanged in the late afternoon when they had all been lulled by the turkey, potatoes, creamed spinach and gravy, wine, pudding and pavlova; when the picking at chocolates, cheese and florentines was slowing. Audrey gave Sienna and Scott the little clothes.

'It's a mixture of boys' and girls' stuff. Most of it can go either way.'

'Audrey Mendes, you always *go too far!*' said Rita. 'Making my gifts look shabby!' Sienna was awash with the little clothes as she unwrapped them and laid them on her belly and on the couch and the coffee table in front of her.

'Audrey. These are the most beautiful little clothes I have ever seen,' said Sienna. 'Thank you so, so much.'

Chapter 15

Alec was not overly gracious or generous when he brought Audrey to the negotiating table. Yet he got her there with relative ease and she was offered a partnership and an office, both of which she accepted. A celebratory lunch followed in the weeks after Christmas.

'I never go back to Michael's anymore, after that last time. This is way better. Wait till you try the CopperTree steak tartare. Heidi loves it!'

'Heidi?'

'Yes. Heidi. She loves it.'

Alec was greeted lavishly by the maître d', which pleased him. He checked to make sure Audrey noted the lavish welcome.

'They always save my table.'

'You and Erin?'

'Yes. Of course. As much as Erin enjoys anything these days.'

Alec and Audrey were shown to an opulent blue velvet banquette, where Alec's wine was being chilled.

'Thank you, Mario. We'll start with a bottle of the Pol Roger Sir Winston Churchill, and the steak tartare for two, and then we'll work out where to go from there.'

Several diners recognised Alec, or at least the apparent

The Little Clothes

level of importance bestowed upon him on his entrance. They turned and craned for a while, until they couldn't place him.

'So, how is Erin? I haven't really spoken to her since all the hoopla.'

'Busy with the kids. Still up at Palm Beach with my mother. Been there since before Christmas.'

'Okay. Still doing her slides and sandals?'

'Who would know?'

'Well, Alec, *you* would know.'

'I can't be across her every little scheme.'

'She was doing so well with that business.'

'Who would know? I just write the cheques.'

'Well, I think she was impressive, getting that business up and going.'

'It was a hobby paid for by me,' Alec dismissed the compliment.

He put his spectacles on the rim of his nose and held the bottle of champagne with an outstretched arm before nodding to the sommelier with an inner-circle understanding of their important inner-circle business.

'So, Audrey, good to get you back where you belong. We've missed you.' Alec clinked glasses with her.

'Alec, you come here with Heidi?'

'No. Yes. Not really. But sometimes with other people from the office. Heidi comes along to be pleasant. The clients and barristers like her.'

'Okay.'

'Have you sorted yourself out, Audrey?'

'Yes. Completely sorted.'

'We'll have the lamb tagine between us please, Mario. And the boiled savoy and broccolini.'

Audrey's heart sank. She wasn't fond of fruit, let alone in her savoury course. She had hoped for steak frites and an opportunity to order her own meal. Definitely not the cabbage.

'It's so wonderful you'll be back on Monday. I have a number of cases for you to start on. I would like you to mentor Hanna. I think you should avoid Daniel and we'll work to keep you apart.'

'Suits me.'

'Good. That's settled.'

'So, Alec, talk to me about the important stuff. The kids, Erin. How was Christmas?'

'Aud, who would know? Erin has gone bonkers. She fusses over those children to the point of neurosis. She can't control Carter. She's always miserable. She should just buck up. Look at what she's got. My saintly mother did everything for Christmas. Erin's taken over the east wing of my mother's house at Palm Beach and even brought her own mother up to help with the children.'

'Okay. So perhaps take a break together? Spend some time together? While the two grandmas are there.'

'Well, for a start my mother is not Grandma. She's Sylvie or Skit to all of us, including her grandchildren. And second, Erin is on a permanent break. I am the one who needs a break. In February I'm flying out to London for work and I hope to get a week in Venice after. Plus, my mother is hardly going to be best friends with Sue. I mean, really?'

'Sure. It was just a suggestion. Is Erin going to join you? In Venice?'

'God, no. It's work and then a break.'

'A break? On your own?'

'So, come in on Monday and Nadine will get all the

The Little Clothes

paperwork done and off we'll go again. Cheers to you, Audrey. Well played.'

'I didn't play you, Alec. I just asked for a partnership.'

'It's okay, Aud. You've done well.'

'Please don't patronise me, Alec. I earned the partnership.'

'And the pay rise.'

'Yes. All of it.'

'Well, we're in furious agreement then. No need to get hot under the collar.'

The arrival of the conical pot and steaming bowl of couscous halted the simmering tit for tat at the table.

•

When Audrey arrived in the office on Monday morning there was an atmosphere. She immediately questioned her decision to return. Her guts clenched.

Nadine found Audrey in the foyer and frantically beckoned her to follow, then locked them in the Colton Room.

'Thank god you're here, Audrey.'

'What's going on?'

'Alec has been having an affair with Heidi, and Erin found out and has hired the best divorce lawyer in the country. Michelle Gurkas.'

'Okay. Gurkas is good. I'd go to her for sure. Clever Erin.'

'Well, you'll never have the need.'

'Sorry?'

'I simply mean you're not married.'

'I may be one day.'

Nadine looked pained.

'Richard and all the other partners have moved against Alec and want him out. He didn't see it coming. Well, he is out. Alec is gone. It's hard to believe. I've always thought Alec *is* the company. His father founded the company. The partners met in secret yesterday and voted. Just as well you did your deal. Here, sign these now.'

'Hang on a minute.'

'Sign the bloody documents, Audrey. I'm helping you. You need to have them signed. Put Friday's date.'

Audrey took the stolen pen from her bag and signed.

'Okay, follow me and I'll show you to your new office. Dinah will be there. She's excited about working for you.'

'With me.'

•

Audrey placed a silver-framed photo of Joni and one of Henry on the window ledge and unwrapped her purpose-bought Conran cup and saucer. She would start with that, at least, but probably graduate to a chipped communal mug or takeaway. She tested the chair she had requested in her deal memo. She gazed out the window onto Hyde Park and St Mary's Cathedral, and beyond, on a big blue-sky Sydney day.

'Erin!'

'Oh my god, Aud, I knew you'd call.'

'Where are you? How are you?'

'I'm at home. I've been at Alec's mother's house for weeks and then I found out about Heidi. Well, I'd suspected for a while but confirmed it by getting into his private email. So I moved back home again. Mum's here helping. Sylvie

The Little Clothes

told my mother to tell me not to wait around for Alec and then disappeared into the house while we packed up and left. Heidi can have him, but I'm going to get what I can to secure things for my children.'

'The partnership's moved against him.'

'I know. Hanna keeps me updated. He took Heidi to a formal dinner with all the heavy hitters and he openly flirted in front of everyone. He fully kissed her at the Christmas party. Hanna says they arrived together and left together. He told me he was going back to our house that night. I was already up at Palm Beach. Anyway, apparently very loud alarm bells rang for the partners. Plus, all his expenses and other indiscretions. His crazy behaviour. He even had the office book a first-class ticket to London for Heidi. And then a flight to Venice and rooms at the Cipriani. Idiot. He gave them everything they needed to move him out. They're cutting the bottom line, and he is a big overhead. Richard has been plotting for a very long time and Alec took his eye off the ball. He doesn't bring much new work in anymore. That's probably more to the point. Every dog has its day.'

'I'm sorry, Erin.'

'Don't worry. He'll pay. I've got Michelle Gurkas.'

'I heard. Well done. You sure you're okay?'

'Wouldn't mind some company.'

'I can't come right now. There's a lot on my plate. I've just started my new partnership. There's going to be a lot of work to do with this upheaval. You must be busy too. But you can call me any time about anything. We no longer have a conflict of interest.'

'Okay. Lunch soon.'

'Definitely.'

'Hello Audrey,' said Hanna, sidling into Audrey's office. 'Welcome back. Nice office. Better than mine. What a day to arrive on. Where did you get that chair? And a bar fridge! How did that happen?'

'Yeah, pretty weird day.'

'Alec promised you'd mentor me.'

'I just don't think I have time for that right now given all the changes, but I'll mention it to the directors when I see them this morning. And we'll work something out. Okay?'

'You're seeing the board?'

'Sorry, Hanna, I really have to get going. We'll have plenty of time to catch up soon.'

Audrey walked the Ape Run on her way home. Past the pub. She didn't glance in. Her *For Auction* sign had been erected since she'd left for work. Summer was full-blown and blowsy. The herbs had gone to seed. Now she sat on her back verandah with Joni and the fat Holland Lop, Chester, and watched the last rays glow and shimmer on a technicolour sky and felt a glimmer of hope for the year ahead. That was new.

Acknowledgements

This book was written on Wangal Country and on Jerrinja and Wandi Wandian Country.

Thank you to my agent, Jane Novak, a steady pair of hands and an all-round smart and lovely person who read my manuscript and took it on with unfaltering determination. She is also an excellent mimic and raconteur, which I love.

And thanks to my publisher, the marvellous Meredith Curnow, who had a passion for Audrey from the beginning, and has looked after me and my writing so well. And to Melissa Lane, who edited the manuscript with skill and care. Bella Arnott-Hoare and Bek Chereshsky are on the shore giving my novel a big push out into the choppy waters of publicity and marketing and I am grateful to them. Also, thanks to the whole PRH team who have embraced this novel and made it hum.

Thank you to Sarah Lutyens of Lutyens & Rubenstein Agency, who took Audrey under her wing in the UK and found her a home with Bedford Square Publishers. And thank you to the Bedford Square crew; Carolyn Mays has been a generous and attentive publisher and always made me feel supported from the other side of the world. Jamie

Hodder-Williams, CEO of Bedford Square, has shown his enthusiasm for my book and it turns out we share a short list of favourite novels. I also thank Polly Halsey in production, Holly McDevitt in publicity and Anastasia Boama-Aboagye in marketing.

Thank you, Amanda O'Connell, for being a very early encourager, reader, editor, listener and clever commentator on not only this novel but for an earlier manuscript that is, for now, tucked away in a drawer.

And thank you:

Mark Dapin, friend and fellow traveller, who read part of my first manuscript and gave the praise that kept me going. And he has been there ever since making me laugh. Often at his own expense. We will always have Aldershot and Broken Hill.

Hilary Keily, my dear clever friend who didn't roll her eyes when I said one sunny Sydney morning, 'I'm going to write a novel.' She said, 'That's a great idea.' And meant it. Although she did move interstate around the time I started reading bits out loud to her.

Cressida Campbell, friend of so many decades, who talks to me about the creative process and has never betrayed the fact in our conversations that her talent and accomplishments far exceed mine.

And thanks to David Watson, Joan Sauers, Linda Funnell, Felicity Driscoll, Terry Hudson, Pam Fowell, Jon Fowell, Garry Linnell, Louise Upton, Renee Polomski, Michael Polomski, Libby Leach, David McKay, Wayne Chick, Angela Kargilis, Kitty Callaghan, Brigitte Oberlander, Edna Warren-Taylor, Angela Hibbard, Katrina Brangwin, Daina Fletcher, Jenni Bruce, Chris Leach, Tina Leach and Bernadette Foley, who were all in my corner one way or another at different stages of the writing of this book. Encouragers all, I am in your debt.

Thanks, and love, to Rose Callaghan and to Tess Callaghan who often listened to me reading out the 'new bits' with good grace. You're everything I ever wished for and far, far more. I hope your own creative pursuits will always be a source of joy and a safe harbour for you.

And big love and thanks to Rory Callaghan, without whom there is no writing.

About the Author

Photo credit © Tony Mott

Deborah Callaghan worked as an interstate train stewardess, a librarian and freelance journalist before starting a thirty-five-year publishing career. She was a book publicist, a publisher and a literary agent. She lives in Sydney with her husband, two daughters and three lovely dogs.

Bedford Square Publishers

Bedford Square Publishers is an independent publisher of fiction and non-fiction, founded in 2022 in the historic streets of Bedford Square London and the sea mist shrouded green of Bedford Square Brighton.

Our goal is to discover irresistible stories and voices that illuminate our world.

We are passionate about connecting our authors to readers across the globe and our independence allows us to do this in original and nimble ways.

The team at Bedford Square Publishers has years of experience and we aim to use that knowledge and creative insight, alongside evolving technology, to reach the right readers for our books. From the ones who read a lot, to the ones who don't consider themselves readers, we aim to find those who will love our books and talk about them as much as we do.

We are hunting for vital new voices from all backgrounds – with books that take the reader to new places and transform perceptions of the world we live in.

Follow us on social media for the latest Bedford Square Publishers news.

@bedsqpublishers
facebook.com/bedfordsq.publishers
@bedfordsq.publishers

bedfordsquarepublishers.co.uk